Signs of Cupidity

HEART HASSLE
Book
1

RAVEN KENNEDY

Cover Design by A.T. Cover Designs
Edited by Polished Perfection

AUTHOR'S NOTE

This is a slow-burn *why choose* fantasy romcom, where the female main character will end up with multiple mates. It includes explicit language and sexual situations, and is intended for audiences 18 years and older. This series is complete.

To all the people who have been screwed over by cupids sticking their arrows where they don't belong. May your book lovers be way more satisfying.

CHAPTER 1

"*H*ey there, gorgeous. Did you sit on a pile of sugar? Because you have a sweet ass," the guy says, leaning an elbow on the bar beside the girl wearing a skintight dress.

His eyes glide up and down her body like he's ready to enter an eye-fucking contest. The woman turns around from her bar stool and flashes him a grin.

I roll my eyes and sigh at her. "Really? That's going to work on you? That's just sad," I mumble. "Don't fall for it, girl. He's an asshole, trust me."

I'm sitting right next to her, but she doesn't hear me. Well, I'm not really *sitting* next to her. It's more like I'm hovering over the empty barstool. Because I'm not *physically* here.

Although, I'm still here enough to be utterly annoyed when the woman gets to her feet and leads Mr. Terrible-Pick-Up-Line to the dance floor. They don't really dance, if I'm being honest. They just sort of rub against each other and hop around. There's a lot of ass holding, too. This one's an ass man for sure. And yeah, okay, he looks like he's an excellent ass handler, but that's not the point. The point is, I was *just* here last night, and this same Mr. Terrible-Pick-Up-Line was grinding on somebody else's ass, using equally awful pick up lines. It's just not right.

"Why does this always happen?" I ask aloud to the crowd. No one answers me. No one has answered me in decades. I guess it's not their fault, since they can't actually hear or see me, but that doesn't stop me from glaring at everyone.

"You guys should really be better than this," I say, focusing my lecture on the barman. "I mean as a species. Can't you evolve to be better at love? Because this is exhausting. And disheartening. And other words I can't even think of right now," I say.

The barman continues pouring drinks and ignores me. I wish I could have a drink. I put my hand in front of the glass as he slides it down the bar to someone else. It goes right through me like always.

I lift a hand to scratch the itch I feel on the back of my arm. It's just instinct to try to scratch. But of course, my hand goes right through my arm without touching it.

"Dammit!" I say through gritted teeth. "Five decades of this phantom itch!"

I try to slam my hand down on the bar in frustration, but it also passes right through. I can't even throw a satisfactory hissy fit. I'd love to really punch or kick something. Then eat and drink something. And then scratch this itch that has been plaguing me for so long. I must've died right when this damn itch cropped up on my arm, and then never got the chance to satisfy it.

"You have no idea how annoying this is," I whine to the person beside me as I continue trying to touch my arm. The man takes a drink and ignores me. "Lucky bastard," I say, eyeing him as he drains his glass.

I glance over my shoulder to look at my red wings. I wish I could touch these bad boys, too. My feathers look so soft, and the color is so vibrant, even in this dark bar. My wings are one of the perks of being what I am. Also the pink hair. I like my pink hair. I have no idea what my face looks like or what color my eyes are, since I don't have a reflection. I'm kind of like a ghost like that. But I'm not a ghost, because they're a drag, and I'm actually pretty fun.

I guess it's not important what I look like, since no one can see me, anyway. But at least I like my silver dress. It kind of shimmers over my pale form, and if I could look in a mirror, I think it would probably look pretty damn good on me, too, hugging my curves as it does. It makes me feel better to be dressed nicely, even if no one can see me. At least I'm not wearing something embarrassing like dirty sweatpants and an oversized T-shirt. Or a Halloween costume. Or workout gear from the eighties. Or a stripper getup. On second thought, those might be pretty fun.

I wonder if ghosts think of things like this. I can't ask one, because they're terrible company. Not that I haven't tried. The thing about ghosts is that they're really confused. They don't really know where or who they are, so they just kind of sulk and float around in a daze. It's like they get afterlife dementia or something. They mope around, completely bewildered as they mumble to themselves. If you try to strike up a conversation with them, they trail off after only a few seconds and forget what you were talking about. Not great conversationalists.

Ghosts are clumsy, too. They're always running into things, sometimes with enough juice to actually move something in the physical plane. The wilder ones often fly around in a frenzy until they get sucked into the plumbing pipes or electrical sockets. Knocking pipes and flickering lights? Yep, just another confused ghost. So yeah, ghosts do me no good.

Besides the loneliness, it's also *boring* being invisible. I'm stuck in the Veil, where I can see the physical world, but I'm not really a part of it. I'm an invisible observer, because I am here for one purpose and one purpose only: to spread love and desire.

Someone walks forward and sits down on my barstool, their body going right through my lap. "Rude," I say with a huff.

I jump off the barstool and fly across the bar, floating right through people as I go. They don't know the difference, so I don't feel bad about invading their personal space at all.

I pick a spot against the wall and hover-lean against it as I watch the dance floor, utterly annoyed. These humans are so disappointing sometimes. Many times. Nearly all the times. Where's the loyalty? Where's the love? Where's the romance? Or, to be more honest about where my bitterness really lies, where's mine?

See, this is what I get. When I died, I was this innocent, naïve, hopelessly romantic girl. So when the angels asked me what job I wanted to take up in the afterlife, I chose to become a cupid.

Stupid fucking cupid.

I thought it was going to be awesome. What better job for a romantic than to help bloom other budding romances around the world and coax them into love? Who wouldn't like to give a good Lust-Breath to some crazy kids looking for a nice tumble? Sign me up, right?

Well, it was nice for the first decade or two. But if there's one thing I've learned, it's that this job has a lose-lose scenario for me. Lose Scenario Number One: I go to all this trouble of singling someone out, following him or her around and finding a compatible match. Then I help coax their relationship along. You know, some Flirt-Touches here, some Lust-Breaths there, and then bang: the Love Arrow. I think, job well done, right? Wrong. One of them ends up doing something stupid and ruins everything. Maybe not right away, but eventually. They get selfish. They get lazy. They get bored. They cheat. They lie. They fall out of love. So, lose.

Then there's Lose Scenario Number Two: I do all of that and it succeeds. They fall in love and then stay in love. My small

4

pushes along the way help solidify their connection. Sounds like a win, doesn't it? I thought so, too, for a long time. But guess what happens to a hopeless romantic cupid watching as these couples love and lust and live? That's right. Just call me Pining Cupid. Or Super Jealous Cupid. Or Bitter Cupid.

I failed to realize when I signed up for this job just how painful it would be to my own non-corporeal heart. My couples either fail miserably, breaking the love I worked so hard on, or they succeed, and I'm left alone with no hope for myself of ever getting love or getting laid.

Like I said. Stupid fucking cupid.

Mr. Terrible-Pick-Up-Line and his new girl are leaving out the back already. They barely made it through two songs. They certainly didn't need any of my Lust-Breaths to help them along. Not that I would give it to them anyway. I'm still pissed as hell that he was here again picking up someone new. It's just greedy.

I push off the wall and fly out the door to go outside. The sidewalk is busy with people waiting to go inside, but I ignore them and fly down the street. Bars, clubs, restaurants, parks, gyms, offices—I go everywhere.

I've been flying around this human realm for so long now, setting people up for love, getting them some great sex, encouraging romantic acts, fueling affection. It's the loneliest job imaginable.

I'm hurt about Mr. Terrible-Pick-Up-Line. Probably more than I should be, if I'm being honest. When I saw him last night with that other girl, I thought I was witnessing one of those rare love-at-first-sight kinds of scenarios. He slid in and made his moves, and I barely had to use my magic for any encouragement at all. I could feel the chemistry spark between them. I'd followed them back to his place just because their desire was that palpable. It drew me in.

It was sexy and exciting and yes, even romantic. Everything I crave. But it was all for show, apparently. All those lines he used, all those whispered promises groaned above her, and he hadn't even meant any of it. It pisses me off. If he wanted a one-night stand, he should've just been honest about it. I don't need to track the girl down to know he's blown her off. I should probably track her down anyway and try to help her move on, but I just can't do it. I don't have it in me.

See? I shouldn't be a cupid. This job has really run me down. There's not even a retirement plan. This job? It's for life. Or second life, anyway.

If I did the whole stress-aging thing, I'd have too many wrinkles to count. I'd look like one of those sheets that get tangled up in the dryer and when you finally unravel it, it has about a million creases in it. I'd have a head full of gray hair, too. But, now that I think about it, I could probably rock gray hair. Gray hair could be pretty awesome looking with my red wings. Maybe second place to my pink hair, anyway.

As I fly down the street, I point an accusatory finger in people's unaware faces. "No Lust for you," I tell one drunk guy before moving on to another. "No Love Arrows for you," I say to a girl. "And nothing for you, either," I add to someone else. "Nothing for any of you!" I yell at the sidewalk full of people. "You guys seriously disrespect the name of love." I cross my arms to stop myself from pointing at more faces and then nod to myself as they all walk humbly by. "That's right. Keep walking. This cupid is done pandering to your needs."

Because what about my needs, right? Right.

When I fly by a theater and hear music, I decide to go inside. The audience sits in high-backed chairs as they watch a couple singing on the stage. The lighting is low, the music soft. It's the perfect recipe for romance stew, and I'm the only one left without a spoon. Or a bowl. Or tangible hands.

I stop flying down the aisle when I spot a guy on an end seat. He's dressed nicely and is splitting his attention between the singers on stage and the woman beside him. He's handsome, and when he reaches over and places his hand gently on the woman's leg, I sigh. I don't remember what it feels like to be touched. I don't even remember what my old life was before I became this. Hell, I don't even remember my name.

Since becoming a cupid, all I have is my assigned number. It's marked on the inside of my right arm, right below the wrist. It looks like a silvery-white tattoo and shows the Roman numerals for one thousand and fifty: ML. I do, however, have a pretty sweet set of bow and arrows that reside in the quiver slung over my back. They hold my most powerful tool: Love Arrows. I can't deny the rush I get when I shoot someone with one of those bad boys. I have perfect aim, too. When I first started out, my aim was terrible. But I've had plenty of target practice since then, and probably thousands of misplaced romances because of it, but oh well.

The second my arrow hits someone, it bursts in a cloud of color before disappearing. It's all different colors—depending on the person. The arrow pushes the person's like right into love. Of course, just like my Lust-Breaths, there has to already be some sort of connection there. It's not like I can force love or desire. I just help it along. Think of me as the gardener. I don't make the seed, I just tend it to help it take root and sprout.

Inside the theater, I settle myself down on the floor beside his chair and listen to the singers as they croon to each other. It's a sappy love song, and my cupid-senses are tingling with the need to throw out some Flirt-Touches and Lust-Breaths until the room explodes into one giant orgy. Yes, I've done that before. Don't judge. They're fun to watch. There's nothing quite like passing the time in the middle of an orgy. So many hands and tongues and other bits just sliding around like a carousel.

Besides, since my powers only work if there's already some desire and want there already, it's not really wrong. The ones that don't wish to partake usually get out of there real quick like. I don't interfere with free will. I just give them a push. But no, no pushing tonight. I'm mad at all of humankind with their stupid physical bodies and their stupid voices that can be heard.

Using my wings, I pick myself up and float out of the theater again into the night. My wings are really the only things I like about my job anymore. Well, besides the Love Arrows. Those things are downright fun to shoot. But I haven't used one in years. Why should I hand out love left and right when I can't get any for myself? I know, I know. I'm petty like that. But seriously, the angels should've given me a heads-up or thrown a Cupid Orientation or something before letting me take the job. I blame them for their oversight. I meander around the streets, blowing a few Lust-Breaths in people's faces as I go along, just because. I don't even wait to find people with a connection like I'm supposed to. Nope, I just fly by and blast people. I like watching them get all hot and bothered. Usually they find someplace to be very quickly, to either take care of business themselves or to find someone to do it with them. But sometimes, if I gave them an extra-strong dose, I get to see them make a complete ass of themselves as they sidle up and make a move on someone nearby. My favorite is when it's a stranger. Then I get to enjoy them getting told off or beaten up. Once, I Lusted this huge MMA-fighter-looking dude, and he practically jumped this poor accountant as he came strolling out of his office. I thought he was going to suffocate the poor guy. It was hilarious.

As I continue to fly, I spot a group of teenagers and zero in on the third wheel. He's a pimply-faced guy made of all limbs, his elbows and knees jutting out like doorknobs. It's so clear that he's the pity friend, that my heart kind of hurts for him. There's a suave-looking bad boy with his arm slung over the girl who walks between them. He has a cigarette illegally perched in his too-young mouth to really round out his whole leather jacket, too-cool-for-school look. The girl looks up at him adoringly even as he blatantly checks out other girls' asses and blows cigarette smoke in her face. The third wheel looks on, hands in his pockets, unrequited love in his eyes as he watches her.

Why should the good guy lose out? So he's a little awkward looking. So what? I'm sure he'd treat the girl way better than this other joker. Plus, I'm sick of the cocky jackasses tonight. I'm already feeling frisky because of earlier, so just as the cocky jackass in question turns yet again to stare at another girl that walks by (and actually gives her a wink), I lose it. I hit him with a Love Arrow so quick that he stumbles right there on the sidewalk like he ran into a pole. The James Dean poseur immediately ditches the girl he's with and runs after the other one. His girl, or rather ex-girl now, screams his name (which is Brad, because of course he has a name like that), and then she bursts into tears when leather-jacket-Brad sticks his tongue down the other girl's throat. Whew. I always forget how fast teen love settles in. It's like normal love, except it's on hyper-drive. They can't help it. Their hormones overpower their brain cells.

Brad continues to feel up his newfound love while his poor forgotten ex watches from the sidelines, now clutching onto Mr. Lanky Third Wheel. He can barely contain his grin as he comforts her and leads her away. I swipe a nice Flirt-Touch across each of them as they walk by me. That should set things in motion nicely.

"Ha. Plot twist," I say, pleased with myself. "For all the friend-zoned nice guys out there!" I call out to their retreating backs. "You're welcome!"

I nod and decide that I'll just go around screwing up more predictable toxic pairings and give a leg up to third wheels everywhere. It'll be great fun to shake things up a bit. Almost like the year of '91 when I made an entire town fall in love with themselves. It didn't last long, and it sure as hell wasn't easy to do, but man, just watching the dates they took themselves on made it worth it. Entire restaurants full of singles, staring daggers at anyone that walked by, treating themselves to whatever they wanted. Vibrator sales went through the roof.

I chuckle darkly to myself, and just when I'm about to break up another trio of unbalanced proportions consisting of a nerdy girl looking longingly at the oblivious guy, the unbelievable happens: I feel the tug.

Uh-oh.

Before I can blink, I'm yanked out of the human realm and thrown into Cupidville. And there's only one reason I'd be yanked back there.

Yep. I'm in trouble.

CHAPTER 2

*O*kay, it's not actually called Cupidville. It's actually a higher part of existence in the Veil, where all the in-between entities go for direction or assignment or whatever the hell else. I've only been to the part that other cupids inhabit, and I'm only allowed to go when I'm summoned. Like right now. Summoning is actually just a nicer way of saying pulled away from your duties because your superiors are pissed off at you. Yeah. I've been here before. Shocker, right? It's kind of like getting called to the principal's office. Except scarier.

I'm yanked away from the human realm, and before I can mutter a string of curses from the stomach-roiling sensation of flying through space and time, my body is dumped into a seat in a brightly lit room full of other cupids. It's like a giant doctor's office, except instead of getting a checkup, we're all getting promotions, demotions, assignments, or…terminated. And termination for us means ceasing to exist. Gone. The End. Game Over. Snap of the fingers, just like that.

That part isn't on the brochure. No, really. There were brochures when I first signed up, complete with a happy pink font that made being a cupid sound like the best job in existence. The devil is in the fine print. I really should've read it all before choosing this as my after-life occupation instead of getting caught up in the romance and a corny slogan: "Become a Cupid: Spread Love, Sex, and Desire!"

What? I was zero years old in the afterlife at the time. And it's not like I was the only one who fell for it, considering the other pink-haired, red-winged people around me. Of course, we're all still incorporeal, even here, so no change there. The only difference is that we can actually hear and talk to each other. And it's the only time I ever get to see other cupids. Surprise, surprise, there aren't that many of us. Considering how many realms we have to serve, it's very, very, very rare to see another cupid when you're working. So, yeah, as scary as it is to be sucked into Cupidville, it's also kind of awesome because I can see and talk to other cupids. It's like a high school reunion where you kind of recognize everyone but have no idea what the hell to talk about.

Inside the room, there's a huge reception area with some of the cupid superiors sitting behind glass, bustling around and looking extra busy. Every once in a while, a huge number displays on the wall with magic, lighting up to announce the next cupid in line to go forward. Right now, XLLL is on the screen. It won't go in numerical order. Just by some strange unknown system.

To my immediate right is a twenty-something male cupid. I think I'm around the same age. Without being able to see my reflection, I'm guessing I look somewhere between twenty and thirty. The only reason I think this is because the last time I was yanked here, this other cupid called me "hot and ripe as hell." I'm pretty sure he was terminated later, but the compliment was nice. I'm also pretty sure that twenty to thirty is a probable age range for "ripe." Unless I'm a cougar. And let's be honest, who doesn't want to be a cougar?

Anyway, the cupid guy sitting next to me is looking over at

the wall where a huge poster hangs with the stupid cupid slogan. I hear him muttering under his breath. "Fooking pile of steaming shite, that is."

I like him immediately. I lean over to get more into his personal space. "I know, right? They trick you into believing it's all fun and arrows and hearts, but in the real world, watching love and sex really starts to suck."

He looks over at me and nods. "Tell me about it. Had me for a fooking ride, they did," he says in the most entertaining accent I've ever heard. "The superior sold me like a bag of ice to a dry lake. Drank that shite right up."

"How'd they get you?" I ask. It's so nice being able to talk to someone. It's almost worth getting in trouble. It's been years and years since the last time I was yanked. I can't even remember how long ago it was. "For me, I was convinced it would be the most romantic job in all the realms. I was practically salivating for love when I signed up," I admit. "Couldn't wait to get started."

He raises a black brow. For some reason, our eyebrows aren't pink like our hair. I have no idea why. I also have no idea what color my eyebrows are, or my eyes. Cupid problems.

"Told me I'd be spreadin' all the sex I wanted, didn't they? Sold it like a fooking porno. Didn't realize not bein' able to join in would be its own sort of torture. I'm a virile guy, get it? I ain't cut out for this celibate shite. And the ghosts are seriously a drag. Fooking morose sons o' bitches."

I nod seriously. "I know, man. Believe me, I know."

He shakes his head, swearing under his breath about what a pain it is to be a cupid. But boy, this guy is pretty. Luscious lips, thick curly lashes, and cheekbones to die for. His pink hair sets his tan off rather nicely, too. I wish I had a tan. My skin is super pale. Like ghost pale.

We both look up as the next number flashes up on the wall. Another cupid, a little old lady, sees it and sighs. She floats toward the reception area looking perfectly guilty. I wonder what trouble she was making to get yanked. She looks too sweet to be in trouble, like she should be somewhere baking cookies and knitting ugly socks that no one will wear.

"Once, I went on a Love-Strike in my city," I say to my new cupid friend. "I didn't give out any Love for a month straight. I was yanked here for it. As punishment, they tripled my Love quota for an entire decade," I say, shaking my head at the memory. "A decade! By the time I was done, I was so sick of shooting arrows that I would've run myself straight through with one of them if I could." I tried. Didn't work. I've tried all my powers on myself. I'm sure every cupid here has. Our powers don't work on ourselves.

He shudders at my story, because he knows how giving out a surplus of Love can get complicated quick. "They can shove their fooking Love quotas right up their hairy arses," he says, making me laugh loudly. I get the stink eye from one of the superiors. Yeah, apparently they like the cupids to be quiet and demure.

"I got sent to the troll realm as punishment once."

I swivel to look at him again and gasp. "No!"

He nods with a grimace on his pretty face. "Yup. I wasn't givin' anyone the Lust, you get it? I was on a strike of my own, if you catch my drift. If I couldn't get any, no one else would, neither. When the superiors caught on, they sent me to the troll realm for an entire year. Those gobshites are the ugliest motherfookers I've ever eyed. I had to Lust 'em, and believe me, their idea of fooking ain't pretty. Plus, they lay eggs after. And I don't mean months later; I mean *right* after. Covered in sex juices and steaming." It's my turn to shudder. It makes my decade-long Love-Surplus seem tame in comparison.

"These cupid superiors are sadists."

"What did you do to land you here this time?"

"Nothing!" I say defensively. "Well, barely anything," I

amend. "I *almost* did something, maybe. I didn't even get a chance to really start, though. And *maybe* I haven't been giving Love out, either. But geez, they're so touchy these days."

"Yep. New management, I heard."

"Shit."

He nods. "You're tellin' me."

Before I can ask him what he did, I see my Roman numeral, ML, pop up on the screen. "Shit," I say again. "That's me."

"Good luck, cupid thousand fifty," he says with a nod.

I look down at his wrist where the letters DCCXX are. "You too, seven hundred twenty." I want to give him a fist bump, but since we don't have real bodies, it would turn awkward quickly. So instead, I just raise a fist in bitter cupid solidarity. "Keep it real."

"Aye. You fooking know it."

I float my way toward reception and stop in front of the glass where a superior cupid with a pinched face glowers at me. Her pink hair is in an updo that looks like a soft serve ice cream cone. "Cupid one thousand fifty?"

I nod and show her my arm. "Yep, that's me."

She looks at some papers and trails her finger down a column of writing. "Cupid one thousand fifty, report to room forty-three. Take door number one, go down the hall to the left. Follow the numbers. Thank you for your Loving service. Have a Cupidly good day."

She says everything with zero expression and in complete monotone, so naturally, a giggle bursts out of me unbidden. She glares daggers at me. "Sorry," I mock whisper, mimicking a motion to zip my mouth closed.

I quickly turn and find the door with the number one on it and go inside, heading down the hallway. Everything is white, and just like she said, there's door after door, all of them numbered. The doors are shaped like hearts, just in case we forgot we were cupids or something. The propaganda around here just doesn't end.

Finally, I reach door number forty-three. I announce myself and hear someone call for me to enter. At least I think he does. He could've just cursed me out or read out an ingredient from the recipe for the perfect chocolate chip cookies. I wouldn't know either way. But now I really wish I had a tangible tongue so I could eat a chocolate chip cookie. Those things look delicious.

Inside is a small office, where a superior cupid sits behind a desk. He's middle-aged, and his wings are tucked in tightly against his back as he watches me enter. There are piles of papers all over the desk and an hourglass trickling sand down its center. The pieces of sand are shaped like hearts, because of course they are. The propaganda, remember? It's Cupidville.

"Please, sit."

I do, but it's not really sitting since my body is still ghost-like. I just manage to make it look like I'm hovering over the chair. He makes it look much easier, but then, since he's a superior, his body is more corporeal than mine, letting him actually touch the papers on his desk. I'm super jealous. I wonder if he can touch a chocolate chip cookie. Wait, can he eat a chocolate chip cookie?

"Cupid one thousand fifty," he says, interrupting my thoughts. He picks up a file folder with my number on it and starts flipping through it. "Human realm. In service for fifty-six years."

"That's me," I say brightly, plastering a huge smile on my face. Because he can't be too mad at me if I'm super-friendly, right?

He looks up at me and cocks a brow. Okay, so maybe I crossed over from super-friendly to semi-crazy with my too-wide smile. I quickly take it down a notch.

"You've been disciplined five times in the past. This is your sixth visit," he says, looking up at me from the file.

"Which is pretty good, right? That's, like, only once a decade on average," I point out, still smiling.

"Is that amusing to you?"

I wipe the smile from my face. "No, nope. Definitely not, sir."

"Hmm. Well, despite your transgressions, you've been somewhat of a success in your duties," he says, surprising me. "Nothing remarkable, but you're a decent cupid."

I'm decent? I wonder who the real screw-ups are if he thinks I'm decent.

"Still, considering the number of purposeful transgressions you've been guilty of, we've decided to move you into another realm."

My eyes widen and I gasp. "Don't send me to the trolls!" I blurt out before I can stop myself. "I don't want to see their steaming sex eggs!"

He pauses his perusal of my file. "Who said anything about trolls?" he asks with exasperation.

I clear my throat and force myself to sit back down. *When did I jump out of the seat?* I am terrible at playing it cool. "Sorry. No one. I mean, I heard about them. The trolls, that is. Sometimes they're used as punishment, right? But you didn't say trolls. I hope you don't say trolls in the future. Because I don't want to go to the troll realm. You weren't going to say that, were you? I'd even take another Love-Surplus over the troll realm. Oh, gods, I'm giving you ideas, aren't I? I'm just going to shut up now."

I'm finally able to shut my yapping mouth. It's embarrassing how long it took.

The superior clears his throat. "Are you done?"

I nod like a madwoman, not trusting myself to open my mouth again in fear of more word vomit.

He eyes me for a moment longer, as if to make sure I really

am going to keep my trap shut. After a moment, he puts my papers back inside my file and puts it down on the desk, folding his hands over it all official-like. I'm so nervous that I'm frozen in place.

Finally, he says, "You're being sent to the fae realm."

I blink at him several times. I open my mouth and then close it again. I blink some more. "I'm sorry, what?"

"The. Fae. Realm," he says slowly, like I'm an idiot. "You'll no longer be serving humans."

"The fae…but…I mean, isn't that a promotion? Like, lots of cupids ask to be transferred to the fae realm, right?" I ask, and my nervousness takes control of my mouth again. "I don't know why. Humans are just fine. Not that I'm saying I don't want to go to the fae realm. The fae realm is awesome. Really great. I've heard super things about the fae realm. Much better than the troll realm. I'd love to go to the fae realm. I just thought…I was getting disciplined? Or maybe terminated? Not that I want that! I don't want to go poof. Or at least, I heard there's a poof. Like we just disappear in a pink cloud and we cease to exist. Not that I'm asking for a termination demonstration. I'm not. You won't poof me, right? No, because you're sending me to the fae realm. Wow. The fae. Am I not in trouble?"

Gods. It's like I just can't help myself.

He looks like he's completely done with me. If there were a magic button on his desk that said, "Get Her Away From Me," he'd press it. We sit in awkward silence, staring at each other for several minutes until he composes himself enough to deign to speak to me again.

"Cupid one thousand fifty. You are hereby transferred to the fae realm. Don't screw up, or you may be in line for termination for your next disciplinary meeting. And yes, you'd go 'poof,'" he says, leaning forward slightly, making me lean back.

If I had a heart, it would've just tripped and fallen down in my chest. "Oh, you got it, sir. No trouble from me. You can bet your wings on it. I'll be too busy spreading Love and Lust around to be getting into any trouble. I'll get them sexing and loving in no time. I'm all over it, sir. You can count on me. No need for poofing."

He just shakes his head at me and sighs. Then he *does* press a button, but this one says "Fae," and just like that, I'm being yanked out of the cupid office and thrown into the fae realm.

CHAPTER 3

*W*ell, I'm certainly not on Earth anymore.

That's my first thought the moment my incorporeal self pops into the fae realm. I'm actually hovering in midair, right smack in the sky. There are clouds above, around, and below me. The sun is straight up, but has more of a pink glow than the one on Earth. But the biggest difference? This place is made up of floating islands. Yep. Floating. Islands. Believe me, it looks stranger and more beautiful than it sounds. And there are *hundreds* of them. Some are barely a stone's throw away from another. Some are thousands of feet apart. Some are up, some are down, some are huge, some are tiny.

I soak in the sight. The fae realm. I never thought I'd find myself here. I'm pretty sure I was human in my former life, although that's just a guess. I just felt a general connection to humans. But being here fills me with a sort of awe. I can almost *feel* the magic that I know is ripe in the air.

The fae are the most magically powerful beings in all the realms, and their realm is also one of the largest. There's a reason lots of cupids want to land a gig here. Fae are supposedly freaky. Freakier than the freakiest of humans. There aren't the same inhibitions with fae as there are in other realms. So it's fun for cupids to get in here and spread some desire, because the fae are down for pretty much anything. And, unlike most realms, there are a ton of different species in this realm, which breaks up the monotony of things.

I don't know why I was sent here, but I'm pretty freaking excited.

I decide to fly to the different islands and look around. There are so many; I just want to explore for a while. I head below to the lowest islands first and scour the skies. One island that I fly over is made purely of water. No land to speak of. It looks like a diamond, hovering there in the sky, and I'm pretty sure I see some merpeople splashing around.

I also see an island with a huge volcano that seems to be stuck in a never-ending eruption. Lava drips off the sides and into the sky, landing gods only knows where far below. A lot of the islands are made up of cities. Some have humble-looking huts, and some have sprawling mansions and town squares. I watch them all from high above, just getting my bearings.

I fly for a long time, not getting close to any island in particular, until I find a smallish one that's set apart from the heavily populated areas. In fact, it looks almost untouched and is heavily forested. I decide this is the one to take a closer look at, though I don't know why I'm drawn to it. Maybe it's because it's so green and serene looking, so different from the human city I came from. Or maybe it's because after getting yanked from the cupid meeting, I'm feeling about a million times lonelier than I was before.

That's what happens every time I get yanked. It's nice while I'm there (when I'm not getting disciplined) because I can actually talk to others. But it doesn't last nearly long enough, and then I'm put back out for however many years with no one but myself for company again. That short visit I had made me feel real, but it's so painful to be cut off from all interaction again. I needed more. I always need more.

So it's my own lonely depression that draws me down to the island that looks just as lonely as me. I float through the trees and touch down on the grass, and then I stare out over the side of the island. If I were real and if I were to take a step, I'd fall right over the edge of it. I wonder how long I'd fall. I can't see anything below except a lilac sky and puffy clouds.

Gods, it's so pretty here.

Gods, I'm so lonely.

If I could produce tears, I'd cry.

Still looking out at the sky, I hear a noise behind me and I swivel around.

There, standing in the forest under the speckled sunlight filtering through the trees, is a shirtless god of a man. Or fae. Whatever.

"Good goddess and all that is sexy," I say under my breath.

He's shirtless and *huge.* I mean, he's at least a foot and a half taller than me, with more muscles than I even knew existed on a body, and every single one of those muscles is ripped. His bicep is bigger than my head, no joke. He's carrying a stack of wood in his arms as he walks toward me. He stops and drops the wood in a pile on the forest floor. Then he looks up and stares *right at me.*

He stalks forward. Like a predator. Like he's coming to devour me. Part of me is like, *hell yes, let's do this,* while the other part is like, *wait, how can he see me?* But mostly, I'm getting ready to climb him like a tree, because this guy is all kinds of sexy.

He continues to walk forward and then, right when I'm about to ask him how he can see me, the guy walks right through me. Yeah. Mood killer. He wasn't looking at me. He was looking at the sky, of course. You'd think I'd have learned by now.

I don't even want to examine how disappointed I feel.

I turn around to study him closer. I look at his back, his broad shoulders, his strong forearms and callused hands, and his...tail. Yep, he's not happy to see me—that's a tail poking out from his pants. It's a sexy tail, though. Like a lion's. *Meow.*

I circle around him to study him closer. His brow is covered with a sheen of sweat, like he's been hard at work all day. He has shaggy brown hair that hangs over his ears, and eyes so black that I can't see his pupils. He has a strong jaw, a shaggy beard, and a thick, low brow line. The guy oozes alpha manliness, and I want to get all up in that. He'd look human if it weren't for the tail and his pointed fae ears. His tail swoops down the back of his legs, flicking left to right lazily, with a tuft of hair on the bottom that matches the hair on his head. It adds to his sexiness.

"You're just all sorts of strong and capable, aren't you?" I ask him. "I'd let you protect me all day, any day, big boy," I say, getting close to his face. He's big and scary, but there's something in his eyes as he watches the horizon—a sad sort of look that makes something inside me squeeze.

I use my wings to hover in the air so that our faces are within inches of each other. If I hover at just the right angle, it's almost like he's looking at me again. That thing inside me squeezes harder. I carefully hover my hands on either side of his face, wishing I could feel him. I'm so damn lonely. This is a new low, even for me. I don't usually go around face hover-touching people. But maybe it's the sad look in his eyes that makes me do it. Maybe I feel a strange sort of kinship with him. Or maybe it's just because he really is the sexiest thing I've ever seen.

Still fake holding him, I whisper, "If I could kiss anyone in all the realms, I'd kiss you first."

I wish I could be heard, just this once. I wish I could feel, just this once. But of course I'm not and I can't.

I drop my hands and sigh sadly. "It's okay, First. It's not your fault."

A noise sounds behind us, and I turn to see two more guys

walking this way. Huh. So much for this forest island being uninhabited. The sad, vulnerable look on First's face vanishes and is covered up with a hardened, blank expression instead. "The pile's right there," he says, nodding his head in the direction of the wood he stacked.

I float over to the other two guys and notice that they also have tails. "Good goddess, you two are handsome, too," I say. And they are. It's like I landed on Sexy-Guy-Island, population: three.

I fly up to the one with blond hair. "Well, hello there. I'd kiss you second, for sure," I tell him as he starts to pick up pieces of wood. He has soft brown eyes, and aside from being so handsome, it's almost hard to look at him. He also looks kind. Like he'd rub my feet after a hard day or just let me hug him.

I look over my shoulder at the other one. He has black hair, pale skin, and stunning blue eyes. He's hot and has that arrogant air about him that makes him all the more irresistible. "Oh, don't worry, I'll kiss you third," I assure him.

The three guys collect the wood and then make their way through the forest away from me. I sigh as they go. I need to leave now. I should probably head to one of the busy city islands to get to work. I don't want to get yanked back and accused of slacking. I have no doubt the superiors would poof my cupid ass.

I look back longingly at the sexy guys and shoot up into the air. The sunlight is already fading, so night will be here soon. And if there's any such thing as crunch-hour for a cupid, it's during the night. That's when lust and love surge, no matter the realm. There's something about the cover of night that lets people shed their worries and get down to the heart of things. Or get down to their birthday suits by stripping off their clothes.

I fly around, heading for the higher islands until I see it: a massive island, the biggest one I've seen yet. Complete with a huge, glittering city made up of stone streets and polished stone buildings. A flowing river falls right off the side of the island, casting off mist and rainbows, and behind it are green gardens and then a huge castle on a hill. It's complete with turrets and towers and a thick, shiny wall surrounding it.

I'm right in the heart of the realm. I've found the fae palace.

CHAPTER 4

*T*he city on the kingdom's island, I've come to find out, is called Highvale, and the people are beautiful, terrifying, and downright crazy.

Barely two weeks in, and I've already seen pixies setting a pub on fire because they got cold, dryads swinging naked from the trees and doing…rather inappropriate things with those said trees, a dwarf fighting a bogle over a piece of string, a sidhee purposely digging under a tavern to make it collapse, and sex. A lot of sex.

Flying fae humping in the clouds, orgies in the water, couplings on the rooftops, and exhibitionists in storefronts. I mean, these fae really like sex. The only thing I've seen more of than sex is fighting. Bickering, fist brawls, combat training, magical skirmishes—they like it all.

Things are a bit mellower the closer you get to the palace, since the high fae are the ones to rule the realm. All the fae species are as different from each other as they are terrifying. Some look more human-like, while other species, like the dryads, with their bark-like skin and vines for hair, are one hundred percent fae. But it isn't just their appearance that makes me feel wary. It's their unmistakable viciousness and their unmitigated power.

The high fae are arguably the most powerful. They aren't limited to a single thread of power like some of the other fae. Ashrays, for instance, only have power over the water they live in. Goblins have super strength. Elves are super good at growing things. But with the high fae, they can pull on multiple threads of power and can have several magical affinities. It's probably why they rule the realm.

As far as appearance, they're tall, taller than humans, with slender, graceful bodies that come in all sorts of pastel hues. But their huge iridescent eyes give them a feral look, and it turns their natural gracefulness into a terrifying beauty. It's clear by the actions of all the other fae species that they all defer to the high fae, albeit grudgingly. No one crosses a high fae. The social hierarchy is clear in that regard.

I've also learned that the realm is governed by King Beluar Silverlash and his son, Prince Elphar. And rumor has it that the prince is due to marry.

I haven't been inside the castle yet. I've been too busy trying to figure out all the different fae species and get my feel for how things work here. It's also taken me that long to get out of my rut. But since it's been a couple of weeks now, and I've tested my magic on some of the different species, I feel like I have my bearings. So when news comes of a royal ball to announce whom Prince Elphar will take for a wife, I know it's my time to shine.

Arranged marriage? I can work with that. The way I see it, if I can get the betrotheds to fall in love, or at least in like, I can work my magic and get the couple happily affable toward each other. As long as they don't completely despise each other, it shouldn't be too hard. All I need is a tiny spark of attraction, and I can nudge it in the right direction.

And let's face it, I like the sound of being responsible for the good of the realm. Cupid'ing the most famous couple in all the realm is exactly the kind of purpose I need.

When I get to the castle, it's even bigger than I thought when I first saw it from the skies. It looks like it's made of opals. It's white when you first glimpse it, but when the sun hits it a certain way, it sparkles with a rainbow of different colors. Bottom line: it's gorgeous. I decide it will be my new home. No more slumming it in the city for me, no sir. The palace is officially going to be my new haunt. In fact, the opal walls are so pretty that I wish I could hack off a piece to carry in my pocket —or possibly pawn for a butt load of money.

Maybe I was a princess in another life, because as soon as I walk through the doors (okay, I float through them), I feel like the luxury is calling to me. "You belong here, cupid one thousand fifty," it seems to say.

Arched ceilings, armed guards, polished floors, scurrying servants, and gilded paintings everywhere. This place screams wealth. There are tiny trees growing out of pots everywhere I look, too. Lining the walls, branches crawling up to the ceiling, leaves arching over hallways. The vibrant energy of them is a stark juxtaposition against the cold, lifeless marble.

The palace is a hub of activity, too. I've never been in a palace before, but it seems like things are busier than usual when I first get inside.

I follow the action, partly because I'm nosy and partly because…okay, so there isn't another reason besides me being nosy. I follow the servants to the one place I know I can find the gossip. It doesn't matter if it's a tiny stick hut or a sprawling castle; if you want the scandals and the rumors, you go to the kitchen. Everyone talks in the kitchen. I think it's the food's fault. People go in there ready to open their mouths.

It's a dizzying trip through the servant's corridors, but as soon as I pass through the walls and see the steam and smoke in the air, I know I've made it. The palace kitchen is bigger than most houses, and it's packed with all types of fae. They're chopping vegetables, stirring pots, kneading dough, lighting stoves, and shouting obscenities or instructions. I hover over a counter in the corner, making myself comfortable to listen.

"I said to steam the greens, not to drown them!"

"You serve that crooked cake, and it'll be the last thing you do, idiot."

"Where's my copper pot? Who stole my fucking copper pot?"

"I need that fire lit!"

"Where'd that water boy get off to?"

"That chicken ain't gonna pluck itself!"

I love listening to and watching all the action. The food looks yummy, too. Too bad I can't smell it. Or taste it. It's a real downer.

After a few minutes, I notice a group of three girls huddled in the corner, whispering. Perfect. I float over to them, invading their space so I can listen in on the good stuff. The girls are feeorin, by the looks of them. Feeorin have dark green skin and red hair and wings that look like fish fins. They're busy polishing silverware.

"I don't know what all the fuss is about. I heard that she's not even that pretty."

One of the other feeorin snorts. "Please. You're just jealous because you tipped your skirt for the prince two months ago, and he doesn't even remember your face, let alone your name."

Before the girl can respond, feeorin number three cuts in to diffuse the oncoming girl-fight. "Well, I think it's good he's finally going to marry. The king is old. It's time the prince marries and has his coronation. Who cares if she's pretty or not?"

"Oh, she's pretty. Trust me. The prince wouldn't marry a boggart."

The skirt-tipping girl bristles. "My second cousin is a boggart."

29

"Then you know how hideous they can be," the girl counters.

The peacemaker interferes again, holding up a carving knife between them. It's a good thing she's standing in the middle. "Shut it, both of you. The engagement ball is in six hours, and we still have to finish all the silver, plus the crystal, and then help Cook with the wine! It won't matter what you think of the princess if you serve her with tarnished silver, because the prince will have your heads!"

The girls grumble under their breaths, but much to my chagrin, the gossiping and arguing stops. Oh, well. At least I know when the engagement ball is. My arrival couldn't be more perfect. Now all I have to do is wait until tonight, find Prince Elphar and his princess-to-be, and work my magic. Should be easy, right?

CHAPTER 5

*T*he ballroom is even more exquisite than the rest of the palace. Chandeliers drip with honey flames, a fae ensemble performs lilting music, the ceilings are covered with arched vines, and everywhere I look, there are all types of fae drinking, dancing, laughing, and reveling. The females' gowns are magnificent, in barely-there fabric that looks like they could be spun from spiders' webs.

And right there, on the raised dais, overlooking it all, is King Beluar Silverlash. He's ancient looking. His lilac-colored skin has more lines than a map. I'm guessing his hair was once a color to complement his skin, but it's long since turned white. He's wearing something akin to a nightdress, and it's ugly as all get out, but I'm sure it costs more than most houses. The guy is the richest fae in the realm, and he's wearing pajamas to his own party. Gotta love it.

When he shifts on his throne, his clothes ride up, and I catch a glimpse of his gnarled, bony knees. Not what I was expecting. I mean, who imagines the most powerful monarch in the realm with knobby knees? Every time I see him move in his seat, I try

31

to steal another look. I don't know why, but I can't help but fixate on them.

"Gods, they stick out like doorknobs," I tell him as I sit on the dais at his feet. I'm in prime knee-looking territory. He reaches forward to take a drink of wine, and his kingly robe moves again, giving me another glimpse. "You could turn one of those suckers and open a door to another world."

I stay there, staring at his knees for an embarrassing amount of time before I force myself to move along. The prince and his betrothed still haven't shown up to their own party yet. I'd go look for them, except I don't know where they are. Also, I don't feel like it. That's mostly the reason; I'm actually enjoying myself, watching the party—and the king's knees.

I decide to meander over to the refreshment table because drunk people are funny to watch, and damn, do these fae like to drink their wine. I think reveling must be a part of their DNA. They're excellent at parties. Attending them, throwing them, crashing them. There's always a party going on somewhere on this island, no matter the time.

It's not until the clock strikes midnight that a hush falls over the crowd. The music stops, the dancers flit back to the walls, and the crowd parts to reveal the most handsome high fae I've seen yet.

The golden circlet that sits on his smooth, navy blue hair gives it away, but even if he weren't wearing that crown, I'd know he was royalty. It's in his straight posture and his clothes that look like they were spun from gold, but mostly, it's in his cool, pompous expression. On his arm is an equally beautiful high fae with lavender skin and hair. Together, they look like a majestic, perfect couple.

An announcer's voice rings out from somewhere saying, "Presenting the Crown Prince Elphar Silverlash and his betrothed, Lady Soora Wyndice."

Applause fills the ballroom, and the prince leads his lady

toward the dais to sit next to his father. Once they're seated, the party resumes, music and all.

"Okay," I say to myself. "Showtime."

I float past the dozens of dancers, right up the dais, and plop myself on the armrest of Lady Soora's seat. "You two are a cute couple," I tell her. Soora's expression is serene, but I can tell she's nervous by the hurried pulse that shows on her neck and the way her hands fidget slightly in her lap.

Beside her, the prince leans over, brushing his lips against her ear. "Have I told you how lovely you look, my dear?"

I didn't know someone with purple skin could blush, but she does, her cheeks blooming like a violet. "Yes, my prince."

He brushes a piece of her hair back over her shoulder, his handsome face smiling. "Well, it bears repeating. You are the loveliest creature in the room."

I whistle through my teeth. "Man, you're good," I tell him. "Very suave. You two don't even seem to need my help at all," I admit, taking in the scene.

Using my powers, I'm glad when I sense their attraction for one another. If I focus, I can see it dancing around them like ribbons on a maypole, wrapping around the other. Yeah, it's a cupid thing. I can sense romantic connections between people. I don't usually use it, because it's difficult to discern in a crowd.

I decide I might as well focus on her since she seems nervous. I lean in close to her and brush my incorporeal finger along her arm. She blinks as the magic of my Flirt-Touch sinks into her skin.

I watch her shy, worried demeanor slip away, replaced with a coy grin. "My prince, I'm sure you say that to all the girls," she says. "As it is, your reputation precedes you."

His friendly smile turns mischievous. "Oh? What reputation might that be?" he asks.

"You're called the Heartbreak Prince."

"Is that so?" he asks. "Well, then I suppose I'll have to take extra care when handling your heart."

"What makes you think I'd give it to you in the first place?" she asks demurely, a brow arched in challenge.

Huh. Who knew she'd be so good at playing hard to get?

His eyes light up and his voice drops down to a panty-melting whisper. "Oh, my lady. Believe me, once I get my hands on you, you'll be begging for me to take it."

Great flying fae, this guy is good (I'm trying out new fae realm expressions. When in Rome and all that.).

Lady Soora tilts her head and laughs as another blush rushes to her face, and he settles back in his seat, seemingly satisfied that he's won the round.

I shrug at them. "Well, I was hoping for a bit more of a challenge, to be honest," I tell them. They continue to watch the party, but I can feel the sexual tension building between them like humidity. This is almost too easy. I'm going to nail this. Suck it, cupid superior! No troll realm or termination poof for me. I got this.

It's after dawn when the king, prince, and Lady Soora finally leave the ballroom, bringing an end to the party. From what I've heard, the wedding is set for just two weeks from today. I follow Prince Elphar as he accompanies his betrothed to her rooms. I'm not surprised in the least when she invites him inside.

He shuts the door before I can get in there, and I catch the knowing look passed between the guards as they stand watch in the hall. I float through the door and into the room where Prince Elphar and Lady Soora are already busy dancing...with their tongues. Down each other's pastel-colored throats.

It's pretty hot and heavy, and I relax on the bed to watch. Yeah, yeah. Voyeurism, right? What can I say? I like watching because it's hot. I hate watching because I'm jealous. I'm a glutton for punishment.

After a few minutes, Lady Soora turns her head and pushes

the prince lightly on the chest. They're both panting for breath.

"My prince," she says in her soft, melodic voice. "We should wait until the wedding."

"Why?" he asks, holding her elbows. "The marriage contracts are signed; we're all but legally married. All that's left is the pomp of the public ceremony. We're as good as married, my dear."

"Yes, but my father..."

"Your father wants his daughter to be cared for. As my princess, and one day my queen, I will see to your every want and need," he says, moving his arms to the small of her back and then even lower. "Just as I know you will see to my every want and need," he adds huskily.

She smiles, and his mouth claims hers again as he walks her back toward the bed.

I have to admit, as I sit on the bouncing mattress, sex looks good on the prince. He seems like a regular sex-pro. Some of the moves he pulls makes his heartbreak title believable. And while it's clear he's no virgin, Lady Soora certainly is. I can tell the moment he plunges in and splits her open, because her moan turns into a cry of pain.

Too soon, it's all over, and the prince is redressing to return to his rooms. I stay with Lady Soora as she bids him goodnight and crawls back to her bed, collapsing into sleep almost as soon as her purple head touches the pillow. I wonder what the maids will say in the morning, when they see the bloodstained sheets. As free as the fae are about sex, it seems there are still some reservations, at least as far as what is expected for nobility and royalty. They're all about appearances, after all.

The prince has wooed his betrothed, the lady is sated, and the future of the monarchy seems bright. As I lie on the bed beside Lady Soora, I sigh in melancholic relief. For the first time in a long time, I'm feeling optimistic about watching a love story play out.

CHAPTER 6

"*Y*eah! Give it to him good!"

I look to my left and laugh at the shouting man. He's a...well, I'm not really exactly sure what kind of fae he is, to be honest. He looks like a bulbous mini-troll. He has more warts on his face than hair on his head. And he's just one of hundreds of fae gathered together to watch the royal tournament.

Currently, there are two contestants going head-to-head using blunted long swords. I know, I know. The sexual innuendos are practically erupting out of me. Especially when I have bystanders watching the tournament and shouting things like, "Stick your long sword in him!"

I look to my right at the female pixie who's responsible for my giggling fit this time. Watching tournaments is super fun.

I float around the bystanders, huffing some Lust-Breaths here and there as I go in the crowd. I watch pair after pair of contestants leave the arena, one as the victor and one as the sore loser.

Sometimes, they're allowed to use their magic, and that makes the fighting even more exciting. I fly invisible amongst the crowd until the royals finally arrive. I wing it right up to them, taking my spot on the arm of the throne for the soon-to-be-princess as she takes her seat beside the prince.

It's been a week since I came to the castle, and everything is going smoothly. This tournament is being held as part of the wedding festivities, no doubt chosen by the prince. It doesn't matter which realm it is, guys like watching people kick the shit out of each other.

Lady Soora watches with polite interest, clapping when a victor emerges and grimacing when a loser gets knocked around a bit too roughly. Prince Elphar, on the other hand, shouts with vigor, claps like he's trying to mimic thunder, and curses like a pissed off drunk when his chosen fae loses. "Rip his wings off!" he yells during a particularly gruesome match between two high fae.

"He's a bloodthirsty one, isn't he?" I say to Lady Soora from my perch.

I notice her stealing looks at him from the corner of her eye every time he shouts down at the arena. I've grown quite fond of the lady. It's obvious why she was matched with the prince. She's going to be the perfect princess. She always looks flawless, her back is straighter than a leveled wall, she has impeccable table manners, she's tactful when she speaks, she's kind, and, based on more kitchen gossip, her father is loaded. With only a week until the wedding, this cupid is sitting pretty on the match of the century.

Yeah, I'm taking credit for it even though I haven't really done anything. So what? There aren't any other cupids around to know any better. There never are. After the tournament, I follow Lady Soora and her maids back to the palace as they get ready for dinner in the great hall. There will be another party tonight, just like there has been every night since their betrothal was announced.

Tonight, there's apparently going to be a play put on. Since

I'm practically a professional spectator, I'm great at going to things like tournaments and plays and musicals. It's kind of my thing. I can watch like everyone else, making it feel a little less lonely.

After Lady Soora is dressed and then after sitting through an excruciatingly long dinner where all I can do is look longingly at all the delicious food being shoved into mouths that are not mine, it's finally time for the play.

Instead of sitting next to Lady Soora in the royal box constructed just for tonight's festivities, I go right to the front of the stage where I can see everything up close and personal. I want to get right in on the action. I want to see the sweat on the actor's upper lip, the stagehands running around frantically, the actresses throwing hissy fits behind the curtain. I love the hidden drama behind the stage drama.

The play has a little bit of everything. Romance, revenge, fighting, death, redemption. By the end, I'm trying to clap my non-physical hands together and whooping shouts of praise with the rest of the crowd.

"Bravo!" I yell to the actress who played the part of making two guys fall in love with her and then leaving them both for another female.

It was epic.

By the time I get back to the royal box, Lady Soora is already gone. Knowing she probably went back to her rooms, I decide to follow Prince Elphar instead. I haven't followed him unless he happened to be with Lady Soora, because I didn't want to get bored. There are only so many political talks I can sit through in the king's council room before I want to stab my ears from boredom.

But I decide to follow him now since he's probably on his way to an after-party. One thing I've learned while here at the palace—he's always up for an after-party. Prince Elphar walks through the great hall, his guards in front of him, ensuring that the crowd parts.

Everywhere he goes, fae tilt their heads in recognition. One high fae female smiles at the prince, and her dress is so low cut that I fear her breasts will fall right out and make her topple over. I'm not the only one who notices, either. The guard and the prince eye her display with pleasure.

"Alright, move it along, hussy. The prince is betrothed," I hiss in her ear.

She just smiles wider when she lifts her head and catches the prince's eye. But he passes by her without a word, making me sigh in relief. I really did win the jackpot with this betrothal. I'm not sure how I got so lucky.

The prince heads upstairs to his wing in the palace. It's ridiculously fancy. We're talking plush carpet, a fireplace I could jump up and down in, a huge bed and seating area, and a balcony. I fly over to his bed and hover on top of it, spreading my arms out and pretending to feel the soft covers.

"This is the life, eh, princey pants?"

He goes through a doorway to where he keeps his clothes and comes out wearing just a loose tunic and pants. For some reason, seeing the prince of the fae realm without shoes on makes me feel all giddy. It's kind of like seeing the king's knees.

Maybe I have a thing for hidden royal body parts. I sit up and join him when he goes over to one of his plush chairs by the fire and sits down, pouring himself a glass of liquor. When a knock sounds on his door, he kicks back the glass, swallowing the contents in one large gulp.

"Enter," he calls out.

"Yeah, enter," I call out. "Wow. Being royal is fun," I say to him. "You don't even have to answer the door. You can just yell across the room at it and someone else will open it for you."

I longingly look at the crystal decanter of alcohol, wishing I could take a swig. I bet it's nice and smooth. I hear the guard open and close the door behind me, and when the prince gets to his feet and walks over, I turn around to see the hussy from the hall standing there.

"Oh, hell no," I hiss, jumping up.

I march over, but before I can reach them, the prince already has her shoved up against the door and his tongue shoved down her throat.

"Hey!" I yell at him. "Stop that!"

I clap my hands together to try to get their attention, which is a horrible instinct that I should have broken by now because my hands go right through each other. I wish I had a spray bottle so I could spritz them with water. It worked on old Mrs. Bunson's cats when they were going at it.

"Your wedding is next week!" I remind him. "You're hopelessly in love with your betrothed."

Standing beside them, I'm shorter than both, so I'm really just staring as their jaws unhinge like they're trying to see who can swallow whom first. I'm pissed. I wave my arm at their faces, but that does absolutely nothing. It's times like this that really suck to be a cupid. All I have in my arsenal are things that will help further ignite the lust. I have nothing to douse it with. And it's not fair, because what about poor Lady Soora? What about their marriage?

If he's already hopping beds, and they aren't even married yet, there's no hope for a happy marriage later on. Not when he so obviously takes people from his court, and the whole palace seems to know about it, except, you know, Lady Soora and the Stupid Cupid.

"Gods, I hate this job," I say with my hands on my hips.

I watch disdainfully as he rips the dress from her body and screws her right there up against the door. It's fast and, if you ask me, there are a lot of exaggerated noises coming from the hussy. Seems like she's really faking it. The prince either doesn't care or doesn't notice. He finishes in four minutes flat. He didn't even take off his pants—just loosed the ties.

When he slips out of her, he tightens his trousers again and goes back to his seat to pour himself another glass of liquor. The female is busy trying to straighten her dress, but it's obviously ruined.

"That's hopeless," I tell her as she tries to hold her bodice together. "Should've thought about that before coming in here and cheating with the prince. Maybe next time you go for a betrothed man, you'll bring a change of clothes."

The prince knocks another drink back and then turns to the female when she makes a small noise, like he forgot she was there. I think she might've sighed, because she's just realized that she'll be doing a hell of a walk of shame 'with her breasts popping out all over. I don't envy her at all.

You might not think it, but the guards here are terrible gossipers. I mean, even worse than the ladies' maids, if you can believe it. In all fairness, the prince does supply a lot of juicy tidbits. Case in point.

"Why are you still here?" Prince Elphar says to her with contempt. The female blanches, and even I feel bad for her.

"I…umm…my prince?"

"Get out," he says with the tilt of his chin. Both of our mouths open in surprise.

"What an ass," I say.

She recovers quickly, spinning on her heel and throwing open the door. I poke my head through to watch as she hurries down the corridor, her arms holding her ruined dress together. The guards laugh at her retreat.

I flip around and stalk over to the prince. I slap my hand at his cup, because he's poured another drink for himself. I envision my hand hitting the cup and causing it to fly out of his hand and shatter against the wall.

Of course, that doesn't happen, so I throw a slightly embarrassing hissy fit instead. "You are a jackass," I say, punching through his face. "What the hell was that? Don't do that again."

But we both know he will. I glare at him as he continues to drink, and my glare follows him until he flops down on his bed and passes out. One thing is clear. This is *not* the easy win I thought it was.

Dammit.

CHAPTER 7

*T*he wedding happened two weeks ago. It was everything a royal wedding should be. Opulent. Lavish. Ridiculously expensive. The bride looked stunning, the groom was handsome. There were so many toasts to the beautiful couple that the king eventually cut it off because he wanted to "get on with it." I shared his sentiment.

I watched them consummate their marriage on their wedding night, and Princess Soora went to sleep that night feeling happy and loved. It's like that saying, "ignorance is bliss." It's totally true in her case. I dreaded to see that look wash away when she found out the truth.

Since the prince's indiscretion against his bedroom door, I've been on him like a beetle on dung. And he's screwed a total of fifteen other females. *Fifteen.* Five and ten, in only two weeks! I've never felt like such a failure.

I've done everything I can think of to make things better. Every single time he's with Princess Soora, I pounce on him with Flirt-Touches until I'm sure my invisible fingertips would be bleeding from contact. I've exhaled enough Lust into them both to impregnate the world. And don't even get me started on the Love Arrows. I've lost count on how many of them I've let loose.

It doesn't seem to matter. As soon as he's away from her, the hound goes sniffing, and the hares spread their legs and go belly up for him to devour them. I watch the prince at dinner, ever the cool, pretentious royal. When I see him look at a female down the table, I know he's plucked his fruit for the night. He glances at his guard with the barest of nods to let him know. If I hadn't learned to pay such close attention, I never would have noticed the exchange.

Sure enough, when the meal is over, he kisses his princess sweetly on the cheek and then retreats to his room. At a decided timeframe later, the guard escorts the female to the prince's rooms. I sigh and wait in the corridor as she disappears behind his bedroom door. I'm depressed. I really wanted this realm to be different. I wanted to at least be the reason for one perfect love. Just one perfect love. Couldn't I have that? I mean, what kind of cupid am I? I suck.

I slump to the floor in front of the prince's door and shake my head at one of the guards. "You're a handsome fae, aren't you," I say thoughtfully. "Are you cheating on your spouse, too?"

One of the other guards starts telling him a story about last night's drinking debacles that involved a magical brew responsible for giving someone named Himiny uncontrollable glitter flatulence. Yep. Sparkle farts. Apparently, it's a thing.

"I don't understand," I say miserably, ignoring their laughter. "If you want to sex around, that's fine. Just be honest about it. There's plenty of love to go around. But I can't get on board with the secrecy stuff. The disloyalty. The lies. I thought you guys were better at this here," I say with a sigh.

They might not be human, but I was wrong when I thought they were really any better at love. They just have a lot more adventurous sex.

The guards are still chuckling about the glitter farts, totally

44

messing up my brooding, so I blow an uncomfortable amount of Lust at one of their faces. He gets all sorts of uncomfortable looking and quickly makes an excuse to leave his post. He practically runs down the corridor with his armored hands covering the front of his pants, while his compatriots howl in laughter. I hope he gets blue balls. Prince Elphar doesn't get that. His balls get more attention than nipples in a wet T-shirt contest.

"I've only been here for four weeks, and you guys have already pissed me off," I say. "I could really use some cupid backup."

I tilt my head in thought. Yeah, that would actually be awesome. Maybe I should try to get yanked and make the suggestion to a superior? Instead of singles, they could start assigning us in pairs. Cupid Couples. Partners in Love. Desire Duos. It would make this whole job so much more tolerable if I had someone to do it with. Too bad the superiors wouldn't listen to a thing I say.

I'm still considering my brilliant idea when I hear the worst sound in the world. "Princess Soora?"

I snap my head up and look in horror at the princess coming this way. "Oh no."

The guards standing outside the prince's rooms exchange a look. "Princess Soora," one of them says again. "How can we be of assistance?"

The princess stops in front of him. "I've come to call on my husband," she says with a shy smile.

The guard clears his throat uncomfortably. "The prince is indisposed, my princess. He has asked for no visitors."

Right at that moment, a very feminine squeal comes from behind the closed door. I see it happen. I watch Princess Soora's eyes flick from the guard to the closed door and then back again. I see the embarrassed flush that floods her body, turning her a deep purple. I see the look of betrayal that fills water in her eyes. And thanks to my cupid powers, I can feel her heart breaking right there in front of me.

It's a struggle to keep her composure, but she manages it somehow, because that's how princess-like she really is.

She lets out a low breath. "I see," she finally says.

"You're too good for him," I tell her. "Don't give that dog another thought. I mean, you didn't even orgasm last time," I remind her. "So that means he's greedy. And inattentive. You could do *so* much better."

"I'll come at a later time," she says.

I can't help but snort with laughter at the double entendre. "That's the spirit. Take care of yourself. You don't need no man."

She turns around and walks away, her two ladies trailing behind her. When she disappears around the corner, the guard visibly relaxes and turns back to the others.

"Shit," he says.

The second guard shakes his head. "That didn't take long, did it?"

"Feel bad for her."

The third guard shrugs. "She would've found out sooner or later."

The first guard slaps him upside the head. "That's our princess. Show some respect."

Just then, the prince's door opens, and all three guards jump to refill their proper positions by the wall. The female slips out of the prince's rooms with a giggle, winking at the guards as she goes.

"Hope you're proud of yourself!" I yell at her retreating back.

I float through the wall and go into the prince's rooms. With my hands on my hips, I scowl at him, ruffling my feathers, and I fly toward him. Of course, he's drinking again.

"You suck, you know that? You have a lovely, beautiful, nice princess, and you go around screwing anything with a skirt and break her heart! If I could, I'd punch you right in your dangly bits."

As usual, he just pours himself another drink. The following weeks are terrible. Now that the princess knows, it's like the prince cares even less for being discreet. Not that he was terribly discreet to begin with. But now, he openly flirts with the females around the palace. I'm forced to watch Princess Soora retreat into herself, like a drooping flower.

During the days, she keeps up her polite princess duties, oftentimes forced to be in the company of the females who have cheated with her husband. During the nights, I watch her cry herself to sleep.

When he visits her, their exchange is quick and completely one-sided. She participates only as part of her duty to produce an heir. I do whatever I can to make the princess feel better, but I really can't do much. She isn't responsive to his flirting anymore, and lust is totally rejected.

I even try to get the princess to fall in love with someone else, but she isn't interested in that, either. No matter what I do to try to help her broken heart, I can't keep the pieces from falling.

I watch her weighed down with betrayal, hurt, and embarrassment. The dark circles under her eyes are proof of her sleepless nights. Instead of bringing in marital bliss to the monarchy, I'm watching matrimonial disaster. I've had it. I thought I was bitter in the human realm, but this ordeal has taken me to a whole new level of resentment.

Why do so many take love for granted? If I were corporeal, I'd love the shit out of someone. I'd take care of that love. I certainly wouldn't toss aside someone's love to have secret trysts in my bedroom.

It's early afternoon, and I'm standing in one of the prince's studies where he's set to have tea with the princess soon. Their conversations lately have been stilted and uncomfortable, although that's mostly because of Princess Soora's lack of talking.

The prince, of course, acts as unmoved as ever, even though he knows she knows. I think he might be some kind of sociopath. Sometimes, it almost seems as if he likes rubbing his indiscretions in her face, like he's daring her to say something. She doesn't.

I seriously consider leaving several times. I've even gotten so far as to fly out of the palace, but I keep coming back. I don't know why. It's not like I can do anything at this point.

The prince arrives in the study first, followed by another high fae. He's around the prince a lot. I think he might be his advisor, although I don't know his name. He's slightly older, with a pointy chin and cheekbones that make him look harsh. He has hair the color of pine needles and light green skin. The princess still hasn't arrived, so the prince and his advisor talk about some politics. Something to do with a race of unruly fae called alven. Apparently, they've decided to try to break away from the high fae's rule. I decide I like the alven immediately.

Kitchen maids come inside the study and start setting the table for tea. One of them is a particularly pretty fae. Of course, as soon as he sees her, the prince stops the political talk and goes right over to her. His advisor pretends not to notice as he busies himself with a book from the shelf.

Prince Elphar corners the maid by the wall and soon has her giggling and blushing. But it's when he stops a second maid that I really lose it.

"Are you kidding me?"

He has them both by the wall now, probably whispering all sorts of debauched things.

I can't take it anymore. Something inside of me snaps. No. It explodes.

Screaming with all the terrible, consuming anger that's been slowly boiling inside of me, I snatch up my bow and Love

Arrows. Without hesitation, I aim and shoot. One after another. Set, pull, release, hit. Set, pull, release, hit.

Over and over and over again, all of them hitting him right in the chest. The arrows explode in puffs of black smoke, probably to match the color of his heart. I see them affecting him, but I'm too far gone to stop.

Every time I loose an arrow, my quiver fills with another. I see him shaking his head, as if trying to clear it. He stumbles away from the maids, but I keep aiming for him. I see two of his guards rush over to him.

His advisor shouts something, but I don't hear anything, because I'm still screaming, and I'm still shooting. I hate him. I hate everything he does to love. I hate how many people love him, when he doesn't deserve it at all. I hate everyone I've ever watched ruin love and take it for granted.

The prince has a murderous look on his face, and the next thing I know, he's standing up with his arms raised and sending a hurtling blast of high fae magic right in my direction.

The power smashes into me.

Not through me. *Into* me.

I *feel* it.

Prince Elphar's immense power crashes into me, and I career backwards, hitting the wall behind me like a rock. A loud crack fills my ears as I crumple to the ground, my bow and quiver crunching beneath me.

Taking a painful breath, I shake my head to try to clear it. That's when I realize that my hands are touching the floor. I can feel pieces of splintered wood and broken glass stuck to my palms.

I push against the floor and try to stand, but my limbs are shaky, the weight of my body completely foreign to me. I manage to stand on unsteady legs as I stare wide-eyed at my now solid body. There are sparks of white light crackling beneath my skin, running up and down my limbs like lightning bolts.

"Holy shit," I whisper.

I realize people are shouting. I look up to see the fae prince staring right at me. "You can see me?" I ask.

My voice cracks, my throat raw and new. I look toward the doorway and see Princess Soora standing there, gaping at me. By the look on her face, I know she saw everything.

The prince snaps me back to attention when he shouts, "Guards! Arrest her!"

Oh, shit.

The guards across the room run for me. I don't waste any time turning to the doorway to make a getaway, but the princess is blocking my way. In a split second, I see her make a very deliberate decision as she takes an intentional step to the left to let me pass.

Relief washes over me, but I don't have time to stop and thank her. I launch myself out of the room and skid into the open corridor. My legs don't work properly, and I stumble several steps, but I can't stop going, because they'll catch me and probably kill me. They probably don't take kindly to people attacking the prince.

I reach the stairs just as one of the guards makes it into the corridor. My inexperienced feet falter on the steps, and I fall and go rolling all the way down the marble stairs, landing in a painful heap at the bottom. The only good thing about my fall is that it's given me a head start from the other guards, but they're already running down the steps after me.

I scramble to my feet and rush to the end of the corridor. I hear shouting as more guards start coming at me from downstairs, too. I'll be surrounded in seconds. I can't go that way, and even if I could, I wouldn't be able to handle going down another set of stairs, anyway. My legs are too new, my balance too inexperienced. But, seeing the window at the end of the corridor, I hope that maybe I can fare better with my wings. I trip again, my legs shaking with exertion, and I slam into the wall.

The guards are just a step behind me now. I hear a shout, and I know they're reaching for me, but I take one more running step even as my legs wobble and falter. With all the strength my legs have left, I jump and launch myself through the window. Glass shatters all around me, cutting into my arms, legs, and wings, and then I'm falling.

And falling.

And falling.

And falling.

CHAPTER 8

*O*f course, the window I launched myself out of just happened to be at the very edge of the floating island. It couldn't have been one that conveniently opened up to a nice grassy garden, oh no.

Nope, I watch helplessly as the castle and then the base of the island whizzes past. Wind whips around me, tangling my hair and pushing against my skin as if it wants to punish me.

I look back and try to flex my wings, but I realize how much harder they are to control now that they're corporeal. Of course, I would realize this *after* I've already jumped through a window.

I grit my teeth and strain to stretch them out. My back muscles scream in protest, but I somehow manage to do it. The wind catches them instantly, and I'm yanked sideways.

I try to straighten myself out, but I can't get the hang of it, and I start to spin sickeningly fast. The kingdom's floating island is already far above me. I can see other floating islands all around, too, but I have no hope of reaching any of them if I can't learn how to fly in my new physical body.

I scream into the air in frustration as I continue to rotate, my stomach ready to heave. I flap my arms out to my sides and force my wings to spread further out, even as the muscles in my back burn with an agonizing tightness. I spread my legs out straight and clench my teeth in concentration.

I feel the air pushing at me relentlessly, wanting to control me, wanting to blow me wherever it wants, but I know that if I don't stop falling, I will either fall forever or crash to my death. I don't like either of those options.

With another ear-splitting scream that burns my throat, I lift my wings and flap against the punishing wind.

Up, down. Up, down. Up, down.

Finally, I manage to stop spinning, and I straighten out. I've been falling for a long time now, and the kingdom island is no longer in view. At least there's that.

I turn forward again and am relieved when I see an island far below. I know I can't fly for much longer, because my muscles are screaming, and my wings feel weak, so I flap toward it with all the strength that I have left.

All I can see are green trees. No cities, no houses. It's a much smaller island, maybe only about a tenth of the size of the kingdom island, and with a lurch, I recognize it immediately. The island where I saw the three very kissable sexy tail-guys.

I fly-fall toward the trees as I near the island. I know I need to slow down, but I don't know how. I keep trying to flap, but my muscles are shaking so badly now that they don't want to lift anymore. A cry wrenches from my throat as I try, but it's no use.

My wings can't hold me anymore or fight against the incessant gravity that is so new to them. I watch as the ground comes closer and closer. Just before I hit the line of trees, I see something whizz toward me. I scream as an arrow pierces through my right wing.

I fall.

And fall.

And fall.

I'm really sick of falling.

I crash into the trees. Every branch that hits me on the way down is like a punishing whip. I try to tuck my wings in, but I scream again because the arrow is still stuck in it, and every movement is agony. I feel every scratch that cuts into me as the branches flay me from all directions. The trees rip me apart, and yet every bit of resistance helps to slow me down.

Talk about a silver lining. It's barely silver. More like really, really, really dark gray.

Just when I'm sure I can't take any more of a beating, I crash to the ground. I land on my arms and knees, tucked into a ball, and my chin slams against the dirt, jarring my teeth together. Whoa. Being corporeal hurts.

I roll over onto my back and stay there breathing, feeling every ounce of pain as it ripples through me. I can't move my wings, and I can't reach where the arrow pierced me, either. All I can see are black dots that swim in front of me, and my heart hammers against my chest so hard that I'm sure it's about to explode.

My vision is just beginning to clear when hands pounce on me. In a split second, multiple sets are holding me down. As if I'm in any condition to move. But the moment their hands touch my skin, something happens.

The strange white lightning that has been stuck under my skin ever since the prince launched his magical attack on me suddenly transfers to the people pinning me down. There's a painful jolt at their touch, and then the hands snatch away from me.

"What did you do to us?" one of the voices above me yells.

I blink several times to rid the blurry tears from my eyes, trying to make sense of his words. When my vision clears, I see them.

The three guys that I first saw when I came to this realm. It's

First, Second and Third. The sexy tail-guys in all their gorgeous, muscled glory. They're staring down at me with fierce scowls.

"You can see me?" I ask shakily, because I need to know for sure.

My mind realizes that they touched me, that they're looking at me, but I need to hear them say it. My heart is in my throat as I wait for an answer. Whatever the prince did to me, it's surely about to end and I'll go invisible and unfeeling again.

It would be my luck to be turned physical only to fall down stairs, trip over my feet, crash through a window, plummet through the sky, be hit by an arrow, and then crash through trees and fall to the ground before turning intangible again.

Seriously. I'm waiting for it.

"What did you do to us?" Third asks.

"What?" I croak.

Sexy strong First grabs my face so that his thumb and fingers are clamped down on my jaw. It's not very polite.

"What. Did. You. Do?"

I swallow because he looks crazy scary. "I-I didn't do anything."

His grip digs into me painfully, but Second leans forward. The nice one. You can just tell he's nice by the look in his brown eyes. Except he doesn't look so nice right now.

"Something happened when we touched you," he explains.

He lifts a hand, and I see that the strange crackling light that had been under my skin is now beneath theirs. After a moment, I watch as it fizzles out. "What did you do?"

"I don't know," I say, watching as his palm returns to normal. "I don't know what that was."

It's difficult to talk with my jaw being held, so I jerk my face out of First's grip.

"I say we tie her up," First says to the others.

"What?" I squeak. "Tie me up? For what?"

He ignores me. Okay, so Mister Strong and Sexy is a jerk. Surprise, surprise.

I snap my fingers in front of his face to get his attention. Except I can't really snap since I've never done it before, so my fingers make a weird, fumbling motion minus the sound. Still, it makes First look back down at me, so that's a win.

"Hey. I asked you a question. Tie me up for what? I don't want to be tied up," I tell him. Then I consider it. "Well, unless it's for, like, some hot bondage-type stuff. I might be okay with that. Except you'll have to go easy on me for the first time. I'm new at all this. Plus I'm injured. We'll need a safe word. How about pineapple?" Because it's always pineapple.

I'm rambling, right? I think I'm rambling. Ouch, I hurt everywhere.

He just stares at me. And stares. And stares. Someone whistles under his breath.

"Bloody hell," Third says with a salacious smirk. "Where you been all my life?"

"Shut up," First snaps at him. "She's an enemy. We're tying her up and then I'll interrogate her. We'll get answers by any means necessary."

Whoa. So definitely not the fun kind of tying up, then.

Well, in that case, he's definitely not the first one I'd kiss anymore. He's just dropped himself right into last place.

Asshole.

When he turns to look at the others, I notice that he has a quiver and bow strapped to his back.

I gasp in outrage. "*You* shot me with an arrow!"

He turns and glares down at me. "You were infiltrating our island."

I narrow my eyes. "*Infiltrating?* What is this, a war zone? I was *falling.* I couldn't help where I landed."

"Sure," he says, as if he doesn't believe me at all.

Yep. He's definitely in last place.

I try to roll over, but even that is too much, and I end up stuck on my side, breathing through the pain as my head spins. Damn.

Third kneels in front of me. His eyes run up and down over me, assessing. "What are you?"

I hear First scoff behind me. "Isn't it obvious? She's a demon."

I whip my head around to glare at him. "Excuse me? I am *not* a demon!"

"You have red wings."

"They're feathered," I counter defensively. "Demons don't have feathers, and their wings are black. Besides, I have pink hair. Have you ever seen a demon with pink hair?"

First crosses his massive arms in front of him. "I'm seeing one now."

I open my mouth to tell him off when Third cuts across me. "What are you?" he asks again.

"What does it matter?" I snap. "You've shot me with an arrow, and now you're going to tie me up. I haven't done anything to any of you. You can all go to hell."

First snorts. "Spoken like a true demon."

"Enough, Ronak," Second says.

I give First—Ronak—a triumphant look. "Yeah, enough," I say, glad to finally get someone who's talking some sense. "You're not first anymore."

He scowls down at me. "What?"

"You were first, but that was before I knew you were such a giant ass. You're definitely not first anymore. I strip you of the honor. I'll call you Not-First from now on."

Not-First—Ronak—stares at me like I'm insane and then lets out a long-suffering sigh. "What's she spewing about?"

Third smirks. "I like her."

"Nobody asked you," Not-First snaps.

"Fuck off, Ronak."

"Yeah, fuck off, Not-First," I add.

All three of them frown at me. Whoops. I guess I'm not allowed to say that.

Second pinches the bridge of his nose and closes his eyes, like he's really trying to keep the situation under control. "Could you two not start?" he says to them. He opens his eyes to look back at me. "What are you talking about with Ronak being first?"

I begin to explain their ranking. "First, Second, Third," I say, pointing to each one of them in correct order. "Except *he's* not in first place anymore," I say, pointing back at Ronak. "His attitude is deplorable."

"You put us in order?" Third asks, his lips twitching up to betray his amusement.

"Of course."

Seriously, who wouldn't?

"In order of what?"

I open my mouth to tell them about my kissing order, but stop myself just in time. "Wouldn't you like to know," I taunt.

Second sighs. "Okay, okay. We aren't getting anywhere, and she's bleeding all over our island. Evert, help me pick her up. We'll take her to the cabin and see to her wounds."

"Are you out of your mind?" Ronak snaps. "She's an enemy."

"Oh, screw off," Third says. "Do you ever pull the stick out of your ass?"

Not-First glares back at him like he wants to melt his face off.

Second gets between them before things can escalate. He's obviously the peacekeeper of the group. "Look at her, Ronak," he says quietly. "She's weak and hurt. She's not going anywhere. I don't think she's like the other ones."

That has me perking up, despite the pain I'm in. "What other ones?" I ask.

I don't get an answer. Does he mean other cupids? No, that doesn't make sense. But then what does he mean?

"What's your name?" Second asks.

Well, if they won't answer my questions, I won't answer theirs.

I raise my chin in a show of obstinacy. "I don't have a name, but I wish I did just so that I could refuse to give it to you," I snap.

Third laughs. "Yep. I was right. I do like her."

"Shut the fuck up, Evert!" Ronak snarls.

"Get her back and tie her up. Now." He turns and stalks away, the bow and quiver slapping against his massive back as he stomps away from us.

Third—Evert—rolls his eyes. "You really going along with this?"

Second sighs. "You know how this looks, Evert. Maybe Ronak's right—"

"Yeah, I'm gonna stop you right there, because right and Ronak don't go together."

"You're just arguing for the sake of arguing," Second says quietly. "No matter what Ronak would have said, you would've taken the opposite side, like you always do."

Third just shrugs at the accusation, like that's exactly what he'd do, and he doesn't give a damn who knows it.

"Don't be like this. Ronak could be right about her. When has someone come to our island that didn't mean us harm? Never," he says, answering his own question. "In all the years we've been here, there's never been one person or creature that was sent here unless it was to hurt us. Be smart about this."

"Smart? Is that what you are for kissing his ass?"

"I don't kiss his ass. I just don't hold a grudge like you."

This would all be terribly fascinating if, you know, I wasn't bleeding out and curled up in agony. "Can you guys argue later?

Whatever you're going to do, just do it. Everything hurts," I grit out between clenched teeth.

That brings their attention back to me. "Help me bring her back to the cabin," Second says, coming forward.

Third—Evert—sighs. "If it was up to me, I'd take you back to my bed and tie you up under very different circumstances, but it seems I'm overruled," he says, making my heart do this weird flip-flop thing. "So just try and be a good little enemy bird, won't you?"

I have no idea what to say to that.

CHAPTER 9

*S*econd and Third kneel on either side of me. Evert slips an arm on one side of my back, while Second slips his arm around my other side. Together, they heft me in the air, each of them taking a side, supporting me under my armpits and thighs.

I cry out when Second jostles my hurt wing, and he grimaces before catching himself. See? He's the nice one, even if he's trying to hide it.

Despite me being dubbed Enemy Number One, they carry me carefully, their matching strides long and even and surprisingly smooth for their bulky size.

I realize that the reason the two of them are carrying me instead of just one is because they don't want to move my wings. That's...oddly thoughtful of them, considering the vastly different vibes I keep getting.

Still, even with them being careful, the gravity pulling at my heavy wings is painful in more ways than one. I can't tuck my wings in either, because of the arrow. Damn Not-First for shooting me. If I had my bow and arrow, I'd shoot him right in the ass.

Despite the pain I'm in, I can't help but be desperately aware of their touch. Where their callused fingers hold under my arms and legs, my skin tingles and jumps, like my nerves are overexcited puppies. I'm pretty sure my thighs would try to melt in their hands if they could. Even my armpits are excited about being touched. Who knew being hoisted up by the pits could feel so good?

When Second moves his hand to get a better grip on my thigh, I nearly shudder. If I weren't in pain and bleeding, I'd grab that hand and rub myself on it like a cat. Speaking of cats, I look over his shoulder and stare at his wheat-colored tail with the blond tuft at the end. It's trailing behind him, flipping back and forth every so often like it's bored.

Third's tail is sleek and black, with a tuft of thicker black fur on the end. I really want to grab one and see what they feel like, maybe rub my cheek against it. Hmm, would that be a social faux pas? I stop myself from doing anything crazy—like reaching back and yanking on one—and decide to study their faces instead.

Third—Evert—has black hair and stormy blue eyes. Like the others, his jaw is covered in a thick beard that makes him look rugged and sexy. But on his cheeks, pretending to hide under his beard, are the sexiest dimples I have ever seen.

Oh, gods, those dimples. I want to reach up and poke my tongue in the indent.

Honestly, I don't know what I was thinking making him Third. He's definitely first place material. Plus, you know, he's the only one who seems to not think I'm some crazed enemy sent here to lead them to their demise.

When he notices me looking at him, he shoots me a smirk, putting one of those dimples on display, and I swear, my whole body flushes.

"You keep looking at me like that, and we might not make it back to the cabin after all."

"Evert," Second scolds.

Second has blond hair that glistens in the sun and those nice brown eyes of his. His skin has a dark, healthy tan, and he's slightly smaller in build than the others. Everything about him gives off a calm, friendly vibe.

"What's your name, Second?" I ask.

He arches a brow at me before answering, "Sylred."

"Sylred," I taste the word on my tongue. "I like it," I say.

"You gonna tell us why you ranked us yet?" Third asks.

"No. But I have to tell you, things aren't looking good, what with the decision to tie me up and all."

"So basically what you're saying is that I'm your new favorite."

"Definitely," I say with complete seriousness.

He flashes me that full-dimpled smile, and I'm ready to bow down before him and declare myself his sex nymph if he'll just keep looking at me like that.

Also, sidenote, I've seen the real fae nymphs. They really are obsessed with sex. It's all they do and talk about. Even I got sick of them after a couple of days. And they aren't what you'd call attractive, either. They're tiny, made up of mostly skin and bones, and have faces like bats. So yeah, pretty disappointing overall.

We're still walking through the forest, and even though I know they're being as gentle as possible, the jostling is starting to make all my aches and pains even worse.

Then I feel something. On my arm. My itch.

I shriek loudly, nearly making Evert and Sylred drop me. Their tails flick around and they crouch into a protective stance, trying to see where the threat lies. But I'm too busy staring at my arm to reassure them.

Without taking my eyes off my arm, I bring my hand to the spot that has plagued me for decades. I curl my fingers and drag my nails across my skin.

"Oh. My. Gods."

I tilt my head back in complete ecstasy and flutter my eyelids shut. I finally, finally, *finally* can scratch this motherfucking itch. And it's *amazing.*

"What the hell?" Evert says.

But I don't answer him. I am in my own little itch-fantasy world.

I keep scratching, and high heavens, does it feel good. I scratch and scratch and scratch. I make that itch my bitch.

"Umm, do you have a rash or something?" Sylred asks.

I finally look up at them, still perched in their arms, and both pairs of eyes are watching me with confusion.

I laugh. "You have no idea how long I've waited to scratch this itch."

Sylred clears his throat and nods at my arm. "Uh, okay," he says, drawing out the word. "But you're making your skin raw."

I wave a hand at him dismissively. Raw shmaw. Who cares? I'm finally rid of the itch! I keep going.

"Alright, Scratch, I think you got it," Evert says.

I realize right then that it is sort of hurting, so I reluctantly stop scratching. Very reluctantly. My skin is bright red with fingernail tracks, and I've peeled a layer of the skin away. But the itch is gone. Gone! That's all that matters.

I shrug and put my hands back in my lap, poised and ready for the guys to continue carrying me. "As you were," I say as politely as a princess. Evert snorts as they start walking me again.

"Don't think I'm not watching you, itch. You come back and I'll be all over you like rain in a puddle," I say to my arm.

Evert grins. "She's talking to her itch."

Sylred's lips twitch. "So I heard."

"Maybe she's daft?"

I laugh, but then I realize that's probably what a crazy

person would do, so I quickly stop. The guys shake their heads at me.

"Are we almost there? My wing hurts," I tell them, and yes, my voice is a bit whiny, but it can't be helped. I've had a very taxing day.

They don't answer, but a few minutes later, we break into a clearing, and I see a large cabin before us. It's made of the same wood as the forest trees, and it looks somewhat crude, with uneven cuts, branches and dried mud for a roof, and a door made of tree branches. The windows are covered with ropes of vines, and there's a chimney jutting from the side made of stacked stones.

"Did you all...build this?"

"Yes."

"Wow," I say, impressed.

But then Mister Not-First-Anymore-Because-He's-A-Big-(not fat)-Jerk-Who-Shot-Me steps out from behind a tree with a rope in his hands, and my stomach falls. I guess they weren't kidding about the whole tying up thing.

Not-First points to a tree nearby, and I see Second and Third share a look before they set me down, putting my back to the tree. Ronak wastes no time coming over to start wrapping the rope around me.

"Hey!"

He ignores me, continuing to tie me up to the tree, and I'm forced to stop struggling because my wing and shoulder are killing me.

"I didn't do anything!" I tell him. It falls on deaf ears. "Why are you doing this?" I ask, my voice catching.

Second—Sylred—stands behind Not-First with his mouth turned down. "Is this really necessary? She's a female and she's injured."

"Quiet," Ronak snaps.

Apparently, it's not up for discussion.

"Typical," Evert mutters under his breath. "I'm out of this."

With that, Third turns around and stalks away, disappearing from sight. Guess I just lost my ally.

Ronak pulls on the rope, ensuring it's tight enough that I can't escape. Then he sits back on his heels and stares hard. "What are you?"

He's tied me so that my hands are caught in my lap, and my back is held against the rough bark of the tree without an inch of give.

"You shot me with an arrow, and now you're tying me up like a prisoner. Why would I tell you anything?"

"Because if you don't, that arrow in your wing will be the least of your problems."

"You enjoy hurting a defenseless female?"

"I'll bet your wings that you aren't defenseless," he replies, unconcerned. "But whatever plan you have against us won't work."

At this moment, he has no idea how wrong he is about me not being defenseless, although I'd never admit it. I'm completely at his mercy. If he was a bit closer, I might be able to breathe some Lust his way, but even if it could reach him, it wouldn't work unless he felt at least a sliver of desire for me, and considering the hatred that burns in his black eyes, I highly doubt it.

Besides, I don't even know if my cupid powers still work with me like this. I don't want to test it out with an audience. I might need it later, and the element of surprise is good to have on my side.

"Who sent you?"

"Your mother."

Not-First takes hold of my injured wing and yanks. Hard. I cry out and try to kick him, but he pins my legs under his and pulls me forward until our faces are only inches apart.

From this close, I can see now how black his eyes really are;

it's like looking down into a bottomless pit. I can't help the tears that trickle out of my eyes from the pain in my wing. Hate burns through me, and I swear, if I had something to stab him with, I wouldn't hesitate.

"Now you listen to me," he says in a low voice. "You will tell me what you are, who sent you, and what you're doing here."

I grit my teeth in both pain and hate. "Let. Go."

"Ronak..." Sylred says from behind him.

Not-First ignores him. "Tell me now," he orders me, letting go of my wing with a painful lurch.

I know I've lost. I'm in terrible pain all over, my body is way too new to be effective in any sort of escape, and there's no way I can get out of these bindings. But I hate him so much that even though I know he has all the power over me, I won't give him what he wants. Why should I?

I turn my head away from him, refusing to answer. Ronak stands up and looms over me, but I don't look at him. I try to make myself stop crying, but the throbbing pain in my wing along with the emotional stress won't let the tears stop falling.

"Fine. You can rot here, tied to this tree, until you're ready to confess."

I snort derisively. Confess. As if I have anything to confess to. Idiot.

Without warning, I take a deep breath and then scream for help at the top of my lungs. Not-First just laughs cruelly, cutting my shrieks short.

He looks down at me with contempt. "Scream all you want, demon. There's no one on this gods-forsaken island but us."

Ronak turns on his heels and stomps away into the forest. I turn to glare at Second, no longer caring that tear tracks stain my face.

"Better go follow your master like a good little kitty."

Sylred tenses. "Ronak is not my master."

"Really? Could've fooled me the way you jump when he

snaps his fingers. Looks like Evert was right. Will you help him torture me later, too? Or will your kitty paws be too busy kneading his back?"

I know I shouldn't antagonize him, but I can't help myself. Third revealed the issues between them, and I'm going to exploit it.

"Let me remove the arrow," Sylred said, kneeling in front of me.

"Don't touch me."

Surprised, he holds his hands up in a placating gesture. "I was just..."

"I don't care. Don't try to do the bare minimum to pacify your guilty conscience. Go away."

Sylred stares at me for a moment, his lips in a thin line, and then nods tersely. He turns and walks to the cabin, tail swishing behind him.

Their cabin is at least a hundred feet away, and the way I'm angled, I can see the side of it and the front door, and I watch as he disappears inside. As soon as he does, I start looking on the ground for anything sharp—a stick, a rock, anything—but there's nothing but grass and dirt.

My wing hurts, and now that the adrenaline is leaving me, I can tell just how banged up I really am. There's a sharp pain in my shoulder that rivals the arrow in my wing, and I have too many scrapes, bruises, and cuts to count. Plus, my muscles hurt. The strain from suddenly turning corporeal and having a physical body is intense.

"Great. This is just great," I mutter to myself. "Out of all the islands to crash land on, it has to be the one where people would tie me to a tree."

I can hear their voices inside the cabin. If Not-First was telling the truth about there being no one else on this island, I wonder what the reason is. Three guys on an island all alone, without any of the world's comforts. There must be a reason for

it. I don't know what type of fae they are. I haven't seen anyone else with tails like them.

I settle back against the rough bark, wincing when a particularly jagged piece presses into my hip. I carefully curl my good arm behind me to feel for it and realize that it's a pretty good size piece of bark.

I quickly start to work it, trying to peel it off. If it's strong and sharp enough, maybe I can use it to shred through the rope.

It's slow going. I don't have a lot of range that I can move, and every time I peel it one way, it inevitably digs into my back. But I keep working it back and forth, trying to pull it free. It's not like I have anything better to do, anyway.

I seriously regret not letting Sylred take the arrow out now. Call it a flare of my stupid cupid stubbornness. What was I thinking? I'm not meant for pain and captivity. I'm a cupid. I wasn't made for this crap. I don't have the best sense of time since I've never had to go by it, but the light from the sun has grown dim by the time I get the piece of bark free, and my shoulder is no longer just throbbing. It's killing me.

The pain in my wing has also amped up, but no matter how I try to maneuver my body against the bindings, I can't reach the arrow to pull it out. Even if one of the guys came out right now and gave me the perfect opportunity to stab this piece of bark in their eye, I wouldn't have the strength to do it.

Somehow, despite the pain, or perhaps because of it, I slump against the tree and fall asleep.

CHAPTER 10

"*W*ake up."

My eyes snap open, and I jerk my neck upright, only to get a painful twinge from the awkward way my head has been lolled to the side all night.

I look up and see Sylred kneeling in front of me. In the early morning light, his blond hair shines. His brown eyes take in my condition, and his lips draw into a grim line.

When I try to shift my weight, I realize that someone wrapped a heavy fur pelt over me sometime in the night. Probably Sylred, but Evert is a possibility, too.

Sylred moves it off of me and then reaches to his leather belt and pulls out a knife. I automatically flinch back.

Sylred catches the movement and pauses, his brown eyes softening. "I'm not going to hurt you."

I try to swallow, but my tongue sticks to the roof of my dry mouth. "I'm already hurt," I croak out.

I'm still clutching the piece of bark that I pried off, and I hide it under my arm. Sylred grabs a part of the rope and starts cutting through my bindings. As soon as his blade is through it, he starts unwrapping me.

"What are you doing, Syl?" Evert asks, coming up behind him.

Sylred shakes his head to himself. "This is not how we treat females."

"No shit," Evert replies, crossing his arms in front of him. "Where'd dickhead go?"

"Hunting."

"Good," he says with a nod. "He's going to be pissed."

Sylred sighs. "Yeah."

Evert smirks. "Well, I'm in. You know I'll take every opportunity to piss him off."

Sylred doesn't reply to that but finishes releasing me. Then he gathers me in his arms—as if I weigh nothing—and carries me toward the cabin. The sudden pull of gravity on my hurt wing causes me to cry out.

"Come on, Evert. You can heal her."

"Why do you think I came out here in the first place?"

Sylred carries me inside the cabin. The inside is lighter than I thought it would be, with sunlight streaming in through the windows. The fireplace is crackling with flames, and there are pieces of handmade furniture scattered around the large room. There's a large pot of water on a wooden table, three chairs in different styles, and a large bench in front of the fire. There are also fur pelts scattered around the wooden floor. At the far end of the room are three doors made with the same leaves and branches as the front entry.

I'm amazed at everything that has so clearly been made by their hands, because it is both rough and yet perfect in its simplicity.

Carefully, Sylred sets me down on the fur pelt that sits in front of the fire. I grimace at the movement, but Sylred doesn't let me go, because I'd surely be too weak to hold myself upright. Instead, he keeps his arm around my back, under my wings, and lets me lean on him.

"Are those your rooms?"

"Why?" Evert says, coming up to my other side. "Already wanting to visit us in our bedrooms, Scratch?"

"No. You wish," I scoff as if it's the most ridiculous thing I've ever heard. I try to shift my arm, but the movement brings me a hiss of pain that radiates up my arm.

"I think you dislocated your shoulder," Sylred says. "And we need to take that arrow out of your wing."

I groan. "Okay."

Sylred looks at Evert and nods once. I feel Evert come up behind me and take hold of my injured wing. I close my eyes tight.

"Okay, Scratch," Evert says. "One...two..." Without finishing his count, he snaps the end of the arrow and then rips it cleanly from my wing.

I cry out in pain and bite my lip so hard that I draw blood. I can taste its coppery tang as it fills my mouth. I realize that it's the first thing I've ever tasted. All I can focus on is the blood in my mouth and the stabbing pain in my wing, but after a few moments, I feel a strong hand rubbing the back of my neck. Up and down, down and up. It's steady and sure and makes me shiver in pleasure. I try to focus on the movement of that hand instead of the angry pain in my wing.

When I open my eyes, I realize that I'm crying again. It seems like I've done way too much of that since becoming physical. Being alive is brutal.

Tears slide down my cheeks, and I can feel each one as they trail down my skin. They're so soft—like wet whispers—and when I lick my bloodied lip again, the taste is now mingled with salt.

"I need to set her shoulder," Evert says. "Syl?"

Sylred braces me in his hold and gives a quick nod.

"Wait—" I begin, but with one excruciating *pop*, Evert snaps my shoulder back into place.

I scream.

It hurts so horribly bad that my vision bubbles with darkness. I collapse against Sylred, my head lolling to the side.

I'm sobbing now. My whole face feels like it's been filled up with thick, syrupy tears, and my head throbs with them.

Still, that hand rubs my neck. Up and down, down and up. When my thundering heart calms, I can hear Sylred whispering in my ear. "There, there. It's alright. It's all over."

He croons soothing words to me, his voice soft and kind. I'm still crying, because I can't help it. Maybe if I hadn't been unfeeling for so many decades, I would be tougher. But I've never felt pain before today and yesterday, and it's all so overwhelming.

"I'm going to lay you down now so Evert can heal your wounds."

Sylred takes extra care with my injured wing as he gently brings my body down so that I'm flush against the fur on the floor. He keeps a hand on my arm and runs his fingers up and down it, continuing his sweet distraction. The pleasure of his touch mixed with the pain of my wounds is almost too much to bear.

"Gods, I never knew this is what it meant to feel," I admit in a sob-sodden whisper.

"What do you mean?" Sylred asks, pausing his ministrations.

"Feeling. Touching. It's so…intense."

He and Evert exchange a look. They probably think I've gone crazy. Maybe I have. I should probably shut up and stop talking, but the sensory overload seems to have unhinged my jaw.

Evert kneels beside me and touches my wing again. I can't see him, but I feel a tug on the arrow wound. It's not pleasant, but it isn't painful, either. It's a strange pulling sensation.

"What are you doing?"

"He's healing you."

"Do I need stitches?"

Evert chuckles. "I am the Stitch."

In a few moments, the tug on my wing fades away, and then he's moving his hands over the rest of my injured body.

When he moves in front of me where I can see, I watch with wide eyes as he gently touches every cut and scrape. Everywhere he touches, my skin stitches together, healing completely and leaving only dried blood and bruises behind. My mouth drops open in surprise.

He pauses when he gets to my hand, which still clutches the piece of bark. "What's this? Planning on giving us splinters, Scratch?" he asks, his lips twitching.

"I was hoping I could jam it into Not-First's eyeball."

Evert laughs and moves on to heal my legs. Everywhere he touches, my skin tingles, and I don't think it's just from the healing. He touches my face next, and I can feel the scrapes there start to heal with the same tugging feeling as before.

I look up at his face and see his blue eyes lock onto mine. Our faces are only inches apart, and I can feel his breath against my cheek. My heart does a somersault when he brings his finger up to touch my sore lip. He traces his finger across it, pulling it away bloody.

"We can't have these pretty lips hurt," he says quietly.

He gently grazes his index finger along my lower lip to heal it, and my eyes flutter closed at the intimate contact. I feel it stitching together even as he continues to trace his finger across my mouth. And then, I'm embarrassed to admit, a moan slips out of me.

Yeah, a moan. I can't help it. His touch feels amazing. If he can do that to me with a single finger, just imagine what the rest of him can do.

"Enough, Evert," Sylred says.

You know, because I'm the enemy and all that.

Suddenly Evert's finger is gone, and I open my eyes with a frown. "No, not enough, Evert," I counter.

Evert laughs and sits back on his heels. "Maybe you really are a demon," he says, his eyes studying my face. "A too-beautiful, too-tempting demon enchantress, sent here to ruin us once and for all."

Again with the demon talk. It really kills the mood. But I'll use it if I have to. I lick my bottom lip slowly, watching with satisfaction as Evert's gaze follows the movement.

"If I were, would you let me? Ruin you?" I ask quietly.

I know exactly what I'm doing. My seductive tone, my suggestive words. I'm a cupid, after all. I pretty much specialize in lusty language. You better believe I'm going to use that to my advantage, too.

Evert grimaces and looks over at Sylred. "This is a test from the gods. I haven't seen a female in five years, and this is what lands on our island? Tell me you aren't thinking the same thing."

Sylred glares at him.

"Fine, fine." Evert waves a hand at him. "I'll go get water. *You* watch her," Evert says. "And good luck with that," he adds with a chuckle.

Evert stands and walks out the door. My lips are still tingling from his touch, and I notice how much better the rest of my body feels, too. The pain from the arrow in my wing is completely gone. As for the rest of my injuries, all that's left is the aches in my muscles and joints, and the painful pulse of my reset shoulder. I try to sit up, and my head swims with the effort. I groan, clenching my eyes closed tight.

"Easy," Sylred says, grabbing my arm again. "Let me help you."

After a few seconds, my head stops spinning. I look down at my bloodied and dirty body, but even under all that grime, I can see that every scrape and scratch that I had is now healed over.

"Wow," I breathe. Even my lip is smooth and unhurt.

"Yeah, that's why his nickname is Stitch."

"He can heal anything?"

"No, he can just stitch flesh back together again. But he does it so well now that he doesn't even leave behind a scar. His magic couldn't have healed your shoulder, though. That's why he had to pop it back into place himself."

"Do all of you have powers?"

Sylred nods slowly but doesn't elaborate. I have a feeling he doesn't want to tell me, but I ask anyway. "What can you do?"

He doesn't answer me. I guess they don't want the maybe-enemy knowing their secrets.

"So you and Third, I mean Evert, you're the nice ones."

This forces the corner of his lips to tilt up. "The nice ones?"

I nod and wave my hand to the direction of the doors. "Yeah. Not-First is the asshole of the group."

Sylred laughs despite himself, and it lights up his whole face, making his eyes crinkle at the sides. It's incredibly sexy.

"Do you think you can stand?"

I have no idea. "Yeah, *of course* I can stand."

With a grip on my waist, he helps lift me to my feet. I wobble, but he steadies me. I can feel the gentleness of his touch through my dress. It's making me all sorts of worked up. Good gods, I'm sensitive.

"Okay?"

No. I'll fall down soon, that's for sure. "Yep, yes. Definitely."

He smiles and lets go, and I'm proud of myself when I manage to keep standing on my own. For about two seconds.

Sylred catches me before my knees hit the floor. "Whoa there."

I huff out in frustration, but he just swoops me into his arms in one fluid motion.

"Yeah, this is better for sure. I should just hire a professional carrier. Then I won't have to worry about sore muscles or tripping or anything," I say.

He chuckles, and the eye crinkle returns. Gods, who knew crinkles could be so charming?

"It's not just standing, I'm terrible at running, too. I've never had to stand before yesterday, though. I can't believe I was able to run away as far as I did. But when I jumped through the window, that was probably my limit," I explain, because word vomit is a real medical condition.

Sylred stares at me incredulously. "...What?"

I snap my mouth closed. I need to get a grip on my runaway tongue. I try to think of some way to lie or distract him from this conversation, and for once, my mouth actually helps me out when I blurt, "Hey! What color are my eyebrows?"

He shakes his head slightly, like he's trying to keep the random sentences from bobbing inside his skull. "Umm... brown?" he answers like it's a question.

"Huh," I say thoughtfully. I always figured I'd be a flirty blonde-browed girl. But I can work with brunette. "Okay, what about my eyes?"

He blinks a couple of times as he stares. "Bluish? ...With some gray?"

Again, he answers like he's unsure.

"Okay, so like a coy blue," I say, envisioning it. "Not like an in-your-face-blue, not a flashy or an obnoxious blue, but like a cool, demure, understated blue. The kind of blue you have to really look at to see. I can dig that."

"Umm, okay."

I'm suddenly reminded that he's still holding me in his arms, and my hands are still wrapped around his neck. We're incredibly close, and his arms feel so solid and perfect wrapped around me that I have the strongest urge to lean forward and kiss him. I think he must sense this change in me, because he looks down at my lips and swallows. Right then, the front door swings open and Evert reappears.

He stops and smirks when he sees Sylred holding me. "Well, well, well. Isn't this interesting?"

"Shut up," Sylred says, quickly turning his head away from me. "She can barely stand."

Evert raises a mocking brow. "Sure. Win her over with that nice-guy shit later."

"So you *are* the nice ones," I say.

"He is. I'm not," Evert says. "Now come on, I filled the tub with water."

Sylred casts me one more look before turning and carrying me out of the house. We follow behind Evert, but we don't go far. At the back of the house is a garden, and at the edge of it sits a wooden tub. Sylred sets me down right beside it, but keeps a steadying hand on my arm so I don't topple.

"Time to get clean, Scratch," Evert tells me, passing over a bar of soap. It looks like it's made of animal fat and has pieces of plants inside it to make it smell nice. "I'll trade you for it," he says, motioning to the piece of bark that I'm still holding.

I don't want to give it up, but I know I really have no choice, so I grudgingly pass it over.

"There's a good little prisoner."

I roll my eyes and then study the soap. "Do you guys make everything by hand?" I ask.

"Yeah," Evert answers simply.

"Will you be alright on your own?" Sylred asks.

I have no idea. "Absolutely."

"Right. We'll just give you some privacy, then," Sylred says, letting go of me as if he can't wait to get away. "Holler if you need us. We won't be far."

"Thank you."

"Oh, and Scratch?" Evert says over his shoulder.

"Yeah?"

"Don't even *think* about trying to get away. We don't know why you're here, but we will figure it out. Ronak is out there hunting, and believe me, you don't want that asshole to find you trying to run away. If you try it, I might just let him have you."

They both walk off without waiting for me to reply.

I let out the nervous breath in my chest. "Okay then," I say to myself.

I ignore the hot and cold sexy tail males and study the tub full of water. Time for my very first bath. I'm almost tingling with anticipation. I've watched a lot of people take baths over the years, and it always seemed so awesome.

I'm gonna rock this bath. I'm gonna take the best bath this realm has ever seen. Because I'm real, and because I freaking can, dammit.

CHAPTER 11

I dip my finger into the wooden tub. I've never felt water before. It feels so...strange. I can't wait to sit in it. Now that I have a physical body, I'm excited about trying everything. I want to feel it all.

I look down and see that my silver dress is not so silver anymore. It's covered in blood, mud and grass stains, but at least it's not ripped anywhere. I got lucky in that regard.

I reach my arm around to try to unclasp it, but I realize that I can't manage it with my injured shoulder.

"Damn," I mutter.

I look down at myself, willing an idea to come where I can remove my dress without ripping it. Nothing comes to mind. This is my only dress, though, and I don't want to ruin it. I guess I'll just have to bathe with it on.

With the soap in one hand, I carefully grip the rim of the wooden tub and lift a leg into it. When my foot is securely in the water, I lift my second leg.

I fall. Of course.

With a big splash and a little squeal, I land in the tub hard. My butt smarts from my clumsy entrance, but at least I'm in.

The water bites into my skin. I don't know how else to describe it, but once the bites calm down, I notice that the water helps to soothe my sore muscles.

Having a physical body is painful.

My wings are too big to fit comfortably, so I pull them in tight against my back. My dress becomes like a second skin as it sticks to me, but I lift it up where I need to so that I can wash my entire body. I have to wash everything with one hand since moving my shoulder is a no-go.

The soap smells fresh, and every stroke against my wet skin feels so nice that I give myself shivers. When I've scrubbed off the last of the blood and dirt, I dunk my head and wash my long pink hair.

Once I'm done with that, I work the soap to wash my dress next. Might as well get the stains out of it, since it's in here with me. I can't reach my wings, so I just hope soaking in the water gets off whatever it can. After I'm satisfied that both myself and my dress are as clean as possible, I relax and lean my head against the side of the tub. I close my eyes, allowing the water to ease my tender muscles.

For a moment, I forget about Prince Elphar and how angry I was at him. I forget about poor Princess Soora. I even forget about the asshole Not-First shooting me with an arrow for flying over his island. I have wanted to have a physical body for so long that I'm having a hard time believing this is real. What the hell did the prince do to me? But more importantly, is it going to last?

I peek open an eye to make sure I'm still alone. The garden is private back here, with tall bushes and vines all around, blocking the view of the cabin. The forest surrounds it, and I can hear the breeze way high up in the trees.

When I'm sure that no one else is around, I take a deep breath and try out a Lust-Breath. I watch as my trusty cupid powers blow pink tendrils into the air.

"Yes! I still got it."

So whatever Prince Elphar did to me didn't affect my magic. That's good. Maybe I can go live in a city and open up a love shop. People can come in and pay me for a little bit of this, a little bit of that. I bet I can make a killing.

I sink even further against the tub as I daydream about all the consensual love fests I'll be starting in my super popular storefront while mountains of money roll in. Maybe I can bottle some of my Lust-Breaths and set them on a shelf? That would be efficient *and* awesome. I'll get a cat, too. One that can hang around in my shop and hiss at customers as they walk in because moody cats are hilarious. Also because the sexy males may have given me a craving to pet kitty tails.

I don't know how long I lie in the bath, but I think I must've dozed off, because the next thing I know, I'm jumping awake at the sound of a voice.

"Hey, Scratch! You awake over there?"

The water sloshes around from my startled movements as I blink the heaviness away from my eyes. Evert must see me moving because he says, "Didn't anyone ever tell you it's not a good idea to fall asleep in the tub?"

"No?"

He chuckles. I guess we're back to Nice-Guy-Evert now instead of Making-Threats-Third. "Well, now you know," he says. "I brought you a fur to wrap up in. Come out and get it when you're done. You can sit inside by the fire to dry."

My teeth chatter together. Now that I'm more awake, I notice that my body feels strange and I'm shaking all over.

"I-I'm st-still wearing my dr-dress," I manage to say through my teeth chattering. His head snaps up from his place over by the cabin's back wall. It looks like he doesn't want to come any closer to me. "You're still in...why?"

"C-couldn't get it off by my-myself."

Silence. And then a long, long sigh.

"Shit. Sylred!" I jump again at his shout.

After a moment, Sylred appears around the corner. "What?"

They're too far away for me to hear what they're saying, but they mutter back and forth to each other and cast me looks. I'm not sure what I did wrong now.

I'm still shaking, and I instinctively clasp my arms together and huddle my body close. When I touch my arms, I feel raised bumps across my skin. My nipples pucker painfully against my dress, and my teeth start chattering more and more. It's such a strange sensation, and I stare at my skin as the bumps continue to rise.

I flex my toes and fingers. They feel weird, too. Stiff. Numb.

Finally, both guys come and stand over me, trying to avert their eyes. "Okay, Scratch, Sylred is going to…"

His voice cuts off and he swears violently when he steals a glance at me. His eyes widen. "Fuck, Syl, her lips are blue!"

"Hmm?" I ask. Or at least, I think I do. My head feels fuzzy.

"Shit," Sylred says. He puts his hand in the water and then swears again. "It's freezing. Why didn't you heat the water for her?"

"We never heat the fucking water!" Evert replies defensively. "Hell, we never even use this tub except to wash clothes."

"Well, you should have heated it up for her! Help me get her out."

I feel two sets of arms dunk into the tub and their limbs wrap around me. They lift me out of the water, but as soon as the air hits me, my body shakes even more, and my teeth chatter together so violently that I think I might break a tooth.

"Get it off her, we have to get her warm."

I feel Evert's hands on my back, searching, tugging. "I'm trying! I can't find any fucking buttons or snaps or…dammit."

"Just get it off!"

"Sorry, Scratch. This wet dress has to go."

"Wha—"

In one quick movement, he rips the dress down my back and peels it from my skin. Before I can worry about my nakedness, Sylred wraps me in soft furs and lifts me up to carry me into the house. I want to put my hands around his neck to steady myself, but I can't move my limbs.

I also realize that I can't feel my fingers. Or my toes.

Maybe the prince's magic is wearing off. Maybe I'm about to go incorporeal again. The thought sends me into another shaking fit.

I rest my cheek against Sylred's chest because it feels so nice. Comforting. I want to burrow inside him. He carries me inside the cabin and sets me on the floor right in front of the fire. I lean into it, my body prickling painfully.

I continue to shake and my teeth continue to chatter. "W-What's h-h-happening t-to-to m-me?"

Evert sits down and digs out my feet from under the furs. He starts rubbing my toes while Sylred rubs my arms through the furs, up and down, down and up. He's really good at that.

"Why didn't you tell us you were so cold?" Evert asks. He sounds angry. Furious, even. "You should've gotten out of the bath much sooner, you little fool."

"C-cold?" I stutter.

Because of course, I know what cold means, but I also don't, because I've never *felt* it before. My jaw hurts from the incessant chattering, but I force myself to ask, "Th-this is wha-what c-cold fee-feels like?"

Being cold sucks. No wonder I always saw people bundling up during wintertime.

Evert gives me an incredulous look and then cups my frozen toes in his hands. At first, I don't know what he's going to do, but in the next moment, he leans over and exhales over them.

His breath is moist and close and... "Warm," he says, finishing my train of thought. "We need to get you warm, Scratch."

"She needs something dry to put on."

Evert barely stops his constant exhalations on my prickly toes to say, "Little busy here. Unless you want her toes to fall off."

I shake my head because I definitely *don't* want my toes to fall off. But I don't speak up, because I suddenly feel very, very tired. At least I think it's tired, because my eyes close and I want to fall into the darkness that lives inside that quietness. I've watched enough people over the years as their eyelids drooped and their breaths evened out to realize that's what's happening to me. I kinda just passed out last night, so I didn't really pay attention to what tiredness felt like.

I close my eyes again, and I can see the orange flames dancing behind my lids. Evert's hands continue to massage my toes, and his warm breath continues to thaw them out. It feels so nice. So...nice...

Sylred's hands clap against my cheeks, scaring me. "Stay awake," he says sternly. "Let's get you warm and dry, and then you can sleep. But not yet. Look at me."

I flutter my eyes open and force myself to focus on him. The fire feels nice, and the painful tingling sensation across my skin has started to subside.

"I need to get her dry clothes to wear. She's nearly hypothermic," Sylred says. "Don't let her nod off. I'll be right back."

Evert squeezes my toes harder than necessary as Sylred jumps up and runs into one of the bedrooms. "Stay awake, Scratch."

Sylred comes back into the room bare-chested and with a handful of clothing. Staring at his chest, I'm suddenly not sleepy anymore. Sylred is the smallest in stature of all three guys, but his skin is tan and smooth, and holy cow, every single muscle is toned and lean. I want to run my fingers over his abs and lick his navel.

"I'll hold up the furs so you can dress, okay?" Sylred asks, coming up to me.

I'm still shaking, but not as badly now. Still, I'm not sure I have the strength to dress myself. I don't even know how to dress myself, to be honest. My large wings make things tricky.

"I—I don't know…"

"I'll help her. Hold up the fur, Syl."

Evert drops my feet, and I'm immediately sorry for the loss of contact. "Ready?" Sylred asks, taking a corner of my fur in his hand.

I bite my lip nervously.

"It's alright, Scratch," Evert says. "I won't look."

I relinquish my hold on the fur, and Sylred quickly takes it away from my body and holds it up so that I'm blocked from view. I cross my arms over my chest, but Evert just picks up the clothes and lifts one of my legs. He slowly puts it through the pant leg, drawing it up to my knees, and then lifts my other leg to do the same thing.

"Let's get you to your feet so we can pull these up. Hold on to me," he says quietly.

His voice sounds different when it's quiet like this. I lean forward and wrap my uninjured arm around his neck. He lifts me to a standing position and then pulls up the pants the rest of the way. He rolls them a few times at the top and then uses a drawstring to hold them in place.

My feet are still covered in fabric, so Evert kneels down and rolls the pant cuffs, too, until my toes peek out. The pants are huge on me, but they're dry and warm, and that's what matters.

"Now the shirt. Tuck your wings in, and put your arms up." He holds a steadying hand on my waist. "I won't let you fall."

I nod and raise my arms and tuck my wings in as much as I can. As soon as I do, I'm completely vulnerable. My front is exposed to him, and I hear his breath hitch a bit, and then the scent hits me.

I don't know how to describe it except that I absolutely know it's coming from Evert, and the scent inexplicably means that he's aroused.

The aroma of his arousal permeates the air, and I'm surprised by not only how strong and pleasing it is but also that I can identify it so easily. Maybe it's one of my cupid powers that has evolved since I've become real? I have always just *known* when someone was aroused, but now that I can actually smell things, maybe this is how I've done it.

I don't know what's more exciting: this new cupid ability or the fact that I've got him so worked up. It's quite the compliment since he's super freaking hot. I close my eyes in pleasure when I feel him gently pull the fabric down my arms and then over my head. His touch is soft and sends shivers down my skin. The shirt gets stuck at my shoulder blades, right where my wings jut out.

"One second," he says quietly.

He moves behind me, and I hear the fabric of the shirt tear down the back. He comes back in front of me and pulls the shirt down the rest of the way, covering my breasts and belly. He reaches behind me and ties the torn fabric together, securing it between my wings.

When he's done, he moves his hands from the back of the shirt to hold my arms instead. I raise my eyes to his. I can feel my heartbeat quicken. He leans in closer and brushes a piece of wet hair away from my face. We're still behind the fur that Sylred holds up, and it feels like we're in our own little world.

"I lied," he whispers in my ear.

A confused frown crosses my face. "What?"

"When I said I wouldn't look. I lied."

When his words sink in, my cheeks flame with embarrassment, but I can't look away from his heated gaze.

"You are pretty fucking gorgeous."

No need for trolls. I nearly melt into a puddle of my very own steaming sex juices right here.

"You done?" Sylred asks behind the furs, breaking the spell between us.

In answer, Evert steps away from me and yanks the fur down as if nothing happened. I'm still incapable of speech.

"She still needs to sit in front of the fire. She's not in danger anymore, but she's still not warm enough."

Sylred guides me closer to the fire and sits me down. My hair is still damp, and I can feel it on my back, dripping down my spine. The fire is making my grogginess feel so much better than the cold did.

"So this is heat," I reflect, holding my cold fingers in front of the fire.

Without glancing behind me, I know that Sylred and Evert are sharing a look with each other. I can feel their unspoken questions. But they don't trust me, so I shouldn't trust them. My mouth doesn't seem to realize this, though, because the admissions keep popping out of it. I really need to work on that, now that people can actually hear me.

Evert comes closer and points at my arm. "What's that?"

I look down at the inside of my wrist where my cupid marking is. It's more noticeable in the firelight. "My number."

Evert frowns in confusion. "Your number?"

"Yeah..." I'm not sure how much to tell them, but I figure this part can't hurt. "I don't have a name, but we're assigned numbers. ML is my number. One thousand fifty."

"ML," Evert says. "Em...elle. That's what your name will be then, Scratch."

"Emelle. I like it," Sylred replies, mimicking what I said about his.

I look down at the markings. "Emelle," I say, testing it out. "You think?"

"It's better than what Ronak wants to call you," Evert says.

I frown. "Demon?"

Evert smirks and nods. "Among other things."

I sigh tiredly and shake my head. "I'm not a demon."

"Then what are you, and what the fuck is she doing inside our cabin?"

I jump at the voice behind us and whirl around. Ronak is in the doorway and has his huge, muscular arms crossed in front of his massive chest. Seriously, the guy is *big*. I could literally climb him like a tree.

I clear my throat and force myself to stand up. I stumble a bit and Sylred has to steady me, but at least I manage it. I need to stand up to face Not-First, because he's a bully and I'm pissed at him. If I had the strength to walk over to him, I'd slap his face. Probably. Maybe. I might have to jump up to reach. I might also chicken out.

Out of pure stubbornness, I refuse to admit what I am. It's the only power I have over him, and as small as it is, it's a victory for me to have something he wants and not give it to him.

"I'm *not* a demon."

"No?" he asks. He stalks toward me slowly, like he's getting ready to pounce. His steps are measured and deliberate. "You passed through an impenetrable barrier over our island," he says, surprising me. I don't know anything about a barrier. "You attacked us with magic when we touched you, and you have red wings. If you're not a demon, then what are you?"

I stand my ground and lift my chin. I hate him right now. I hate him so much, because he was the first face I saw in this realm, and my heart jumped when I saw him. I wanted to kiss him. I wanted to trace my fingers down his muscles. I wanted to rub my cheek against his rough beard. When I saw him standing there in the clearing, when his face softened with sadness in his black eyes, I thought that he was a guy I could love. I saw the vulnerability hiding behind his strength, and I wanted to kiss him and make it all better.

But that view I had of him was a lie. A fantasy. He's an ass, and he's mean, and he shot me out of the sky. And I'm going to give him a piece of my mind.

"You're either too dumb or too deaf to understand, but do your best to pay attention, Not-First," I snap. "I'm not a demon. I don't know anything about a barrier, but I fell because I couldn't fly. And I didn't attack you with magic. Someone put a curse on me, or something. I'm not here for any of you. Falling on this island was an accident. Believe me, I wouldn't willingly come here, considering how I've been treated."

Not-First starts to open his stupid mouth, no doubt to say other stupid things, but I cut him off. "And yes, I have red wings. Thank you for pointing out the obvious. But like I told you before, demons don't have red wings like this. Have you ever even seen a demon?"

The look on his face tells me all I need to know.

"I didn't think so. I *have* seen them, and let me tell you, my wings are way too pretty to be from hell. I mean, just look at them!" I say, spreading them out and ruffling. "See these feathers? They're super soft and freaking *lovely*. And this red color is definitely more blooming-flower-red than burning-in-hell-red. Any idiot can see that. You don't even deserve to look at my wings."

We just stare at each other. The guy with the cat tail and the girl with the bird wings. The face-off is tense, and I can tell that Evert and Sylred don't quite know what to do.

I sigh wearily. "Look. I've had a *really* bad couple of days, okay? I was hit with powerful magic, jumped out a window, fell through the sky, got shot with an arrow, dislocated my shoulder, got ripped to shreds by the trees, crash landed, strained all my muscles from moving, was tied to a tree all night, and nearly died from feeling cold for the first time. You're the asshole here, not me. *You* shot me out of the sky. *You* hurt *me*. I didn't do anything to you, and you *hurt me*—" My voice cracks, and I can't speak anymore because tears choke me from the inside out.

Damn. I'm a crier.

I didn't mean to say so much, and I certainly didn't want to cry again, not in front of Not-First, but I can't help it. All three faces stare at me in varying expressions. I'm out of breath, so my chest is kind of heaving, and my face feels almost as hot as the fire, but I don't care. I stare at Not-First with all the hatred I feel for him. He stares back at me with an unreadable expression as he towers over me, but I don't look down. I won't.

My neck hurts from looking up at him. My legs hurt from standing. My shoulder hurts from being dislocated. My entire body hurts from falling out of the sky. My wings hurt from flying. Every muscle hurts just from *moving*. And inside my chest, right where my new beating heart is—that hurts, too. Because I've dreamed for decades about what it would be like to be seen and heard, to have a body where I could feel and touch.

But now that I have that, I'm faced with three ridiculously handsome guys who are either toying with me, wary of me, or downright awful to me. They don't want me here. They don't want me to exist. And it hurts.

Not-First leans down close to my face, and it takes everything in me not to flinch away. His voice is gruff and darkly quiet, but he enunciates every word. "Now you listen to me. I don't trust you. I don't believe you. You can cry and yell and plead, but your lies won't work on me. I'll be watching you, and if you threaten me or my covey, I will kill you."

Without another word, he turns on his heel and stomps away, storming out the door and disappearing outside. I let out a long, shaky breath.

Then I collapse.

CHAPTER 12

hen I open my eyes, it takes several moments for my sight to adjust and take in my surroundings. I'm in a small room and lying on a low pallet made of soft brush and grasses and covered in fur pelts. The walls are plain and unadorned, but there's a small window covered with vines that lets in lines of sunlight that streak across the floor.

So I'm in one of the guys' bedrooms. Obviously not Ronak's. But I wonder if it's Evert's or Sylred's?

I sit up and stretch as I look around. My muscles are still sore, including my strained wings, but I ruffle my feathers a bit to work out the kinks. A couple of my red feathers shed off onto the bed.

I tentatively stand up, careful to keep a hand on the wall so I don't fall. I have no idea how long I slept. My legs are wobbly, but I manage to walk to the door and pull it open. I peek out, but there's no one in the main room.

Maybe I can walk right out the front door and keep going without any of them noticing? Ha. Fat chance of that. I have no doubt that they'd find me in minutes, considering how I can barely walk and that this island is pretty small. I might as well stick around until I'm stronger.

I walk out quietly and take my time looking around the main room. I trace my fingers along the different-styled chairs that sit around the table. I wonder which of the guys each one belongs to. The styles are so different. There's one with carvings, one with inlaid rocks, and one that looks like it was made out of a solid tree trunk. I'm guessing that one, based on its massive size, is Ronak's.

The front door opens, and I turn around to see Sylred walk in with an armful of chopped wood.

He stops when he sees me. "You're awake."

"Yeah. Was that your room?"

He shakes his head. "Evert's." He walks toward the fireplace to throw down the stack of wood beside it.

"You're still not wearing a shirt," I blurt out.

He raises a blond brow. "You have my only one."

I look down. "Oh. Right. I'm sorry about that…" I frown. "Do you want it back?"

A look of dismay crosses his face. "You don't…You're…" He clears his throat. "No. You keep it."

I try to stifle my smile. Poor guy thinks I was just going to strip down right here and now.

I look down at my borrowed pants and then his. Mine are made of soft linen, while his are made of leathers. "But you had extra pants?"

He shrugs. "I wear the leathers over the linen ones."

"Oh," I say, looking at his leather pants again. "Doesn't that make things real sweaty and sticky?" I ask. "That's gotta be uncomfortable, huh? Not that I really know. I've never worn leather before. But I've watched enough bikers and BDSM members to know that things can get muggy down south real quick. Oh, and latex. Like one of those full bodysuits. I went to a party once where everyone wore one. Things got real squeaky."

Sylred just blinks at me for a moment. "...I don't know how to reply to that."

I wave him off. "No need to reply. I'm used to talking to myself. Anyway, I'll give you your pants back soon. I can try to fix my dress, maybe. I don't want to be responsible for sticky balls."

Poor guy blushes. It's really cute the way I can see the tops of his tan cheeks turn darker. His blond beard covers most of it, but it's there.

We're still standing in uncomfortable silence when a noise growls from the pit of my stomach, startling me. I clench a hand across my belly and look up at him in surprise. "What the hell? Am I dying?"

He blinks at me a few times. "I expect you're hungry."

A slow, wide smile spreads across my lips. "Hungry. I'm hungry?"

He nods cagily, like I'm a crazy person, but my smile only gets brighter. "I can actually eat food!" I say breathlessly.

I can't contain my excitement. I can *finally* eat. All those foods and drinks that I've fantasized over and looked at longingly over the years rushes into my mind, and my mouth salivates. I suddenly can't wait a second longer.

"Can I eat now? Please?" I ask desperately.

Because even though they're holding me prisoner and think I'm a demon, I have manners. I'm a lady like that.

"Whatever you have, I don't care. I'll eat literally anything edible."

"Of course. Sit," he orders, motioning toward the table.

He doesn't have to tell me twice. I choose the chair with the carvings, but my wings get in the way. They're too big for me to sit. I try the other two chairs next, but even the largest of the three doesn't quite accommodate my wings.

I decide to give up and sit on the floor instead, settling on top of the fur rug. Sylred doesn't comment on my movements or my choice of seat, but after digging through some wooden boxes and drawers, he plunks down a wooden plate piled high with food and a full cup in front of me. There are fruits and vegetables I've never seen before, plus a large slab of meat. It smells delicious, and my stomach lets out another growling sound, making me laugh.

I dig into the food immediately and moan aloud when I take my first bite of meat. The taste is smoky and spicy, and it practically melts in my mouth. I devour it within minutes.

I eat it all the way to the bone and then move on to the vegetables. They're green and long, with yellow dots on the side. They taste like earth, but I love them because, hello, food! I move on to the fruit last, and I'm so surprised when I bite into it and taste the flood of sweet nectar, that I can't help but moan and laugh again.

Gods, food is delicious. I want to eat more. I want to eat everything. Gimme all the foods. From now on, it's food everywhere, all the time, every kind. I want to constantly stuff my face. Screw relationships, I'll make food my new love. I've clearly been misplacing all my fantasies on love and sex. I should've just focused my pining on food this whole time.

When everything edible is gone, I barely stop myself from licking the plate clean. Barely.

I pick up the wooden cup and tip it back, draining every last drop of water. It tastes so pure and cool that it makes my whole mouth crave more. I sigh in pleasure because I feel so full and good. My taste buds are going berserk at all the new flavors.

"Second, can I have some more wa—" I stop mid-sentence when I look up.

All three guys are standing by the door, staring at me. I didn't hear any of them come in, but I was so engrossed in my meal that I probably wouldn't have heard a stampede run through the cabin. What I also didn't notice, but which is now blatantly obvious, is the thick scent of arousal in the air, and I know I'm new to this and all, but I'm pretty sure it's coming from all three of them.

"Oh. Hey," I say.

I wipe my mouth with my hands, because they continue to stare. Maybe I have a piece of food stuck to my chin or something? When they still don't say anything, I snap, "What?"

Evert shakes his head. "Nothing," he says with a growing smirk, bringing his dimples into the room. "You just…you really enjoyed your meal. You were very…vocal about it."

Sylred coughs.

"Oh, well I've never eaten before," my mouth says before I can stop it. Ronak narrows his eyes at me. Oops. "I mean…I've never eaten something so yummy before," I say quickly, trying to amend my statement to sound less suspicious. "Everything tasted…well, everything *tasted*. It was amazing. All the flavors…I never knew there could be so many."

I'm just going to shut up now.

"I just wonder if she makes those noises during other activities," Evert quips.

Sylred laughs even as his cheeks turn red again. Not-First just glowers.

I narrow my eyes on them all at the implication. "None of you will be lucky enough to find out. You're holding me prisoner, remember? I don't have sex with my jailors."

Ronak crosses his arms. "Someone want to tell me what she's still doing inside?"

Sylred loses his patience and huffs. "She was hurt and starving, Ronak."

"You're an idiot. She's supposed to be our prisoner, not our guest."

Sylred shrugs, as if being the recipient of Ronak's anger doesn't faze him at all. It's pretty sexy to see him going toe-to-toe with Not-First. "Even so. We aren't barbaric. We don't treat females that way."

Ronak looks so angry that I'm afraid he might pull back one of those massive fists and deck Sylred right there. His black eyes flick to me, and I flinch at the hatred I see boiling in them. "Covey meeting. Now."

"What does that mean?" I ask, standing up.

"It means get out," Not-First snaps at me.

Gods, what an asshole.

I bite my tongue to keep from telling him off, because it's no use, anyway. He doesn't like me, and I don't like him. I shoot him a glare, pretending not to be scared of him one bit, even though I definitely *am* afraid of him. I mean, he could probably snap me in half like a twig.

I stomp toward the door so that I can give a nice dramatic exit. Well, I try to stomp. I end up tripping over my feet and nearly bowl right into Sylred. He catches me and sets me back on my feet.

"See? You're the nice one," I tell him, patting him on his chest. His bare chest. I might rub it a little, too. What? I can't help it. He actually has to pry my hand off of him to get me to stop. Whoops.

When I'm steady again, I walk out the front door. I try to slam it shut behind me, but since it's only made of branches, it doesn't give the right effect, and I hear some chuckling for my peevish effort.

"Asshole," I mutter.

"I heard that," Evert says from behind the door.

"Good!" I snap.

I hear him laugh again as I stalk away.

"Stay in the garden," Not-First hollers. "If I have to chase you, it won't end well for you."

"Maybe I'll just fly away!"

"Just fucking try it!" Not-First barks back.

"She won't," Sylred says. "She can barely stand. She's not

97

strong enough to fly or run anywhere." Dammit. I hate that he's right.

I walk to the back of the cabin so that they see me pass by through the windows. I have absolutely no intention of really staying in the garden, though. A secret covey meeting? You can bet your dinner plate that I'll be eavesdropping.

When I'm in the garden, I creep back along the house from the other side. I'm good at spying. I've been doing it for fifty years. I keep my back to the wall of the house as I slink forward, only stopping when I make it to the front, right under the window.

I crouch down to listen. "—and that can't happen," Ronak says.

"One of us was always here to keep an eye on her. I understand your concerns, but you're getting worked up about nothing," Sylred replies.

"Nothing?" Ronak retorts. "You think it's a coincidence that she's here right now? She was sent by someone to sabotage us, and we have no idea what she is or what she's capable of."

"I'm not so sure she really is here to sabotage us, though," Sylred says. "All the others that have come here were clearly sent by the high fae. They came actively trying to kill us. She hasn't done anything hostile."

"Then she's trying to trick us. Get us to lower our defenses."

"The timing is suspicious," Sylred concedes with a sigh.

"Exactly," Ronak agrees. "She won't admit what she is, even as she keeps denying me when I call her a demon. Plus, she just happens to fall from the sky onto our island—passing through an *impassable* barrier, mind you—right before the royal culling trials begin? No, the timing is fishy. I don't believe in coincidences. She's either a distraction or a spy. Or both. And you heard her. She's seen us before—watched us. She even *rated* us. She *admitted* to spying."

"If she was sent here by the high fae, then what was with the barrier?" Sylred asks.

I don't hear all of the mumbled answer. "—to distract us right when it's imperative that we are focused," Ronak says. "We've been banished here for five years, and now, the culling is weeks away. We need our minds on the goal, which is to return home. We can't do that if we're distracted. And we don't know if she can negatively affect our covey link, either. It could sabotage everything we are, everything we want. We can't risk it. We need to watch her very carefully. So keep your dicks in your pants and your minds on our goal so that we can get off this gods-forsaken island, or I'll tie her up where none of you can find her and leave her for the birds."

I see red. And not in the hell-fire-demon red kind of way, because I am definitely not a demon. But in the I'm-so-pissed-I-can't-see-other-colors way. But beneath my anger is also a pit of churning sadness.

Gods, it's like I just can't catch a break. Just when I think they're starting to lighten up around me, Ronak comes back and casts me in the shadows again.

"And what if you're wrong?" Sylred asks. "Then we'd be treating her this way for nothing."

"It's my duty to protect our covey. If it's between hurting her feelings or saving our lives, the choice is easy. Everyone needs to rein it in. We only have a few more weeks to get through. Is the little demon worth risking our future over?"

I don't hear the answers, but I assume they shake their heads.

"Then it's agreed. We watch her, and we take her down if we need to. No distractions, no falling for her tricks or her charms. Now go tie her back up."

I quickly leave my spying spot and run to the back of the cabin and into the garden. I might as well try to stash some food if I'm going to be tied up again. Who knows if Not-First will feed me again. Now that I've had a taste of food, I don't want to miss any meals.

I pluck off the first fruit I see. It's growing on some kind of bush, and the fruit is light purple and about the size and shape of an eye. I stuff a handful into my pants pocket and then turn and grab at another plant where some orange fruit grows and stuff that in as well.

I turn around to see what else I can get my hands on when Sylred rounds the corner and spots me. I see him look down at my dirty hands, and then his blue eyes travel to my bulky pockets.

Just when I think he's about to make me empty them, he jerks his head and says, "Come on."

"What if I don't want to?"

He narrows his eyes at me and stares, so I narrow my eyes and stare right back. I can play this narrow-eye challenge game all day, buddy.

Oops, I blinked. Dammit.

I briefly consider taking off in the other direction, just to piss him off. Hmm. Nah. I've only run once, but I was not a fan.

Okay, so maybe I can just stubbornly stay where I'm standing? Make him physically have to force me back to the tree?

As fun as that seems since he's shirtless, I don't want to crush my precious fruit that I have stockpiled in my pockets. Priorities, you know?

Also, he *is* the nice one, and I don't want to push my luck. I'd rather he continue being nice to me. I also still want to get them to trust me, and the only way to do that is to show them that I'm not the bad guy here.

Sighing, I go to him. "I could've won that eye stare, just so you know."

He smiles and shakes his head at me as he leads me to my tree and motions for me to sit down.

My butt is going to be sore sitting on the hard ground, so I pout a little. "Can't I get something to sit on? Pretty please?" I bat my eyelashes at him.

At first, I think he's going to call me out on my blatant manipulation, but he just sighs and heads back toward the cabin to get something. Huh. Who knew the eyelash trick actually works? When he comes back out, he folds a fur pelt and sets it on the ground for me.

I sit down on it and smile sweetly. "You can be in first place now."

"Well, since you still haven't told us what first place means, I guess I can't get too excited."

"Oh, it's a good thing. Trust me."

"Maybe I could, if you'd tell me who you are."

"Nice try."

He shrugs as he starts to tie the handmade ropes around me. I watch him as he checks that the bindings are secure before standing up again.

"Are you here to spy on us?"

"Nope. I swear on my very pretty, very un-demonic wings that I am not a spy."

"I guess we'll find out."

Without saying anything more, he turns and leaves. When I'm left alone, I test my bindings. They're secure, but they aren't nearly as tight as when Not-First tied me up. I have a fair amount of movement allowed, so I can easily reach the fruit that's stuffed in my pockets.

With more room to move around, I reach my arm around to the tree bark and start trying to break off another piece. Might as well. It's not like I have anything else to do. I'm not sure where my old piece went since Evert confiscated it. Which is a downer, because I worked hard on that piece, dammit. I really liked holding it. Being able to hold and touch things really rocks my world.

I doze off in between sitting against the tree...and sitting against the tree. What can I say? It's boring.

When I come to, it's dark out. Someone has left me a pile of nuts and some more fruit, along with a waterskin. I look over at the cabin and see the soft glow of the fireplace coming through the windows and smoke drifting up from the chimney. I can also smell meat cooking, and my stomach growls. I guess prisoners don't get freshly cooked meat.

I scratch at my arm absently. I don't like to go too long without scratching that spot. It's a tricky, conniving little itch, and I won't let it win again.

I can hear the guys inside, probably eating around the table. I'm sure they're enjoying that nice meat and having a good time, warm by the fire. I really wish I were inside with them. I'm dying to talk to someone. It's a serious addiction.

Besides, it's kind of freaky out here alone at night. What if a bear comes around and decides to eat me? I'm sure I look tasty. Or maybe there's some crazy giant insect in this realm that can paralyze me with its stinger and then drag me away to its nest.

I jump when I hear something rustling behind me. I stare into the dark forest and see a squirrel running away. I let out a relieved sigh. Maybe it's best not to let my imagination run away with me. But my imagination and running commentary are the only things I've had to entertain myself with, so it's my first go-to. I sing some songs from the human realm to pass the time. Those humans have some catchy tunes. And yeah, okay, most of the songs I sing are from nineties boy bands. Don't judge. It was super cool at the time.

I consume all of the food and water in a few short minutes. Being held captive against a tree is hungry work. Luckily, before I dozed off, I'd managed to not only get a new piece of bark off the tree, but I also loosened my ties some more.

A lot more.

Like, I'm technically free, but I'm still sitting here, because I have plans for tonight, and I don't want to get caught.

I wait until I see the firelight die down and the cabin goes quiet. I watch the stars through my little opening in the trees, and I listen to the sounds of the forest. It's peaceful here, and the air is sweet, with a calm breeze that tickles the hair around my face.

When I'm satisfied that I've waited long enough that everyone is asleep, I carefully extract myself from the ropes and stand up, stretching my arms and wings with a satisfying sigh. I have to be careful with my shoulder because it's still tender, but I feel much better already. Maybe I heal faster than normal.

I walk to the cabin and peek in through the window. The main room is dark and empty. All the guys are in their rooms. Their covey meeting revealed a lot, and Ronak's words circle in my mind over and over again.

Sabotage. Spy. Demon.

I know that I'm not any of those things, but that doesn't help me. As much as I hate them distrusting me, I don't want to ruin anything for them. It isn't their fault that I fell on this island. I don't know anything about their covey link or the culling they mentioned, but I don't want to mess up their lives.

What I want is what I've longed to have for so many years: connection.

I want to connect with other people and be wanted. I want to feel and smell and see and hear and taste *everything*. But I'm not going to get what I want here. That much is blindingly clear. Which is why I had an epiphany when I was loosening my bindings. I simply need to get off this island. I need to leave and find someplace I can live with some people who don't look at me as an enemy.

Who knows, maybe there's another hot covey out there that will actually earn my kiss-rankings and become completely devoted to me.

A girl can dream.

I'm going to find my own true love if it kills me. And I'm going to have sex. A lot of hot, steamy sex. Because orgasms. Orgasms seem super great. I want in on that.

The problem is, I can't leave this island until I can properly fly. Which brings me to my plan now. I'll just wait every night until they're all asleep, and then I'll work my ass off until flying is as simple as breathing.

I walk away from the cabin and head to a slight clearing in the forest where some moonlight shows through, careful to keep the cabin still in view. Just in case one of the guys wakes up, I'll use the shadows to my advantage and hurry back to my tree.

In the canopy of the trees, I'm surrounded by the secret noises of night. Animals running, insects chirping, leaves rustling. The forest smells nice, too. I always wondered what was so special about smells. People seemed to talk about them a lot.

They came up with all sorts of ways to describe smells, and honestly, I thought they were exaggerating, but they were right. So many different smells cause so many different reactions. Some smells, like the cooked meat, are enough to make my mouth water. Others, like the scent of the grass, have a calming effect. And some, like the way Sylred smelled when I'd been pressed up against his chest—no.

Nope. Not going there. Stop thinking about how he smelled. No more sniffing the captors, Emelle.

Emelle.

At least, out of this entire situation, I finally have a name. That's something.

I spread my wings a few more times to get the feel of them. Why do they have to be so heavy? I ruffle my red feathers and look down at my feet when I step on a sharp stick. Too bad my cupid attire didn't come with shoes.

My legs clench together instinctively, and I realize that this

o I turn my head and nuzzle my nose against his neck, and
 nip him gently, using my lips and tongue to soothe the
s. I can practically feel him shudder in both surprise and
ger. And I don't mean hunger for food.

Set me free," I whisper in his ear huskily, because I just want
e if he'll do it.

e leans back, and I can see the desire in his clear blue eyes.
attraction between us is obvious. It has been since I first
ed here. His aroused state saturates the air, and I inhale
ly.

here's clearly no need for any cupid power intervention
. We have it in spades. Or maybe hearts—wink, wink.

When he goes to the side of the tree to start undoing the
ings, my mouth opens in surprise. "Wow, that really
ced?"

e chuckles. "Nah. I came out here to let you loose for a
e."

Oh." I quickly pull the ropes tight in my hands, hiding the
on from him. I don't want him to know how loose they
y are, or my jig will be up. When he unties me, I stand up
grimace. Maybe I practiced flying a tad too much last night.
vert misunderstands my expression of pain and frowns.
e the ropes too tight?"

No."

lis frown deepens and his blue eyes trail over my body. "Did
s some of your injuries?"

No, you got them all I think. I'm just sore."

Your shoulder?"

nod, because that's as good an answer as any. "Yeah. And
vings."

e accepts this and then tosses me a piece of round fruit. I'm
ing, so I immediately bite into it. The second my teeth
k through the skin, I wrinkle my nose and pull it back from
nouth.

physical body also requires me to take care of some private business. I quickly dart behind a bush to pee. Ahhh. That's better. Who knew peeing could bring such relief?

Now that that's taken care of, I can practice flying. Because I *will* master my new physical wings and get out of here as soon as possible. There is no other option. I can't stay here. If anything goes wrong for the guys, they'll blame me, and then Ronak will come after me.

"Okay, Emelle," I say quietly to myself. "You can do this."

I smooth my red feathers out and look side to side. My wingspan is longer than my body, maybe about six feet. It was so easy to fly when I was invisible. The instinct is there, I just need to build up the muscles to match it.

With a running start, I leap into the air, forcing my wings out. I flap a few times and then touch back down. I do this over and over and over again. Back and forth in my small clearing.

Run, leap, flap, land, repeat.

My muscles start to burn, and a layer of sweat breaks out over my forehead and my back, but I keep going. I practice like this until I can't lift my wings anymore.

I let them drag on the ground behind me when I walk back to my tree. I'm sure it's terrible wing etiquette, but I'm just that exhausted.

Sweat is soaked through my shirt, and my light pink hair is plastered to my neck. I nearly collapse against the tree, and by the time I slip back into the bindings and down the entire contents of the waterskin, the sky has turned a soft shade of gray.

When the last of the night fades away to concede to morning, I drift away. I dream of the stars. I dream of being one, of dancing alone in the sky, of glittering beside the moon. Being a star is not so different from being a cupid. People wish and the stars try to grant, but even as the stars sacrifice themselves and fall, so many wishes are wasted, just as so much love is lost.

CHAPTER 13

I wake with the sun.

Not true. I actually wake with someone looming over me, blocking the sun from my face.

I jerk awake at his voice and close proximity, my eyes adjusting to see Evert smirking, the sun behind his head like a halo.

"Who knew such a small Scratch could make such loud snores?"

I sit up, groaning at my sore muscles. "I don't snore."

He reaches forward and pulls out a twig stuck from my hair. "And that's not a puddle of drool on your shoulder either, I suppose?"

I jerk to the right and quickly wipe my chin and shoulder from the offending fluid, shooting him a glare at the same time. "I was tired."

"Oh?" he says, playing with the twig in his hand, flipping it between his fingers nimbly.

I have to admit, he has nice looking hands. And he has that nice muscled forearm with the vein... Mmmm.

"Is sitting down all day and night tiring you out, Scratch?"

Oh, if only he knew.

"Maybe being held in captivity doesn't agree with

"Maybe," he concedes, tossing the twig aside. "Ar to tell us who and what you are?"

I try to cross my arms, but I can't do that witho how loose my bindings are, so I just set my arm instead.

"That depends. I'll tell you if you agree to stop and threatening to kill me. I also want more mea fruit. And extra furs to sleep on. Oh, and you have t because it's boring without someone to talk to."

"I'll be sure to let the guys know your terms," he

I roll my eyes. "What you mean is, you're goin First, and he'll decide."

Evert crosses his arms, the smirk falling from h no. But we're a covey. At least for the next few we to work together until then."

"Oh, really?" I ask innocently. "Because it seer he's in charge around here."

I'll just be here, holding a giant spoon and sti I'll stir it all day and cook up something really goo

He narrows his eyes on me. "I know what Scratch."

"I don't know what you mean, Third."

He snorts and leans close to me, making my With him this close, my brain does some crazy se I successfully undress him and jump him in my r good at sex-visualizing.

"Tell me what you are," he says quietly, his li my ear.

Tricky, tricky Third.

If he thinks he can seduce me for answers, thing coming. Because hello, I'm a cupid. If anyo the seducer, it's going to be me.

Evert laughs. "You're supposed to peel it first."

"That would've been good information *before* I bit into the bitter skin."

I put the fruit on my lap and start peeling it. When I get the red skin off, I find a juicy pink fruit inside. It tastes *amazing*. I let a little bit of juice dribble down my lip. I lick the escaping juices slowly, letting my tongue swipe across my bottom lip.

If I thought he was aroused before, it's nothing to the heavy presence of it in the air now. I really like this new addition to my powers. It's quite useful.

I slowly put the last bite of fruit in my mouth and bite down provocatively before swallowing.

I smirk at his expression. "What's the matter, Third?" I ask innocently.

He looks like he wants to devour me, and I'm pretty sure I'd like to be. "You think it's fun tormenting me, Scratch?"

"A little, yeah."

He reaches forward and grabs my hand and then slowly lifts my finger to his mouth. He puts it in his mouth and sucks the rest of the fruit juice off it in a delicious swirl of his hot, wet tongue.

Annnd my love lips just filled with lady lava.

He releases my finger and leans back with a triumphantly smug look on his face. Whatever expression he sees on mine makes him chuckle darkly. "Whatever you do to me, I'll match and raise you, Scratch. Remember that."

Gods, I hope that's a promise.

"Come on. We're taking a walk. Do you need to go first?"

I try to clear my head, because he has me all worked up. It takes me a second to comprehend his words. "Umm, go where?"

"You know...relieve yourself," he says, and, I swear, he blushes.

He just sucked my finger like it was nothing, but he's totally embarrassed by pee.

"Oh, yeah," I answer, realizing that as soon as he mentions it, I do have to go.

These physical bodies sure do take a lot of maintenance.

He points in a general direction behind me. "There's an outhouse about a hundred feet over there. I'll wait here."

An outhouse. That would have been good to know last night before I popped a squat in the forest like a bunny rabbit.

"Thanks."

I walk in the direction he pointed and soon find the small wooden outhouse. Inside is a simple wooden bench with a hole, but the smell makes me promptly plug my nose. I do my business quickly and then return to where Evert waits for me.

When he sees me, he motions me over. "Come on, I'll take you for a walk."

I look up at him suspiciously. "Why are you taking me for a walk?"

"Would you rather stay tied up all day?"

"No."

"That's what I thought." Evert leads the way through the forest, and I follow beside him, careful to watch where I go.

Evert is barefoot, too, but unlike my sensitive and dainty feet, his seem adjusted to the forest floor, and he walks over sticks and rocks as if he doesn't even feel them.

"So. Stitch, huh?"

"Yep. That's me."

"Pretty fancy trick you have."

He chuckles and reaches up to push aside a low hanging branch. "I don't do tricks, Scratch. I perform miracles."

"Gods, you're humble, too."

This time, his laugh echoes around me and fills my belly with warmth. "Just one of my many positive attributes."

"I'm sure."

"Where you from, Scratch?"

I wave a hand dismissively. "Oh, you've never been there."

"Tell me anyway."

"Are you going to set me free?"

He holds his arms up and motions around. "What do you call this?"

"I call this supervised exercise. You know, like what a prisoner gets."

He chuckles. "How'd a pretty little thing like you end up falling over our island, anyway?"

"I jumped out a window," I deadpan.

I pull off a leaf as we walk by, twirling it around in my fingers as I run it across my palm.

"Boyfriend?"

I smile at him. "Why, are you interested in filling the position?"

"What if I were?"

I shrug. "The application process is very selective. You probably wouldn't pass."

"Oh, I'm sure I'd be fine."

Hell yeah, he'd be fine. He and Sylred both. And Ronak. Dammit.

We come to a copse of trees whose branches are hanging heavy with long green fruit in a conical shape.

"What are these?" I ask, trailing forward.

"Bice Horns," he answers, reaching up his arm for one.

I watch his muscular bicep flex as he snaps the fruit from a branch and hands one to me, and that's when I notice the tattoos poking out from his sleeve.

"Try it." He catches me staring at his arm, and his signature smirk returns.

I take the offered fruit. "Are there any secret fruit tricks to this one that I should know about?"

"You're learning," he says, reaching forward.

Our fingers brush, and I try to stop the slight shiver that runs down my arm from the contact, but I don't think I'm successful.

Gods, I don't think I'll ever get used to this touching thing.

Evert snaps back the point of the cone-shaped fruit, and the skin falls away, leaving a smooth, pale green center. He hands it back to me, I take a bite, and my mouth floods with saliva.

I make a face and Evert laughs. "The outside is sour, but once you get closer to the core, it gets sweeter, I promise. Keep chewing."

I decide to take his word for it and keep working on it, while Evert gathers a few for himself. By the time I finish my one, he's eaten three. I wipe my mouth with my hand, making sure there's no residual food on my chin.

"You're right. It had a sweet center," I say. "Is that kind of like you?"

He looks over at me with a glint in his eye, his dimple showing on his cheek. "What?"

"Yeah, you know. You try to be a jerk, but you're really just sweet on the inside."

He scratches at his black beard and laughs. "I hate to break it to you, Scratch, but I'm definitely *not* the sweet one in the covey," he says with a mischievous glint in his blue eyes. "But if you want to stick with your fruit analogies, I won't stop you from trying to taste me to see if your theory holds up."

It's my turn to smirk at him, and I feel a jolt of victory when I realize he's watching my lips curve up. "Be careful, Third. You don't want to start something and get in trouble with your boss."

He scoffs, and we start walking back toward the cabin, our paces slow. "I already told you, he's not the boss."

"Hmm. I don't think he knows that."

I am pot stirrer, hear me whisk.

"Tell me what the ranking means. Why do you call me Third?"

"Fine. Since you took me for a walk and gave me food, I'll

112

tell you. I decided I was going to kiss you thirdly," I confess. "But Ronak turned out to be a complete asshole, so my ranking is clearly flawed."

He chuckles and shakes his head, but there's a decided heat that passes between us, and I can tell that I've dragged his mind right into the gutter. Right where I like it.

When we're quiet for a couple minutes, I take a risk and ask, "Why were you banished to this island?"

The second the question is out of my mouth, I know it's a mistake. Evert's face shutters closed, his expression becoming suddenly cold and unreadable. The friendly flirting that we'd been dancing with immediately ends.

"That's covey business."

"Sorry," I say quickly. "I didn't know it was a big sensitive secret. I heard you mention something about it."

"It has nothing to do with you, so don't bring it up."

Gods, I really struck a nerve.

Evert's pace quickens so much that I nearly have to jog to keep up, which I decidedly can't do because I'm sore, and my body still feels like a newborn foal trying to walk on unsteady legs.

When we get back to the tree, we don't speak as Evert ties me up again. It's tighter than before, but I don't worry about that now. At least it's not as tight as Not-First would have made it.

When Evert stalks off, I'm left alone again. The walk was nice while his good mood lasted, and the fruit was yummy. I just wish I hadn't pissed him off. Maybe I could have talked him into letting me walk around for longer.

Oh, well. Tomorrow is another day, and if I want to sneak out of my bindings again by nightfall, I have a lot of work to do to get them loose again in time.

CHAPTER 14

I doze off sometime around late afternoon, but I jolt
awake at a loud cracking noise that seems to echo
from every direction imaginable.

I automatically try to jump to my feet, but of course, I can't,
so all that happens is I manage to give myself some rope burn. I
look around wildly and see all three guys running toward the
front of the cabin. They all stop right in front of me, looking up
at the sky.

I follow the direction of their gazes and see a strange shimmering dome above us. As we watch, the once invisible barrier
seems to dissolve, starting at the top.

"What's happening?"

Not-First rounds on me, his jaw and fists clenched, his
expression furious. He points a finger in my face as he towers
above me, and I can't help but cower from him.

"That's the barrier coming down, and the only ones who can
do that are the high fae," he snaps, looking at me accusingly.
"They're either sending something else here to kill us, or it has
to do with *you*. So you'd better talk now, demon. Are you doing
something for them?"

My eyes widen in shock, and I look back up at the quickly dissipating barrier, watching as the shimmering dome recedes. I feel all the blood drain from my face. If the high fae find me, they'll imprison me and probably execute me.

I look back at him and my voice becomes shrill. "Please, don't let them find me!" I plead. "If they find me, they'll kill me," I tell him. The guys behind him share a look, but I know the decision will be left up to him. "*Please*, Ronak."

It's the first time I've called him by his name to his face, and his gaze sharpens. Tears pool in my eyes, and my voice cracks, revealing my desperation. He studies me for a moment, kneeling down before my face. We're only inches away, and his dark gaze bores into me like he's trying to dig up every single thought in my head. If it would make him realize I'm telling the truth, I'd let him.

Whatever he sees in my expression solidifies his decision. He reaches back to his holster and grabs his dagger, and for one second, I think he might just slit my throat right here and now and be rid of me. But I let out a huge sigh of relief when he cuts through the ropes instead. He hauls me up roughly to my feet, a firm grip on each of my arms.

"I'll fucking kill you if you're lying to me," he growls in my face.

I have zero doubt he'd follow through with his threat.

"Get into the outhouse and stay there. Do not make a noise, do not move, and do not come out until one of us comes to get you, do you understand?"

All I can do is nod nervously. Quickly, he leads me toward the outhouse. Ronak opens the door and shoves me inside, slamming it shut again without a word as he rejoins the guys.

I squat down on my knees, careful to keep my wings pulled tight against my back. There's not a lot of room in here. From my squatted position, I peer through a crack in one of the boards. After some maneuvering, I manage to just barely see half of Evert's face and Ronak's arm and leg.

I wait for a long time and so do the guys. Sweat drips between my shoulder blades and beads on my forehead. There isn't a lot of airflow in this small confined space, and the smell isn't exactly pleasant, either. I don't know how long I stay huddled in the outhouse, but I finally hear the sound of twigs cracking under heavy footsteps. I can't be sure how many have come, but it's definitely more than a few.

I hear a new voice call out. "Covey Fircrown, I see you're right where we left you," the man's voice says.

His tone is gloating, like the guys being banished here is entertaining to him. "How long has it been now? Nearly five years? My, my how time flies," he laughs, and it's a mean, humorless sound.

"What do you want, Chaucel?" Ronak asks, sounding bored.

"Why do you assume I want anything? Perhaps I've just come to see what you've been reduced to before you head to the royal culling trials. I do like a good slow-burn banishment to really break a soul down before the competition."

"We are neither reduced nor broken," Ronak replies, his voice like steel. "My covey doesn't break."

"Hmm. We shall see."

The male steps closer to the guys, and I can finally see him—well, part of him, at least. Unlike the guys' golden or pale skin, his skin tone is pastel green. His hair is a much darker shade and is pulled back in a metal clasp at his back, and he's wearing a long, dark green robe. When he turns to look at Ronak, I clamp a hand over my mouth. It's *him*.

The high fae advisor to the prince. The one who was there that day I attacked Prince Elphar. My heart pounds in my chest, but I force myself to take steadying breaths. The last thing I want is for this guy to find me. He saw me when the prince slammed his magic into me and made me physical. There was a moment, when our eyes locked, right before I hightailed it out of that room.

There's no doubt in my mind that he's here for me.

His next words steal the breath from my throat.

I see him turn to look over his shoulder. "Search the premises."

I realize with a lurch that there are guards with him. Lots of them.

"What's this about, Chaucel?"

Chaucel turns back to look at him as three guards stream past, heading toward the cabin. I soon hear them knocking things over inside, crashing furniture to the ground in their search.

"The prince...misplaced something," Chaucel answers elusively. "We're searching the surrounding islands for it."

Yep. The "it" is definitely me.

Ronak is going to give me over. He's going to point in my direction, and Chaucel will send the guards my way.

Why wouldn't he? He has no loyalty to me. He's already been banished. I don't know what would happen if Chaucel were to discover that Ronak was hiding me. Ronak wouldn't put his covey's life in danger like that. Not for me.

I steel myself and crouch on the balls of my feet, flexing my wings a bit. I have to be ready to flee. I might not get away, but I have to try.

I see Ronak cross his huge arms in front of his chest. He's not wearing a shirt, and his golden skin glistens, like its sole purpose is to highlight his muscles. "Nothing can get on or off this island. Not with the barrier in place," he says. "You know that, Chaucel."

"I do. And I also know that strange magic is on this island. I can *feel* it. And if I find out that you're hiding what Prince

Elphar seeks...well, let's just say that the culling would seem like a reprieve compared to the execution he'll sentence you to. It will be slow.

"It will last for days and days, maybe even weeks. Every time you beg for it to end, we will stop, and a healer will come. And then when you're healed, we will start all over again. You will go mad with pain. You and the rest of your covey," Chaucel says with menace. "But you, Ronak, you will go last. You will see your covey succumb. And only when you are on your knees, kissing the prince's feet and begging, will he let you die."

Good gods. This guy really has a thing against Ronak. His threats nearly make me pee my pants right there, and he's not even talking about me.

But Ronak simply shrugs at him. The cheeky bastard.

"You always did have an overactive imagination. But I can tell you right now, I don't know what you're looking for, but if it were up to me, I'd make sure you never found it," Ronak says, taking a step forward threateningly. "As for the kissing, well, sorry to disappoint, but you're really not my type."

My heart stutters. Ronak is...not going to give me over. I can't believe it. I have no idea why, but I'm not about to look a gift horse in the mouth. At least, not until he's done chewing.

Maybe he just hates Chaucel more than he hates me. Whatever the reason, I'll take it.

Chaucel takes a step forward until he and Ronak are nearly nose-to-nose. He says something that I can't catch, but I see Ronak's fist clench at his side.

Chaucel lifts his lips into a satisfied smirk. "Guards, keep searching. I want every rock unturned. The prince is nothing if not thorough."

I snort. Yeah, he's thorough alright. He thoroughly made his way through every female fae he came into contact with, leaving no skirt unturned, not caring who he hurt or how he abused his position of power. Pig.

It takes a while for them to continue searching. I can hear guards walking around every once in a while, and every single time, I panic that they'll open the door to the outhouse. But so far, so good. Maybe the smell is enough of a deterrent. It's certainly strong enough.

My wings are sore from being stuffed in the tight space, and my leg muscles have cramped up from my squatted position on the floor.

Leave, leave, leave, I plea silently.

I see two of the guards return, shoving past the guys to face Chaucel. They have similar bluish skin but are wearing armor and holding swords.

"Nothing in the house or garden," a guard reports. "And nothing along the perimeter either."

"Fine," Chaucel says, looking unsurprised but still disappointed.

He swivels his neck around, and then I swear, he looks *right* at me, even though the outhouse is somewhat hidden between the trees. Even though I don't think he can actually see me through the cracks, I don't dare move or breathe.

"What's that?" Chaucel asks, pointing in my direction.

"Our shit shack," Evert answers.

I know it's him speaking, even though I can't see him. I also know by the sound of his voice that he's wearing a shit-eating smirk. "So unless you want one of your guards to wipe your ass for you, I'd say it's time for you to leave our island."

Well. That would've made me laugh under different circumstances. You know, like when I'm not hiding for my life in said shit shack.

I lift a silent prayer to Eros that Chaucel takes Evert's bad attitude in stride and leaves.

Chaucel steps forward, probably to get into Evert's space. "I see you still haven't learned to train your pussy cats, Ronak.

119

Search it," he says over his shoulder, and my stomach plummets right down to my toes.

Oh, shit.

CHAPTER 15

*T*hey can't find me. They just *can't.*

If I get taken, I have no idea what will happen to me. I could run for it, maybe, but I know I'm weak, and even if I managed to run without tripping, it would be seconds before they caught up with me.

I can't fly. Not that well, and I'm already really sore from all the practicing. If I open the outhouse door, the guards will see me right away. I am totally screwed.

I look all around the small outhouse, and my eyes land on the bench and the hole that acts as a makeshift toilet seat.

Shit.

Without giving myself a chance to think about what I'm about to do, I lift up the top of the bench and jump in, letting the top close behind me with a quiet creak. I land a few feet down in a pile of…yeah. Shit and piss.

I immediately start to heave, but I clamp a hand over my mouth and nose. Luckily, I managed to keep my left hand clean when I fell in. My right hand was not so lucky since it helped to break my fall.

The pit is wider and deeper than I thought it would be, and I scramble to the edge and squat down at the dirt wall, huddling close to the sides and bottom and trying to make myself as small as possible, just in case the guard looks down the hole in the bench.

I hear the outhouse door creak open, and I look up. I don't dare breathe. Tears stream down my cheeks as my eyes sting from the revolting filth I'm surrounded in, and my stomach clenches, threatening to throw up all the fruit from earlier.

There's shit and piss squelching under my toes, splattered on my legs and feet, and covering my arm and wings. It's *everywhere.* It's all I can see and smell, even without breathing through my nose, and I squeeze my eyes closed tight to keep myself from panicking.

I hear the guard above me walking, his steps scraping against the wood. I feel him hover over the hole, looking down, and I wonder if I just jumped into this filth for nothing. If he looks down and finds me, I'm going to be so pissed.

The only thing that might be worse is if he drops his trousers and adds to the pile right on top of me. Then I might seriously snap. I'm never going to be able to feel clean after this. I wait for the shouts and the hollers to ring out, all but convinced that I'm about to be taken prisoner.

But instead, I hear footsteps recede, and the door closes again. I let out a huge sigh of relief, except it's not all that relieving since, you know, I'm still trapped in a hovel of shit.

The blood starts to pound in my ears. I need to get out of here. Like *now.* I'm starting to lose it.

I can hear voices again, but I can't make out what anyone is saying. I don't dare move from my spot, and I have no idea of knowing if the guards are still around, so all I can do is sit, huddled in revolting filth, and wait.

It seems like hours go by. My left hand is still held tightly against my nose and mouth, and I can only take in quick little gasping breaths that sound a lot like hyperventilating. I gag some more, but I don't dare move my hand.

Just when I'm sure I can't hold my stomach back any longer, I finally, *finally* hear the door open again and the top of the bench is lifted.

"Bloody fucking shit," I hear above me.

I look up and see Evert holding the lid of the bench up. He reaches an arm down, and I quickly take it with both hands. He lifts me up, my wings snagging on the top of the bench as he pulls me out. I nearly topple into him, but he holds me at arm's length and then backs out of the outhouse.

I stumble out after him, and then I fall down on my hands and knees onto the grass and vomit violently. As if the pee and poop weren't enough, I have to add vomit to the mix.

I hear noises and voices, but my ears are too full of my own brutal heaves to decipher anything. My stomach clenches again and again until there's nothing more to throw up.

Then I'm being doused in cold water. I shriek at the sudden onslaught and cough as water floods my nose and mouth, but I feel bucket after bucket being tossed over me.

When the assault stops, I'm a soaking wet, smelly mess, but at least the clumps of shit have been rinsed off of me. I sit back on my heels and look up at the three guys standing over me, each of them holding a pair of empty buckets in their hands. We stare at each other for a moment, and then Ronak drops his buckets.

"You'd better start talking," he says, his black eyes trained on me.

I glare up at him from my puddle of muck. With as much dignity as I can muster, I get to my feet, my legs shaking so much that my knees nearly knock together, and I turn around. I walk away from them, my face burning with embarrassment, anger, and nausea.

They all just saw me...covered in their own crap.

And even though they didn't give me up to Chaucel, I hate them right now, and I don't want to be anywhere near them.

I'm also desperate to get clean, and I heard the sound of running water last night while I was practicing flying, so that's where I head. It's now my sole mission to find that water and scrub my skin raw.

"Where do you think you're going?" Not-First asks, catching up to me easily and stepping in front of me to block my path.

I sidestep around him and realize that he won't physically stop me because he doesn't want to touch me in my current state. Yay for small victories.

"I just had to jump into a pile of your shit to hide from the high fae, or else I would've been taken prisoner and probably killed. So unless you want me to shove some of this disgusting crap onto you, leave me alone," I snap, continuing to walk away.

I'm surprised when he doesn't try to stop me a second time, and soon, I've left the guys behind and am following my ears to the sound of water getting louder.

After a few more minutes, I come to a small river. The current is strong, so I keep going, walking against its flow until I come to a rocky cliff with a thin waterfall cascading down into a rocky pool. *Perfect.*

I nearly cry out in relief at the sight of it. I quickly strip down and get in the water, careful to walk around the sharp rocks that jut out of the water. I can't swim, so I only wade in until I'm waist deep. I clutch onto one of the rocks coming up the side until I'm directly below the waterfall and stand underneath it, letting the water run over me.

I stay like that for a long time, eyes closed, water rushing over my head and hair and torso, while the bottom half of me just soaks in the cold pool. I let the unending stream of water rinse every bit of grossness off me. Then I take a deep breath and dunk down, plunging my whole body underwater, and scoop up some fine sand from the riverbed to use to scrub my skin and scalp.

I do this several times, rinsing under the waterfall in between each scrubbing session. I rinse my fingernails, mouth, nose and ears, lady bits…everything.

My skin is pink and feels raw by the time I'm satisfied that I have every last trace of filth washed off of me. I drag myself out of the water and rest on the grassy riverbank to let the sun dry my body and hair.

When I stand on the edge, I look down at the water and see my reflection for the first time. I have a heart shaped face, smooth pale skin, thickly arched brown brows, and full lips with a prominent cupid's bow. Because of course I'd have that. It's probably a job requirement.

My long, pastel pink hair nearly reaches my waist, and my wings look even more awesome behind me than I thought they would.

I stare at myself for a while, I'm not gonna lie.

I make every face I can think of, just to see what it looks like. I pretend to laugh, cry, frown, scream, and of course, I try out my resting bitch face. Yep. Totally nailed that one.

When I'm done admiring myself, I lie down and close my eyes, relaxing under the warm sun as it kisses my skin. The cool relief of the air on my sore skin relaxes me.

If it weren't for the three moody members of a certain covey and the fact that the prince is hunting me, I might have wanted to stay here forever. Lying naked under the warm sun with the smell of the grass and the sound of the water is paradise.

"Ah, hell."

My eyes fly open, and I sit up with a shriek. I find Sylred and Evert standing a few feet away, staring at me with wide eyes. My hands fly to my chest, and my wings come up and around to shield my body.

"What are you doing here?" I yelp.

Sylred whirls on his heel to turn around. Evert just stands there.

"Evert!" I snap at him.

"Fine," he says, grudgingly turning around.

I peek through my wings first to make sure they've both turned around, and then I scramble to pull on my clothes, only to realize that there's no way in hell I'm wearing those filthy things again.

Poor Sylred. They're ruined, which means he'll have to go shirtless forever. Well, at least the view will be nice. He has sexy, taut muscles. Even the view of just his bare back is pleasing.

"Dammit," I mutter, not knowing what I can wrap up in.

Before I can explain my dilemma, Evert reaches up and pulls his tunic off, rips it down the middle of the back, and tosses it over his shoulder at me. My face catches it.

I put my arms through the long sleeves but struggle to keep it tucked under my wings. I try to keep the back up, but I fail miserably and have to hold it up against my chest so that it doesn't fall off. At least it's long enough to cover my bottom. The shirt reaches me mid-thigh.

"And pants?"

"Sorry, Scratch. It'll take a bit more effort on your part to get me out of my pants."

"Ha ha," I say dryly. I sigh. "I need help," I admit, hating the words.

I don't want to ask them for anything right now, but I can't just go around with my top falling off every time I move. The guys turn around, and I see both pairs of eyes trail up my bare legs. A smug expression crosses my face at seeing them checking me out.

Evert steps forward and motions for me to turn around. I clutch the back of the shirt and then turn around for him. I keep my wings in and pull my damp hair over my shoulder to allow him full access.

I hear his breath quicken and smell his arousal again. I worry for a second that maybe he can see my butt, but even if he can, oh well. I've checked it out. It's a pretty nice butt.

Evert tugs at the tunic, and I can hear a few quiet rips as he tears a few strips on both sides and then ties them together in the space between my wings. His fingers are warm on my cool skin, and I try to ignore the shiver that threatens my spine.

"There," he says, his voice gruffer than usual. "That should hold."

I arch a brow at him over my shoulder. "Should?"

He gives me a roguish look. "Accidents happen."

"Hmm."

I turn and flip my hair over my shoulder, letting the shirt go. It holds together just fine, and all my goods seem to be covered.

"Thanks," I say, running hands down the shirt. "What are you two doing here?"

"Looking for you."

"Why? Afraid I'll run away and tell your deepest, darkest secrets?"

Admittedly, I'm in a terrible mood. Hiding in a pile of poop will do that to a person.

"No. It's obvious now that you aren't a spy."

I open my mouth and laugh humorlessly, the sound falling flat on my ears. "Oh, *now* it's obvious? When were you tipped off?"

Evert widens his stance and crosses his arms to match my own posture. "Well, I think it was right around the time when you decided it was better to roll around in our shit rather than to let the high fae bastard find you."

"Yeah, well, even though you guys are assholes sometimes, I'd rather take my chances here with you than be taken back to the prince."

"Why were you with the prince?" Sylred asks.

I don't say anything, and he and Evert study me. I don't want to think of Prince Elphar. I don't want to think about how close I came to being caught or about my failure with Princess Soora. Every time a heart breaks on my watch, I feel like even more of a disappointment.

The guys stare me down, trying to intimidate me. They aren't menacing with their size and muscles like Ronak, but they still have a head of height on me and are obviously much stronger with their lean forms and sculpted muscles.

We watch each other for a moment longer until Evert finally sighs and says, "Come on. We're here to bring you back. You're lucky it's us coming to get you and not Ronak."

I snort. "Yeah, I'm *so* lucky," I say, my tone dripping with sarcasm. "And I'm not going back, so you can leave now."

"Yes, you are coming back."

"No. I'm not. I'm grateful to all of you for not turning me in. I really am. But I'm not going back. You don't trust me, you don't like me, and you don't want me there. And believe me, it's probably better if I stay away from you. I don't want to complicate your lives, and I don't want anyone getting beheaded for me, not even Ronak."

Evert rubs a hand down his face. "Look, Scratch, you can't stay out here alone. You need to come back and finally tell us who you are and why the prince is looking for you."

I know he's right, but I realize just how nervous I really am to admit the truth. What will they think?

At my continued silence, Evert tosses his hands up in the air in frustration. "Fine. Stay here, then."

I feel a jolt of triumph, but then he walks toward a rock by the river and sits down, leaning back on it. Sylred chooses to take a seat beside a tree.

I look back and forth between the shirtless guys. "What do you think you're doing?"

Evert looks over at me with a cocked brow. "You won't come back, so we'll stay here."

I shake my head adamantly. "No. Nope. Uh-uh. You need to leave."

"Not happening," Evert says, stretching his hands behind his head and looking as comfortable as a cat in a basket. "We go where you go."

"So that you can spy on the spy?"

"I already told you, I don't think you're a spy anymore. Never really did to begin with, to be honest."

"How observant of you."

I turn around and decide to ignore them. They'll get sick of babysitting me eventually, right? Besides, I can still do what I decided to do, which is to learn how to properly fly and build up my muscles. Now that I'm out of my bindings early, I might as well continue my exercises.

I turn away from the guys and walk through the forest in search of the perfect tree. I pick a yellow flower from one of the branches as I go and run my finger over the soft petals.

For my exercises, I decide that I'll change things up by choosing a sturdy tree branch to jump from. It doesn't take long to find a tree with low-hanging branches. My arms are weak, but I manage to pull myself up on the low branch, hauling my legs over the sides. Hmm, this would probably be better to do when I'm wearing panties...

"What are you doing, Scratch?" Evert calls over.

They haven't moved from their spots, but I can see both of them watching me. I continue to ignore them. I carefully walk to the end of the branch, and then without hesitation, I jump off.

I hear a shout, and both Evert and Sylred are on their feet in an instant and rushing toward me, but I just throw my wings out and catch myself in the air. I flap repeatedly, forcing my wings to hold me up. I manage to circle around the tree once before I drop to the ground. My landing is a little shaky, but I'm able to land on my feet without falling, so I call that a win.

I pass the guys and go back to the tree, pulling myself up again to repeat the act. Just as I'm about to lift myself up on the branch, I feel hands on my waist. Heat from his hands burns into me, even through the shirt.

"Stop it. You could get hurt," Evert demands, holding me in place.

The feeling in my chest makes me want to turn around and bury myself against his neck... What? No. Get a grip, Emelle.

I slap his hands away and turn around to face him. "What do you care?"

He lets me go and shrugs. "I don't want to have to heal you again."

Jerk.

I snort and turn, hoisting myself up on the branch again. "Well, then you're in luck, because I release you from that duty."

Instead of jumping from the first branch, I pull myself up to an even higher branch.

"Emelle," Evert growls.

I'm not going to lie, hearing him say my new name gives me a little thrill.

"Go away, Third. Tell Not-First that you couldn't find me. Tell him that you *did* find me, and I was fraternizing with the enemy. Or tell him that my wings turned black like a demon's, and then I disappeared, cackling into the shadows. Or hell, tell him that you tossed me off the island to get rid of me," I spout off. "I'm not interested in being responsible for screwing up your lives. I'll leave you alone, and you leave me alone. It's better for everyone involved."

As much as I hate it, it's true. I don't want the high fae to find out that the guys hid me. Because if something happened to the guys because of me...I couldn't live with the guilt. I have no doubt that Chaucel was telling the truth about executing them.

"You're being ridiculous."

"No, I'm not. I don't want any of you to get killed because of me," I say quietly.

Evert's eyes soften at my admission.

"So let's just pretend I was never here. I'll leave this island as soon as I can, I promise."

With a deep breath, I walk to the end of the second branch and jump. My wings come out faster this time, even as my muscles hurt sooner. I'm at least twelve feet up, but feeling the air under my wings is freeing, even under the weight of the guys' stares. I catch a breeze and soar for a few seconds before landing on the ground again. I can't help the smile that stretches on my lips. That felt good.

Sylred and Evert are now standing sentinel in front of my tree, trying to block my way, so I simply pick another one. I pull myself up the first branch before they can get to me.

"Dammit, Emelle. Stop it. You're going to get hurt," Evert says, looking up at me from my spot on the branch.

"And like I told you before, it's not your concern if I do."

"Why are you doing this?" Sylred asks. His tone isn't incredulous or frustrated, just curious.

I pull myself up two more branches. I'm twenty feet up now. "Because," I call down to him. "I need to learn how to really fly. I need to exercise my muscles and train my wings so that I can get off this island."

"You're saying you don't know how to fly?"

Oops.

"Umm...I'm just out of practice."

The branches are thinner up here, so I step carefully as I walk to the end. But not carefully enough. When I'm halfway to the edge, the branch suddenly snaps under my feet, and I start to fall.

I hit the branch below me and spin forward. There's not enough space or time to open my wings, but instead of falling to the ground, I'm caught by a pair of strong, warm arms. The air gets knocked out of me.

"Oof." I look up and see that Sylred's the one who caught me. Our eyes lock for a moment, and I swallow. "Thanks."

He makes a noncommittal sound before setting me down, and I try to calm my racing heart. I try to take a step back from him, only to slam into a wall of man-chest behind me.

I turn to Evert with an innocent smile. "Excuse me, you're in the way of my tree. I need to climb again."

"Like hell," Evert snaps.

He has a terrific scowl on his face, and his blue eyes are stormy.

"You're not in charge of me."

"You're going to break your bloody neck. I've had enough of this shit."

Without warning, he bends down and, in one fluid motion, catches his shoulder on my belly and lifts me up, flinging me over his shoulder.

"Hey!" I yelp in surprise, scrambling to pull the tunic down over my ass. "Put me down!"

He ignores me and starts walking, his long strides jostling me with every step. I struggle to keep the shirt tucked over my bottom. Sylred walks behind us, and I glare at him, too, because he's guilty by association. I punch Evert's back, but really, the guy is a solid mass of muscles, and I'm probably just hurting my hand more than I'm hurting him.

I try to kick him instead, but he brings up his other hand and smacks me on the butt. I squeal and try to kick him again, but he just holds my legs together with his free hand so that I can't.

"Don't make me spank you again, Scratch."

My face burns with embarrassment. "I hate you. I hate you both."

Sylred raises his brows. "Why both? I just caught you from falling out of a tree."

"You're letting him manhandle me!"

"I can't control him."

"No, he can't," Evert agrees. "Besides, I'm hungry. You must be, too, after you so colorfully tossed out the contents of your stomach earlier. I gotta say, the fruit looked *much* better going *in* that pretty mouth of yours than it did coming back out."

I knock my fist against his skull. I don't even manage to move his head. It's embarrassing.

"You like food too much to pass on dinner," Sylred agrees.

My stomach growls right then. Traitor.

I sigh dramatically. "Fine. Can you please put me down now?"

"Are you going to follow us back like a good little Scratch?"

I want to retort something sarcastic, but I also want for my butt to not be in immediate danger of flashing anyone. "Fine," I agree with a huff.

When he sets me down, I fix the shirt to make sure it's not riding up anywhere. The guys walk on either side of me like they're waiting for me to break out into a run. But they mentioned food, so I'm not planning on getting away anymore. My stomach has taken over. Maybe I'll try to sneak out when they're sleeping.

Our pace is leisurely as we walk in companionable silence, which is actually nice. It's not until we've been walking for a minute or so that Evert's voice breaks through and says, "Can't keep your hands off me, eh, Scratch?"

I jerk my head to the side and notice that I've got hold of Evert's arm. My hand is clutching his bicep, and my thumb is... stroking his skin back and forth. How embarrassing. I quickly snatch my hand away and glare down at it like the hussy it is.

"Sorry," I mumble under my breath.

But really, I just wish I could reach out and touch him again without him noticing.

Evert laughs. "You always do that," he muses.

"Do what?"

Sylred is the one to answer. "Touch one of us. Or grab something to hold. It's almost like it's subconsciously done."

A blush stains my cheeks. He's right. I keep catching myself reaching out toward them or impulsively grabbing something as I walk by, just so I can remind myself that I can.

But come on. I went *decades* without being able to touch another person. Without being able to feel anything at all. Every time I tried to, my hand would just go right through it. So yeah, maybe I overstep personal boundaries.

I change the subject, because they won't understand, and I don't want to admit how much I crave to feel their warm skin. "What happens when I tell you all everything and you don't believe me?" I ask, because this is what I've been dreading all along.

Evert and Sylred share a look. "Look," Evert says with a sigh, stopping to face me. "This won't be forever. We have the culling in a couple of weeks, and then this will all be over. If you aren't here to bring us harm in any way, then you have nothing to worry about. So just play nice, tell us what we want to know, and I promise we won't let Ronak hurt you."

"But what if you don't believe me?" I repeat.

Evert shrugs. "If you're telling the truth, we'll be able to tell."

I perk up. "Why? Is that someone's power?" I ask, remembering that they all have one.

Evert smirks but doesn't answer. "Wouldn't you like to know?"

I roll my eyes.

As we continue walking toward the cabin, my hand snakes out to grab hold of his arm again. Neither of us comments on it.

CHAPTER 16

I continue to walk beside the guys, absentmindedly scratching my arm where my itch used to be. I like to keep up on it. Just in case.

"You keep doing that and you're not going to have any skin left there," Evert says.

I shrug and stop scratching. "Can't be too careful. I'm telling you, don't ever let an itch go. You have no idea how that oversight can haunt you."

He shakes his head at me like he can't quite get a grasp on the things I do or say. "Do you—"

Evert's words are cut off suddenly as a giant shadow leaps out at us from the side and crashes into him.

I scream and trip, falling backwards on my butt. It takes a few seconds for my mind to catch up with what I'm seeing.

There's a big beast trying to maul Evert as they grapple on the ground. Its fur is dark gray in color, and it has curling horns on its head and huge fangs that stick out of its lips, its hackles raised menacingly.

It has claws like talons and a short, stubby tail. It's bigger than me, and probably at least a hundred pounds heavier.

Where the hell did this thing come from? In a moment, the beast has tackled Evert onto his back, and another one comes running to attack him, too. The beast pins him down, going for his throat with its huge fangs.

But suddenly Sylred is there, grappling with it, trying to get it off Evert. Evert manages to knock the second beast off of him and grabs its throat in a headlock while he reaches for his knife.

I'm still sitting frozen on the spot where I fell down like an idiot until I feel the hairs on the back of my neck rise.

Uh-oh.

I turn my head slowly, and my heart drops when I see two more beasts right behind me.

"Emelle, fly!"

I'm not sure which of them yells it at me, but I don't have to be told twice. I scramble to my feet and bend my knees, launching myself into the air as high as I can just as the beasts launch themselves at me.

I stretch out my wings and flap desperately. Both beasts jump for me, barely missing my feet. I tuck my knees to my chest and keep flapping, gaining pathetic inches up, but it's the best I can do.

I try to use every single breeze to my advantage as I flap frantically, but I'm just not high enough to catch any real wind. It takes everything in me to keep myself off the ground.

I steal a look behind me but wish I hadn't. "Shit." They're following me.

They're right below, running after me and showing no signs of slowing or stopping. I keep going, my heart hammering with fear as they snap their jaws and continue to take running leaps at me that I barely dodge. But I'm tiring. I know I can't keep going like this for much longer.

I maneuver around the trees, twisting and turning around them, desperately trying to not crash into one. I try to gain more height, but I can't manage it with the trees so close together, and I'm unable to spread out to my full wingspan.

I see a huge boulder below me and barely register it before I realize my mistake. One of the beasts runs right for it and launches itself into the air, using it as a jumping point for added height.

Powerful jaws wrap around my ankle, the beast's fangs piercing my skin instantly as it yanks me down. I scream as I fall and land hard on the ground, my head smacking against the rock.

The beast still has hold of my ankle, and the pain is so intense that I can barely breathe. Another beast comes upon me, too, and I know it's over. I'm going to die right here and now.

My screams turn to sobs, but I'm stuck with absolutely no hope of getting away. The second beast runs toward me, and all I can do is lift my arms to block my face before it jumps, its fangs ready to rip me into shreds. But the impact never comes.

I hear a pained shriek and a terrifying growl. Lowering my arms, I look up to see Ronak tackling the beast to the ground. He appeared out of nowhere, all massive muscles and uncontained fury.

Ronak lifts the beast by the scruff of its neck as if it weighs nothing, takes hold of its head, and snaps its neck. He tosses it to the ground in a heap and then turns to me, but the other beast starts pulling on my ankle, trying to drag me away.

I cry out in pain, and I know that if the beast bites down any harder, there's a good chance it will rip my foot clean off. Ronak's tail rises behind him, twitching with warning. His long brown hair and beard looks like a mane around his face, and his eyes flash gold. He looks feral and dangerous.

Locking eyes with the beast, Ronak lets out a low, threatening growl. It makes the hair on my arms rise. The growl doesn't deter the beast at all. It rears up and then clamps down on me even harder than before, making me scream in agony.

In an impossible leap, Ronak is suddenly there. He reaches his huge hands around the beast's jaws and wrenches them open. The moment the fangs leave my leg, I try to crawl backwards on my elbows, but I'm hurt and dizzy from the blood loss, and every movement that drags me along sends a fresh wave of pain so intense that I can't manage more than a couple of feet.

The beast and Ronak are locked in a vicious fight. The beast leaps and clamps down on Ronak's arm, but Ronak rears back to throw a punch, aiming for its side. The beast manages to dodge it at the last second, but Ronak still lands a glancing blow across its ribs, and the sound of snapping bones cracks in the air. If the beast hadn't dodged, Ronak would have killed it with just that single hit.

The beast lands and shakes its head with a dazed shriek. Ronak's massive muscles flex and his tail flicks. As they circle each other, the beast snarls at Ronak, but Ronak snarls right back. The sound is so bestial that I flinch. Then the beast turns to me.

It's like the animal has just realized how big and ferocious Ronak really is, and it knows it's going to lose the fight, so it decides to take me out instead. I flinch back as it leaps for me, but once again, it doesn't reach me.

Ronak is suddenly there in front of me, and the beast crashes into him instead. They land only inches away, and then Ronak straddles it, grabs the beast's head with both hands and *pulls*.

Ronak rips the beast's head from its body with a sickening sound of popping bone and tearing muscle. He tosses it away like garbage and gets to his feet, staggering slightly, and I stare up at him with wide eyes.

His shirt is ripped, his chest is heaving, and he's covered in blood. His nearly seven-foot height towers over me, and even though I know he just saved my life, I can't help but feel fear. The expression on his face is deadly and vicious. His muscles

ior, and I know that as long as I hear it, everything will
y.

n't know how long I drift along with the melody, but it's
e a part of my soul. I don't know when my sobs drain
r when the shaking calms. But before the song ends, it
ie into a deep sleep, and I embrace the darkness with
rms, because even if this is death, it's peaceful, welcom-
d far too tempting to deny.

iis is death, so be it.

are tense, poised with strength ready to strike. He just ripped
the head off a two-hundred pound beast like it was nothing, and
I tremble at the sight of him.

If he wanted to kill me, now would be the perfect time. He
could end me and blame it on the beast, and no one would be
the wiser. But he doesn't. He could've let the beasts have me. But
he didn't. He saved me. *Ronak.* Out of all the guys, Ronak
saved me.

I don't know what to make of it. He takes a step toward me
and then stops himself. We stare at each other without speaking,
and I feel tears falling down my face.

"Please…" I plead.

I don't even know exactly what I'm pleading for. He clenches
his fists, his whole body on edge. I can see the lines of sinews
straining in his neck. Then Sylred comes crashing into the
clearing.

"Ronak," Sylred says, hurrying to stand in front of him,
trying to get his attention.

Ronak still doesn't look like himself. He looks murderous.
Predatory. Animalistic. His normally black eyes are still shiny
and gold, and his lips are still pulled back in a snarl. Ronak
continues to stare at me from over Sylred's shoulder, and I can't
look away.

"Ronak," Sylred snaps, moving closer to block our view.
"Evert is hurt."

This finally seems to snap him out of whatever trance he was
in. He shakes his head as if to clear it, and I watch as his eyes
turn black again.

"Where is he?" he asks, turning to Sylred.

"That way. He's unconscious. You'll have to carry him. He's
too heavy for me. I'll get Emelle."

When Ronak walks away, I realize that I'm still trembling
and crying. My leg looks really, really bad.

Sylred comes and kneels beside me, but I flinch when he

reaches out to touch me. "It's alright," he says quietly. His voice has a natural calming sound to it. "You're okay now. It's all over."

I can't speak. My whole body begins to shake violently. As soon as he says it's over, my mind goes into overdrive, and I keep replaying the terrible scenes. Every second lasts a lifetime.

"I'm going to pick you up now, okay? I need to take care of your leg. You've lost a lot of blood, and Evert isn't well enough to heal you."

I don't answer, but he scoops me up as carefully as he can. Even as gentle as he tries to be, pain explodes in my leg and foot.

"I'm sorry, Emelle," he says, his mouth in a grim line.

As soon as I'm secure in his hold, he takes off, careful not to jostle me too much. I stare at the beasts behind us, their bodies bloody and unmoving. I can't take my eyes off them.

I don't know how long it takes for us to get to the cabin. I don't know what the voices say as the guys speak around me. I just stare at my ruined leg and shake and cry and bleed and hurt.

I'm laid down on furs, and then someone is talking to me, but I don't hear them. I see Evert suddenly laid down beside me. He's covered in blood, and I can't stop staring at his unmoving body. This is all my fault.

I try to reach out to him, but I'm too far away, which only makes me cry more. Gods, if he dies… Another sob escapes my throat.

"Please don't die," I whisper.

Then someone is touching my hurt leg, and I scream again and thrash with pain, but strong arms keep me down. "Emelle, listen to me, you have to stop moving or you're going to hurt your leg even more. I know it hurts, but stop fighting us."

But I can't connect the words to meaning. All I know is that they're hurting me. I hurt so damn bad.

"She's in shock."

"Do something, Sylred."

"She's losing too much blood."

"So is he."

"Dammit!"

"I need more bindings."

"Fuck, Emelle, hold still!"

"Sylred!"

"Give her to me."

All of their voices are a jumbled mess i[n] tell who's saying what. Hands are all over [me] as I scream and thrash. Incoherent word[s] alongside shrieks of agonizing pain.

It hurts.

It hurts so much worse than all my [pains] together. Evert is hurt, and it's all my fault.

I can't stop fighting the hands that hol[d] the pain from consuming me like a ragin[g] me. I can't escape it.

Then I hear something.

My whole body goes still at the sound, [___] my throat. My eyes are sealed shut with [the] darkness, I hear the most beautiful, calmin[g] existed.

It's a low whisper of a melody. A slo[w] immediately smooths over my sharp panic into my ears and burrow into my bones, heartbeat. It swims in my blood. It capt[ures] breathes new air into my lungs. The tune and I feel more peace than I've ever felt in It's a song that you want to fall into and liv[e]

I hear murmurs of voices, but I do[n't] them. I don't even pay attention to th[e] against my ankle or the bindings I feel [___] center of my pain. All I concentrate on is [the]

my s[___]
be o[___]

I
beco[___]
away[___]
pulls[___]
open[___]
ing, a[___]

If [___]

140

141

"Do something, Sylred."

"She's losing too much blood."

"So is he."

"Dammit!"

"I need more bindings."

"Fuck, Emelle, hold still!"

"Sylred!"

"Give her to me."

All of their voices are a jumbled mess in my head, and I can't tell who's saying what. Hands are all over me, holding me down as I scream and thrash. Incoherent words fly from my mouth alongside shrieks of agonizing pain.

It hurts.

It hurts so much worse than all my previous injuries put together. Evert is hurt, and it's all my fault.

I can't stop fighting the hands that hold me, and I can't stop the pain from consuming me like a raging fire. It's going to kill me. I can't escape it.

Then I hear something.

My whole body goes still at the sound, the screams dying in my throat. My eyes are sealed shut with tears, but even in the darkness, I hear the most beautiful, calming sound that has ever existed.

It's a low whisper of a melody. A slow, tranquil tune that immediately smooths over my sharp panic. I feel the song seep into my ears and burrow into my bones. It slows my frantic heartbeat. It swims in my blood. It captures my exhales and breathes new air into my lungs. The tune sings to me, for me, and I feel more peace than I've ever felt in my entire existence. It's a song that you want to fall into and live in forever.

I hear murmurs of voices, but I don't pay attention to them. I don't even pay attention to the hands that move against my ankle or the bindings I feel wrapping around the center of my pain. All I concentrate on is the song, because it's

my savior, and I know that as long as I hear it, everything will be okay.

I don't know how long I drift along with the melody, but it's become a part of my soul. I don't know when my sobs drain away or when the shaking calms. But before the song ends, it pulls me into a deep sleep, and I embrace the darkness with open arms, because even if this is death, it's peaceful, welcoming, and far too tempting to deny.

If this is death, so be it.

CHAPTER 17

J'm vaguely aware of voices as I wash up to shore after swimming for so long in slumber. The voices are waves at first, steady, low, constant.

When I open my eyes, I find myself back in the cabin, in yet another bedroom. The first one I'd awoken in was plain and bare, but that's the complete opposite of this one. This one is full. I sit up carefully and stare.

There are wooden…things. Everywhere. Things carved with a blade and polished to shine. Some creations are as small as my hand, and some are as tall as my body. I have no idea what they all do, but they're beautiful. They're stacked on handmade shelves, tucked into every corner. I want to touch them all. I want to figure out what they're for.

But then I remember. The high fae. Hiding in the outhouse. Bathing the filth off of me. The guys coming to bring me back. The beasts attacking us. Ronak…

I lift the blanket away from me to look at my ankle, expecting to see a bloody mess, but my leg is smooth and as unblemished as before. I can't tell that anything ever happened. Evert must have awoken and healed me.

I remember how badly it had looked. With muscle and bone visible through the gaping slash in my leg. If it's healed like this, Evert must be responsible. I sigh in relief to know that he's alright. I carefully stand up, and the steady sound of voices pulls me forward, so I tiptoe to the door to listen.

"I'm telling you, I *felt* her."

It's Ronak. I frown as I push my ear closer to the door. *Felt* me? What does that mean? He better not have felt me up while I was unconscious, or it'll be my foot that *felt* his balls with a swift kick.

"I knew exactly where she was. I felt her fear and her pain."

My mouth opens in surprise.

"That's not possible," Evert says with a condescending drawl.

"No, I felt her, too," Sylred admits.

So not only Ronak, but Sylred, too? I don't know what to make of this revelation, and I have no idea how it's happened, or what exactly has happened.

"But what does it mean?" Sylred asks. "How did she do it?"

I can only hear mumbles in response and then, "It's the magic that attacked us when we first touched her. It has to be," Ronak says.

"What, like some sort of protective spell?" Sylred asks.

"I don't know," Ronak answers, stupefied.

"You're both fucking tipped in the heads," Evert says.

"You're saying you've never felt that slight tug toward her?" Sylred asks.

"Oh, a part of me is tugging toward her, alright. It just has nothing to do with magic."

I snort silently. What a horn dog.

"Can you think without your cock for one godsdamned second?" Ronak snaps.

"I don't know; can you not ruin our lives with yours?" Evert retorts.

Whoa.

Arguing ensues. There's a lot of swearing.

I've heard enough. I may not know what the hell is going on, but I know that once the arguing dies down, Ronak will figure out how to blame the "tugging" thing on me. Everything gets blamed on me.

Before he can get around to that conclusion, I open the door and walk out, doing my best to stand tall when all three heads swivel to look at me.

I hold up my hands and take a deep breath. "Okay, look. I have no idea why you can feel me. I'm kind of creeped out by it, to be honest. I swear, that magic that touched you when I landed on the island wasn't mine. But before you say anything else...before you start yelling at me about the magic or calling me a demon spy or threatening to kill me or just...generally start acting like assholes and decide to tie me up again, can I say something?"

They all stand perfectly still, and I swallow under their intimidating watch. Ronak doesn't say yes, but he doesn't deny me, either, so I figure this is as good as I'm going to get.

I look at Evert and Sylred first and take a breath. "Thank you. If you hadn't come to get me, I could've been alone in the woods when those beasts attacked, and I wouldn't have escaped. And thank you for carrying me back and calming me, Sylred. I don't know what you did...but I know it was you. Whatever that was, it helped. Like, a lot. Because that bite *hurt*."

"I'm glad it helped," he says with a soft smile. "They have venom in their bites. It's why it hurt so much."

That makes sense. I never want to be bit by one of those beasts again.

Finally, I lift my eyes to Ronak. I tilt my head to study him. I wonder what would have happened if we'd met under different circumstances. This huge mass of muscle and scowls. This male who exudes raw strength. The one I first saw, the one I first wanted to feel. This is the same guy who didn't hesitate to shoot me down and tie me up, but who also hid me from the high fae and then saved me from a terrible death. After what I saw him do with the high fae and the beasts on my behalf, I feel like there's been a shift between us.

The problem is I have to make him admit to that shift, too. And with someone as stubborn as Ronak, that means I have to play this just right.

I let a soft smirk spread on my lips as I continue to look at him. The smile immediately sets him on edge, I can tell. Me, smiling at him is the last thing he expects, and he frowns at me, his brown tail twitching in agitation.

Ignoring my pounding heart, I walk toward him, feigning calm. He tenses, but I keep going until I'm right in front of him. I have to crane my neck to look up at him, because my head only reaches him mid-chest, but I know that eye contact is crucial in this moment.

I can feel the others nervously watching the exchange, wondering what I will do. It's like a stray wolf approaching an alpha. I'll either be accepted into the pack or be attacked.

The more he frowns down at me, the more my smile stretches until I'm practically beaming. It really freaks him out.

"You saved my life," I say in an accusatory tone. He catches it and narrows his eyes on me.

"Yeah, so?" he asks defensively.

"You've been threatening me since I got here. You've been nothing but mean and distrustful. You shot me out of the sky just for falling over your island. You could've let Chaucel take me. You could've let those beasts kill me, but instead, you protected me both times," I say.

I stand up on my tiptoes and lean closer to him so that my face is right in front of his. "You want to know what I think?" I ask, my voice barely above a whisper. "I think you saved me because you *wanted* to. I think that you know I'm not your enemy. You don't hate me, Not-first. Admit it."

146

I swear the color drains from his face. Some people are afraid of snarling beasts in the forest or the threats of beheading, but nope, not Ronak. No, he's afraid of feelings and a smiling girl.

"Yes, I do," he says gruffly, shifting on his feet.

"No, you don't. Deep down, you know that I'm not really any of those bad things you keep accusing me of being. You don't hate me," I say, crossing my arms stubbornly, daring him to admit it.

He waves a hand at me dismissively, but I catch it in mine, and he completely freezes up. I'm talking water-turns-to-ice freezes. The fact that I'm touching him has him in a full-blown panic. It's hilarious, but I don't laugh at him. If I laughed at him now, it would ruin everything.

"You don't trust me yet, but I'll change that. I'll prove to you that I'm not a threat to you or your covey, and then I'm going to break through this whole gruff exterior thing you have going on," I proclaim as I hold his hand, tracing the rough calluses along his palm with my soft fingers. He honest-to-goddess shivers from my touch. I'm going to count it as one of my greatest accomplishments. "I'm going to wear you down until you admit it."

He grunts and starts to turn away. He really wants to escape me. But I stop him, not with strength, but pure surprise factor. I let go of his hand and fling my arms around his middle, squeezing him tight. His whole body seizes up as if he's under attack instead of just receiving a hug.

"I forgive you for shooting me with an arrow. I forgive you for tying me up. I know you were just trying to keep your covey safe. And thank you, Ronak," I say against his chest. "Thank you for saving my life."

The words hover between us, sticking between us like beads of sweat. He still hasn't moved, so I take pity on him, drop my arms, and back a step away. All he can do is stare down at me in shock. When he's not scowling at me, he looks so incredibly handsome.

I've rendered him speechless. It's a nice change on him. Plus, now I know that when he's running his mouth, all I have to do to shut him up is hug him. It's good ammunition to have at my disposal. He closes his mouth with a click and then turns on his heel toward the door. He practically runs out of the cabin.

I listen to his fading footsteps outside before turning to the other guys. They're all staring wide-eyed at me, like I'm some rare animal they've just discovered. Then, all at once, they burst into uproarious laughter.

Sylred bends over, clutching his stomach while his laughs escape him. Evert has his head thrown back, letting his boisterous laugh echo off the ceiling. I join in, too, because their laughter is completely contagious and also because I can still see Ronak's terrified face after I'd hugged him. I soon have tears running down my face from laughing so hard, and my stomach hurts.

"Did you see his face?" Evert asks. "The bastard was petrified of her."

Sylred chuckles. "Who knew the one with the strength power would be so fragile against a pretty girl? Poor guy didn't stand a chance."

"He didn't stand a chance because she cheated."

I scoff and put my hands on my hips. "What? I did not cheat. It was a hug. I was simply showing him the sincerity of my gratitude," I say, pressing a hand to my heart. "Besides, I'm right. He saved my life. Twice. On *purpose*. He definitely likes me." This sends the guys into another laughing fit. "Keep it up," I warn them with mock seriousness. "You're giving Not-First a chance at being first."

They shake their heads at me, smiles still plastered on their faces. "I haven't laughed this hard in…" Sylred trails off. "Gods, I don't even know when I last laughed like that."

Evert pats me on the head. "Come on, Scratch. Let's feed you. You need to eat."

"Yes! Feed me," I say enthusiastically. I love eating. They can feed me all day long if they want to.

The guys move through the room and start gathering up food for me, setting it all on the table. Together, we each make a plate. The guys settle into their chairs, and I sit on the floor again with my legs crossed.

"Why are you sitting on the floor?"

"Her wings," Sylred answers over a mouthful of food.

I nod. "Yeah. My wings don't fit in your chairs, but it's okay. The fur rug is soft," I say, settling in. I start to eat the meat, and once again, I can't contain my moans as I bite into the delicious food. "This is so good," I say with a full mouth.

"At least we'll know if you don't like something," Evert smirks. "You'll be quiet."

"Don't make fun of me for enjoying food. You would too if you hadn't eaten in decades."

They both stop moving. Stop eating. Stop talking.

Whoops.

I desperately try to chew up the huge piece of meat in my mouth to fix my statement. "Umm, I mean..." Dammit. Why did I take such a big bite, and why can't I shut my big mouth?

I finally swallow the huge piece, only to start coughing and choking on it. I flail my arms around in a panic. Oh gods, I'm going to be the first cupid to die by choking on meat. Yeah, I know how that sounds. I definitely don't want to die this way. I'll never hear the end of it in the afterlife. Sylred pops up from his chair and rushes over to me. He delivers several hard slaps against my back. A piece of chewed up meat flies out of my mouth and lands on the floor with a slick slap. Eww.

"Took in a bigger one than you're used to, eh, Scratch?" Evert says with a wink.

I pick up a berry from my plate and launch it at him. I miss. He laughs.

Sylred clears his throat. "Right. Well. I think it's time you give us the full story, Emelle."

I know it's time to tell them everything, so I sigh and then nod. "Okay."

The guys exchange a surprised look. "What?"

"That was…easier than we thought it would be," Sylred says.

I shrug. "I'm not unreasonable. And I don't really have anything to hide. I was just keeping it to myself mostly to irritate Ronak because he was being an ass," I say, making the guys chuckle.

I take a bite of fruit and nearly forget my name because of its juicy taste. "Oh my gods, what is this? It's delicious."

"It's called Red Wings," Sylred says.

I stop eating and look up at him. "Seriously?"

He nods with a smile. "When it grows, the red flower looks like wings. I'll show you sometime."

I smirk and take another bite. I think it's my new favorite food. "Does Ronak like it? Or does he call it Demon Wings?"

They both laugh again and shake their heads at me. I like making them laugh. It fills me with something I can't describe. Who knew I'd go from being tied to a tree to this? I feel accepted for the first time in my existence. This must be what it feels like to have friends.

I don't want to give up this truce between us. I don't want to mess anything up. But I still have a lot to tell them—a lot to explain—and I don't know how they're going to react when I tell them what I am.

But for now, I eat and I talk and I laugh with them, because every moment I get to is awesome, and I don't intend to waste it. Something changed for all of us in the forest when we were attacked. Or maybe it was when they banded together and hid me from Chaucel and the guards? Whatever it was, something significant changed between us.

"Whose room was I in?" I ask as we finish our food and start cleaning up.

They have a pitcher of water and a bowl set up on a kitchen worktable, and they use the food remains for a compost heap outside.

"Mine," Sylred answers, collecting fresh water.

"What are all those wood carvings in there?"

"They're instruments."

This surprises me. "Musical instruments?"

"Yeah, I make all kinds. I invent my own."

"That's incredible. Will you play for me sometime?"

He shoots me a smile, and the eye crinkle is in full effect. "Sure."

"So your gift is music," I say. He looks at me with surprise, so I hurry to explain. "After I was bitten, I was pretty out of it and in a lot of pain. But I heard music that calmed me down and made me sleep. That was you, wasn't it? That's your power?"

Sylred just nods slowly. "Yeah. I'm a Sound Soother."

"He can do more than just calm people. He can cause a lot of emotional responses."

Sylred nods. "Anger, violence, happiness..." he trails off.

"Impressive," I say.

Sylred just shrugs, looking embarrassed by the attention. "Let's have that covey meeting," he suggests, moving the conversation away from himself.

I wrinkle my nose. "Ugh. Already?"

"Scratch..." Evert warns.

I huff. "Fine. I'll call Not-First." I skip over to the door and call out as loudly as I can. "Ronak! I need you!"

When I turn back to the guys, they're laughing again. "What?"

Evert chuckles at me. "Nothing. Nothing at all." He turns to Sylred. "Sixty seconds, tops."

Sylred takes the bet. "It'll be forty, but he'll threaten to wring her neck as soon as he gets here and realizes nothing's wrong."

We wait, no doubt with all of us counting, until Ronak's hurried steps rush inside. Fifty-five seconds. He's panting, searching the room for threats. When his eyes land on me, I smile at him sweetly.

He stalks over to me. "Unless you're dead or dying, *don't* call me like that, or I'll push you over the edge of the island next time," he snaps.

Sylred shoots me a triumphant wink.

"What do you want?" Not-First demands.

"Covey meeting, of course. I'm ready to tell you everything."

CHAPTER 18

"*I*'m sorry, you're a what?"

"A cupid," I repeat.

The guys just stare at me. They're all sitting down in their chairs while I stand. It's nice not to have to strain my neck to look up at them as I talk. I told them everything.

I explained all about becoming a cupid and being in the human realm. I even explained my growing loneliness and bitterness and then how I entered this realm. I go into great detail, explaining my encounter with the fae prince and how I turned physical, including the magic he hit me with that must have somehow transferred to the guys when they grabbed me.

It's the only explanation I can give as to why they claim to be able to sense me. I even admitted to how I first came to this realm and stumbled upon their island. I tell them everything, right up until I crashed on their island. They didn't speak at all the entire time.

This is the first time any of them have spoken, and it's to question the first thing out of my mouth—that I'm a cupid.

Sylred takes the lead first. "So...you died, probably as a human in this other realm, and became a cupid."

"Yes."

"Cupid's aren't real," he says slowly, as if I'm daft.

I raise my brows at him and wave a hand at my body. "Clearly, that's incorrect. I can assure you, we're very real. Everything I told you is true."

"We're having a hard time wrapping our heads around this."

"I understand. Cupids are always invisible entities. We exist in the Veil. We're not *ever* physical. Whatever the prince did to me, he pushed me out of the Veil, and when I fell into the physical world, I became corporeal."

"So that's why you kept talking about not eating food before," Evert says.

"And why she didn't know what cold was," Sylred points out.

I nod. "Yeah."

"And why she seems to be generally bad at flying and running and walking and...standing," Evert says with a smirk.

I scowl at him. "Okay, I think that's enough."

I try not to look at his bare chest as it flexes with laughter. I fail, and he catches me looking and cocks a brow at me. Dammit.

Then, slowly, I watch the smirk fall from his face until he's flat out glaring at me.

"What?" I ask with confusion. I don't like this sudden change in him.

"Wait a fucking minute. Did you...are you using your cupid powers on me? So that I want you? You using your fucking magic on us, Scratch?" he yells.

I shake my head adamantly, nervous at how furious he looks. "No. I swear. I haven't used a single power on you guys. I wouldn't do that, anyway."

Sylred crosses his arms, his own face wary. "Why not? Seems like if I was held captive, I'd use whatever power I had to get free. Is that how you got us to trust you?"

"No. I haven't used it, I swear."

They don't look like they believe me, and I hate Evert's change in demeanor toward me. He's always had an easy, flirtatious way with me that I've come to love. But now, he's actually looking at me the way Ronak first did. My heart breaks a little.

"See, this is why I didn't want to tell you guys!"

"We're trying to process," Sylred says.

"You're trying to figure out if I'm lying."

"So?" Evert snaps. "If you're a fucking cupid and you can do all that shit you said you can do, then why wouldn't we wonder? You could be fucking tricking us right now, using your wiles on us."

I can't help the nervous bubble of laughter that pops out of my mouth. "*Wiles?*"

Evert's scowl only darkens. "You know what I mean. Don't fucking play with me, Scratch. Did you use your magic on me?"

"No!" I snap.

Ronak has his arms crossed as he stares at me, his face unreadable. Before, it would have scared me or pissed me off. But now, every time I look at him, all I see is his face in the forest, when he jumped in front of me to block the attacks from the beasts.

"So when you did your duty as a cupid, you...spread love?" Sylred asks.

"You make it sound like a disease. The god Eros created cupids to do his dirty work. He doesn't want to keep up with everyone these days, so we're his minions. But it's not just about 'spreading' love. That's the goal, but everything that comes with desire—flirtation, longing, craving, anticipation, lust, sex... It's all important, and I cultivated it all. Well, for the most part. Sometimes. Usually."

"Unless you were too bitter and jealous, you mean?" Evert asks.

I shrug. "Yeah, pretty much."

"You wanted in on the action, Scratch?"

I narrow my eyes. "You would too if you had to watch people for as long as I did. I had no one to talk to, no one to touch, no one to touch me..."

I feel the sexual tension rise in the room as my words taper off. My talk of intimacy sets them off, and it's awesome. I like to get reactions from them. I'm reaction-deficient.

"Anyway, as soon as I strengthen my wings, I'll be on my way and get out of your hair. I'll go find love, make some friends, eat as much as I can, because food is seriously amazing, and I'll do... whatever else people do when they're alive. So...are we good here? I've told you everything," I say, starting to walk toward the door.

I really want to escape Evert's suspicious anger and go explore their garden more. I could look for that Red Wings plant Sylred told me about. That stuff is super yummy. "Prove it," Ronak says, stopping me in my tracks.

I look over my shoulder at him. "What?"

"Your story doesn't change anything. You've had plenty of time to come up with a story. Just because you've told us, doesn't mean we believe it. We need proof."

"You want me to prove it to you?"

"Yes. Unless you can't."

I look at him warily. "Fine. But you can't get mad."

I turn and walk toward him slowly, my bare feet soft against the wood as I take deliberate steps. My long pink hair is in soft waves over my shoulders and reaches to the small of my back.

I'm still in Evert's shirt and nothing else, and I'm acutely aware of my bare back and the way my cleavage can be seen from the top of the loose ties of the tunic. My blue eyes lock onto Ronak as I prowl closer, because for once, he's not the predator. He's the prey.

I stop when I'm right in front of his chair and position my legs between his. I lower myself onto his lap and lift my hand to stroke along his cheek and jaw, finally touching that scruffy beard I've longed to feel.

Slowly, I allow shivers of flirtatious desire to escape from my fingertips. The power comes out of my fingers in silvery wisps, nearly translucent. Ronak freezes, reacting just like he did when I hugged him. But this time, I can see smoldering embers in his black eyes. I lick my bottom lip, and he follows the motion, making heat boil in my belly.

I lean in closely, our mouths nearly touching. It's so quiet that all I can hear is my own drumming heartbeat. Then, with exquisite slowness, I loose more power in one long, sensual Lust-Breath. It steams out of my mouth in pink tendrils that wrap around him and then disappear.

The embers in his eyes instantly erupt into hot, out of control flames, and I feel his erection spring to life beneath me. The intense smell of arousal floods my nostrils, making my own eyes dilate with yearning. He makes a low, guttural groan that turns my insides into putty. But I wait, not once breaking eye contact with him. I feel the heat coming off of him as his cock grinds into me.

Then his mouth comes for mine. But just before he can make contact, I jump out of his lap. He's out of his chair so fast that it knocks over and falls to the floor with a crash. He reaches for me, but I anticipate the move, so I leap out of the way before he can grab me.

"Uh uh uh," I reprimand him, wagging my finger coyly. "You're still Not-First, remember?"

I hurry to the other side of the room so that the table stands between us. I can see that it takes everything in him not to chase me down. I have to hand it to him. The guy has self-control—I gave him quite a bit of Lust.

I quirk a brow at him and put my hands on my hips, just because I know it'll infuriate him. Ronak is breathing heavily, the evidence of his desire obvious in his pants. He's trying to control himself, but I can see how...hard it is. Ha!

"You asked for it. Lust-Breaths. Flirt-Touches. And if I still had my bow and quiver, I could shoot you with a Love Arrow, too, but I wouldn't do that to you. Anyway, there's your proof," I say sweetly, waving a hand toward a very lustful Ronak from across the room. "Have fun with the aftereffects of that."

Evert laughs at Ronak's expense. "Oh, shit. No, you never did that to me. I would've seen it. Your power is visible," he muses, more to himself than to anyone else.

"I told you."

"That was awesome. How you feeling, big guy?" Evert taunts.

"I've heard a cold bath will help," I tell Ronak with a wink.

With that, I turn around and saunter away, swaying like a badass with a nice ass. I'm so caught up in my hip action that I forget I'm not incorporeal anymore and I can't go through walls. I smack face-first into the wood.

"Ouch," I say, rubbing my face.

Totally embarrassing. What a way to ruin my exit.

I dart to the door, throw it open and flee outside. As soon as I reach the garden, I hear the guys start laughing hysterically.

I soothe myself with the knowledge that I've left Ronak with a raging hard-on that won't wear off for a good while, not to mention a good knock on his pride. That'll teach him to mess with this cupid. Plus, it showed Evert that I haven't been using my powers on him. I can't help but smile.

Cupid: two, Wall: one. Cupidity at its finest.

CHAPTER 19

I'm up a tree, watching the sun fade. I went through my flying exercises nearly all day. Okay, that's a lie. It was just for an hour, and then I mostly lounged around and ate fruit from the garden. What? I got tired, and my muscles are still learning how to do this whole walk and move thing. But hey, baby steps, right?

The guys were off doing their own thing, so I had the day to myself. After practicing flying, I decided to climb up here and watch the sun fade away. It's different from the human realm. In the human realm, their sun lowers in the sky, taking all the light with it. Here, where there's not just one sphere of earth but a ton of floating islands, it works differently. The sun sort of drifts further and further away, until it's just a pinprick in the darkening sky, and then the stars peek out and the moon comes closer and closer. It's like a dance where one partner moves in as the other glides away.

It's peaceful here on the island, but I can't help but wonder again why the guys were banished. I want to ask them about it, but with the way Evert reacted, I know I need to tread carefully.

They may not want to kill me anymore, and they may believe me about what I am, but I don't have their trust. Not yet.

"Have you learned nothing about climbing up trees?"

I look down and see Evert and Sylred looking up at me through the branches. I hadn't realized before how far up I am, but they're quite a ways down from me. "But it's such a nice view from up here," I tell them. "Don't worry, I promise not to fall this time."

Evert rolls his eyes. "Come down, Scratch. It's time to eat."

They know I can't resist food, even if I did gorge myself on fruit for most of the day. I quickly get up and launch myself off the branch. I hear a shouted curse below me. A rush of air greets me as I fall, and I flap my wings three times, landing on the ground in front of them with a soft thud.

"Fucking hell, female, don't do that."

I point my thumbs over my shoulders. "I have wings," I remind them.

"Which you just confessed to never using before this," Sylred points out.

Evert points in the direction of the house with a scowl. "Go."

I roll my eyes but do as I'm told. I like food too much to stand around and argue. When we get inside, Ronak is already there, sitting at the table. I haven't seen him since this morning when I used my powers on him. I pick up a plate and fill it up with food with a smile on my face. Ronak is doing his best to ignore me, but I'm not going to let him off that easily.

"So. How are you feeling?"

Ronak pins me with a murderous gaze. I smile back.

Evert laughs and sits down next to Ronak. "Don't worry, Scratch. We all believe you now."

When I've piled on as much food as I can fit on my plate, I take my seat on the floor and start digging in. Between mouthfuls, I ask, "So, now that you realize how wrong you were, not to mention rude, assholish—yes, I'm making up a word—unkind, arrogant, thickheaded—"

"That's enough adjectives," Evert cuts me off.

"Anyway, now that you realize how terrible you were to me at first, when I in no way deserved it and am in fact completely innocent of all idiotic accusations, are you going to tell me what the hell you are and why you were banished on this island?"

The guys exchange a look, but it's Ronak who answers. "That's not your concern."

"Well, that's hardly fair. I told you mine, so you should tell me yours. What exactly are you? You're not like any other fae I've seen since I've been here. And if you tell me you're some sort of demons, I am seriously going to throat punch you."

Sylred and Evert laugh. "We're genfins. Not demons. This island is demon-free, apparently," Sylred says. "Well, unless you count those devil-spawned beasts that attacked us."

I give an involuntary shiver. "Those things were horrible."

"Yeah, the island used to be filled with them. We were nearly mauled to death the second we landed on this island, but luckily, we managed to thin their numbers down substantially over the years. We usually know where their dens are, too, but that pack caught us off guard. They aren't normally so close to the cabin."

"What if they come here?" I ask, trying to keep my tone calm and cool but failing miserably. I can't help it. Those things nearly killed me and took my foot off.

"They won't. Ronak took care of them. We'll be eating the bastards from now until we leave."

I wrinkle my nose at that but can't ignore the relief that floods through me.

"So...genfins. I don't know anything about that type of fae," I say, fishing for answers.

Evert crosses his big arms in front of him and leans back in his chair. I see his black tail swishing behind him. "Not surprised. You wouldn't see many of us. Our population is pretty pathetic. Plus, we tend to stick to our main island, which is about thirty islands that way," he says, hooking a thumb over his shoulder.

"I can't imagine why; you're all so friendly to outsiders."

Evert uncrosses his arms and leans forward, his blue eyes alight with mischief. "I'll show you exactly how friendly I can be."

Good gods, I think my lady bits just rolled over and drooled. Down, girl.

I eye him appreciatively. "So…does this mean sex is back on the table?"

Sylred starts choking on the water he'd been drinking, so Evert slaps him on the back, which doesn't help at all.

"I'm good with sex on a table," Evert says with a smirk.

I laugh throatily. Now, this is fun. This is what I've been waiting for since…always. Flirting, playing, desiring. My skin tingles with delight, and I can feel my cupid powers hovering just beneath my skin, begging to be released. My feathers ruffle, drawing Evert's gaze.

"Maybe you are," I say, "but I'm not on the menu yet."

Evert's lips spread out into a wide, wolfish smile. "Hmm. I'll have to remedy that."

I shrug a shoulder. "If you can."

He points a finger at me. "But no cupid magic."

"Psh. Like I even need to use it."

Ronak shakes his head and stands up. "Enough."

Evert snorts. "Please. Like you don't want to tip her over? She's hot as hell, and you know it. But if your limp dick is too hung up to perform, I'm happy to take one for the team."

He thinks I'm hot. He's totally in first place now.

"You'll do no such thing," Ronak says. He's such a cock block. "Just because she's not a spy doesn't mean we can have anything to do with her. We don't risk our covey link."

"Oh, fuck the link. We're talking about breaking it anyway," Evert snaps.

Ronak's jaw grinds, and the room grows tense. They're trying to break their covey link? What does that mean?

Ronak finally turns back to him. His eyes are black with anger. "Yeah, but not until after the culling, Evert. We need our link to get through them, and you know that. Which means we can't fuck it up yet. Which means you can't fuck *her*. Neither of you can."

I bristle and get to my feet to face him. "Excuse me, don't talk about me like I'm not here. And did you not hear me? I'm not on the menu!" I retort haughtily.

I'm *totally* on the menu. I'm just not going to make it that easy on them. "I haven't waited over fifty years to just sleep with someone who doesn't deserve this," I say, motioning up and down my body with my hand.

All three sets of eyes follow my hand, taking in the curves hiding behind Evert's shirt. "And you guys definitely don't deserve this yet. You shot me and tied me up, remember?"

Evert gets hung up on one word. "*Yet?*"

I blow out a flustered breath, making a strand of hair move out of my face. "Are genfins known for being thickheaded?"

Evert cocks a brow. "Depends. Which head are you talking about?"

I try to fight the laugh that wants to break through, but a smile slips out despite my best efforts. "You're a pig."

"You like it."

I really do.

"Evert, enough," Sylred says. "You know Ronak's right. We need our covey link intact if we're going to survive the culling."

Evert rolls his eyes. "Fucking royal culling. I can't wait to be done with this shit."

They all nod at that. It's the first thing they've all agreed on.

"What exactly is the culling?"

Surprisingly, it's Ronak who answers. Probably so he can make sure no one says more than he wants me to know. "The culling trials are a series of public competitions against other banished fae. We'll fight to the death."

My mouth drops open. "To the death?" I squeak out. "But why?"

"You aren't the only one who's pissed off the high fae," Evert says, glowering at Ronak.

"So that's why you were banished here?"

"Yep."

"Why not just kill you? Why banish you and then send you to fight?"

Sylred looks at Ronak, maybe for permission, and then back to me. "Ronak would've been executed, and possibly the two of us by covey association, but high-ranking members of fae court cannot be put to death outright. Fae laws protect those in leadership positions."

I look around at this ill-fitting group of guys. "And you three are in a high position?" I ask dubiously.

"Yes. Our covey is set to be leaders for our people."

I just look at them.

"What? We don't look noble enough for you, Scratch?" Evert taunts.

I press my lips together, refusing to let a sarcastic reply fly out. He likes it too much. I look back to Sylred. "So there's more than one covey that's in charge of the genfins?" I clarify. "Yeah. One other. A group of elders."

I tilt my head at them, taking in their appearances. Two of them shirtless (I'm not complaining), all of them with thick, scruffy beards, a shaggy head of hair, dirt under their fingernails, hardened features, sunned skin. They don't look like members of the fae court at all.

I watched members of the fae court. For the most part, they were soft, pristine prats drunk on power and enamored with political games. These guys in front of me are anything but soft and pristine. They are rugged and wild. They don't look pretentious or snobbish. They just look...hot as hell. I clear my throat, realizing I've been staring.

"So...uh, you did something to piss off the high fae, and instead of executing you, they committed your covey to be banished for five years and then set you to fight in the culling," I summarize.

"Yep, that's the gist of it, Scratch. Now, if we're done with story time, I'm going out to train. Any of you assholes coming?" Evert asks, getting up.

Ronak stands up, too. "We all need to train all day long from now on. We need to be prepared. The culling will be here before we know it."

"Can't come soon enough," Evert mumbles, stalking outside.

I would've missed it if I hadn't already been staring at Ronak —hell, I almost missed it, anyway. But I saw it—the flicker of pain in Ronak's expression as he watched Evert walk out. It was there for an instant, and then he closed it off, fitting his usual cold and expressionless mask over his face once again. But it was there. I have no idea why Evert hates Ronak so much, but based on what I just saw, it hurts Ronak immensely. I wonder if Evert knows. I wonder if he cares.

"You can come with us to the training yard. You wanted to practice flying, right?" Sylred asks.

"Right."

"Come on then," he says, leading the way.

I follow the guys outside. We walk behind the garden and head into the forest. After a few minutes, we reach a clearing, and I stop in my tracks, my mouth hanging open. I thought their handmade cabin and furniture was impressive. But this is just...

"Whoa."

Sylred turns back to look at me and then looks at the training yard, trying to see it through my eyes.

He scratches the back of his neck and shows a sexy smile, bringing the eye crinkles out to play. "Yeah. We train a lot. Being banished gets boring."

I look around at the large, immaculate space they've built. There's a fence along the border, and inside there are several sections designated to practice different types of combat. Wooden dummies for sword practice, soft sand for javelin throwing, huge boulders that I realize Ronak actually uses as weights, chucking them across the yard as if they're nothing. There's even an obstacle course. What's equally as impressive is the open stall with weapons stacked inside, all of them wooden or made from sharpened stone, all of them handmade and deadly.

"You can practice on that far end," Sylred says, pointing. "That's where we usually do our running. The terrain changes, so it's good practice. I know you like to use trees to climb and jump off of, but I have a small set of stairs I made that you can use instead. You'll have more stability that way."

Stability and I don't belong in the same sentence. But hey, at least I'm not tripping over my feet every time I stand up anymore. I'm getting used to this whole physical body thing.

I leave Sylred to go where he pointed out. Ronak is still throwing those huge boulders across the yard. He's taken his shirt off and tied his long brown hair back with a leather strap. Every time he picks up a boulder, his muscles flex and ripple with strength. I choke a little on my drool.

Evert is throwing spears, and I'm pretty sure they're going much farther than should be possible. Sylred has gone on ahead of me as I look around, but when I see what he's doing, I let out an excited squeal, making the guys stop and look over at me. I don't care, I'm already rushing toward Sylred.

My hurried feet get tangled up, and I trip and land on my

butt. That's what I get for getting cocky about not tripping lately. "I'm okay!" I say as I jump to my feet again and hurry over to Sylred. "May I?" I ask.

He nods and hands over his quiver and bow. With a broad smile, I move to get a look at the row of targets set up. The first one starts at about thirty yards away, and the farthest one isn't part of the training yard at all. I can see a line of wooden targets going further and further into the woods, hanging on tree trunks in succession, all at different heights. I take the bow and nock an arrow in it.

The bow is pliant but strong, made of a good, solid wood. It's not what I'm used to with my cupid's bow, but I can tell it's been made with care. The arrows are heavier than I'm used to, too, but that will work in my favor in the physical world, since I now have to contend with things like wind.

With perfect form, I line up and aim. I take the shot at the nearest target and hit it left of the center. I hear Sylred make an approving sound behind me. I just smirk against the bow as I pull out another arrow. I hit the next target, and I'm closer to the center this time. By the third target at about sixty yards away, I have it. I've adjusted to the bow, attuned to the wind and the tilt of the arrows.

I narrow my eyes on the next target and hit it square in the center. Then I move on to the one further away, and further, and further, and further. Each one hits exactly in the center, right where I want them to. Yep. I'm a total badass.

I'm finally in my element. I might not be able to walk or run or fly very well, but I can launch arrows like a professional, because I am one. When I've hit the furthest target I can see, I start hitting the different targets in rapid succession. As soon as I've let one arrow fly, I nock another and let that loose, too.

One after the other, I fire them off, quicker than the breeze that helps carry them. When I reach back and find that all the arrows are gone, I realize I'm breathing fast, my arm muscles are screaming, and my hands are cut and blistered from the bowstring. But I don't care, because that felt damn good. I turn around with the biggest grin on my face, only to find that the guys are now in my lane, staring open-mouthed at me. I toss the empty quiver and bow to Sylred and shrug a shoulder.

"What? I'm a cupid. The bow and arrow is kind of my thing." I give them a wink and then turn around, nearly skipping my way over to the track where I can practice my flying.

"What the fuck?" I hear Evert's incredulous voice behind me. "She just hit every single center target without missing once, including the one over three hundred yards away!"

"Yep," is Sylred's quiet reply.

"She can't even walk without falling, but she can shoot like that?"

"Yeah, so don't piss me off!" I call over my shoulder.

There's silence for a beat, and then, "Well, you're fucked, Ronak." I tilt my head back and laugh. He's not wrong.

s hard enough trying to fly in it without showing off my
bits. I'm gonna flash everyone for sure.

ou'll be fine."

ook down at my feet. "I don't have shoes. I could get
rs."

's good to harden them up."

ok around, trying to find another excuse I can pluck from
r. "Umm…I trip. I trip a lot. I could skin my knees or
hing. That would hurt."

n sure Evert would heal you. Now stop coming up with
s and run."

mmit. I'm losing here. I look around at the other guys, but
e pretending to do their own thing, too busy to rescue me
aving to run. Chivalry is dead.

en a thought pops in my head, and I snap my head back to

obs!" I shout loudly.

looks taken aback at my outburst. I'm pretty sure the
uys are looking over at me, too. That word has a lot of

ak sighs. "What?"

ld my boobs up with my hands as if I'm putting them up
lay for him.

obs. I have them. It'll hurt if I run. They'll be bouncing
like balls," I explain, tilting my head in thought. "Well…
e balls," I say, motioning toward his groin area. "But you
t I'm saying. Or maybe those *do* bounce around when
, too? I have no idea. Do they?"

oks at me as if I've grown two heads. I hear Evert start
. I'm not embarrassed, I'm actually really curious. I
eir pants don't look tight enough to really hold every-
ether. But maybe I'm wrong? Or maybe Ronak has tiny
it doesn't bother him? The way Ronak is watching me
ode well for me to get any answers, though.

I'm lying propped up against the weapons shack, with
my arm slung over my eyes when a shadow crosses
over my form, cutting out my sunlight. I move my arm down a
smidge and peek one eye out to see who is disrupting my sun
soak. Not-First towers over me with his arms crossed, wearing
his usual scowl. Although, maybe it just looks like he's scowling.
Maybe that's just his face. Maybe I wouldn't be able to tell if he
was smiling, because of his crazy thick man-beard. "Can you
shift two steps to the left? You're blocking my sun." He doesn't
move.

"What are you doing?"

I sigh and drop my arm, shifting so that I'm sitting up
straighter as I tilt my head up to look at him. "I'm taking a
break."

"You said that twenty minutes ago."

I blink at him. "Umm, yeah. That's how breaks work. You
just sit and…don't move for an indeterminable amount of time."

He shakes his head. "No. We train all day from now until we
leave. That includes you."

I laugh. "Yeah, no. That's not happening." Quicker than I can flinch, he's taken me by the arm and hauled me up. He settles me firmly on my feet before letting go.

"You can't fly more than a few feet in the air, and your endurance sucks. You have terrible balance, you drag your wings on the ground when you're tired, and I've never seen someone so horrible at walking before you. You need training, and while you're on my island, that's what you'll be doing."

I kick the dirt between my toes, forming a divot. "Geez, I'm not that bad."

"You are," Evert says as he walks by us.

"Yeah, well, you just got yourself back into third place, buddy!"

"Training," Ronak repeats, regaining my attention.

"Oh, come on, I can do super awesome bow and arrow stuff! Surely that gives me a pass. Or like a partial pass. Like half of a pass, at the very least."

"Do you ever stop talking? Now come on," Ronak says, turning on his heel. He doesn't wait to see if I'll follow him. Part of me wants to stand there obstinately, but the other part knows that he'll probably just manhandle me. Not that manhandling would be a bad thing necessarily, but the guy has to earn stuff like that. I follow behind him, my steps as slow as I can possibly make them. He waits for me by the running track, rolling his eyes at my pace.

When I finally make it to him, he says, "Glad you could join me."

"I aim to please," I say dryly. "Now what? My wings are already sore from practicing flying earlier. I'm telling you, I can't do more. I have to practice in small bursts. You might have a cute little kitty cat tail, but these bad boys are heavy and take a lot of work to use."

He looks at me incredulously. "Cute little kitty cat tail?"

"Yeah. It's adorable," I say, watching it flit back and forth behind him. "Can I pet it?"

He makes a weird choking sound.

"Whoa. Are you gonna have a fit or somet[...]

"I…you…"

"What? Is petting your tail like a no-go[...] genfin rulebook. Is it off-limits? Too bad. It l[...] when I get out of here, I'll find some other [...] me pet his tail. Or I bet Evert will let me pet [...]

"Fucking hell."

"What's the big deal?"

He pinches the bridge of his nose with h[...] deep breath. "Just…stop talking."

"Okey dokey, kitty cat."

He shakes his head at me while I try rea[...] "Anyway. You need to push your wings [...] way you'll build up your stamina and [...] now, you won't be flying. You'll be running[...]

I stare at him and blink. I probably mis[...]

When he says nothing more, I copy hi[...] arms. "I'm sorry, did you say run? I can't r[...]

"You told us you ran when you were[...] points out. "You ran from the beasts. A[...] nearly ran to the river when you were co[...]

I scoff. "Well, yeah, those times [...] necessity."

He looks at me, unimpressed. "I coul[...] scenario if you'd like. Would you like m[...] those beasts in the forest and have them[...] get a bucket from the outhouse?"

"I hate you."

"Believe me, the feeling's mutual, [...] running. You can stop when I say."

I look down at my clothes. I'm still [...] nothing else. It's definitely not running [...]

"I'm not dressed for it," I tell him.

CHAPTER 20

I'm lying propped up against the weapons shack, with my arm slung over my eyes when a shadow crosses over my form, cutting out my sunlight. I move my arm down a smidge and peek one eye out to see who is disrupting my sun soak. Not-First towers over me with his arms crossed, wearing his usual scowl. Although, maybe it just looks like he's scowling. Maybe that's just his face. Maybe I wouldn't be able to tell if he was smiling, because of his crazy thick man-beard. "Can you shift two steps to the left? You're blocking my sun." He doesn't move.

"What are you doing?"

I sigh and drop my arm, shifting so that I'm sitting up straighter as I tilt my head up to look at him. "I'm taking a break."

"You said that twenty minutes ago."

I blink at him. "Umm, yeah. That's how breaks work. You just sit and...don't move for an indeterminable amount of time."

He shakes his head. "No. We train all day from now until we leave. That includes you."

I laugh. "Yeah, no. That's not happening." Quicker than I can flinch, he's taken me by the arm and hauled me up. He settles me firmly on my feet before letting go.

"You can't fly more than a few feet in the air, and your endurance sucks. You have terrible balance, you drag your wings on the ground when you're tired, and I've never seen someone so horrible at walking before you. You need training, and while you're on my island, that's what you'll be doing."

I kick the dirt between my toes, forming a divot. "Geez, I'm not that bad."

"You are," Evert says as he walks by us.

"Yeah, well, you just got yourself back into third place, buddy!"

"Training," Ronak repeats, regaining my attention.

"Oh, come on, I can do super awesome bow and arrow stuff! Surely that gives me a pass. Or like a partial pass. Like half of a pass, at the very least."

"Do you ever stop talking? Now come on," Ronak says, turning on his heel. He doesn't wait to see if I'll follow him. Part of me wants to stand there obstinately, but the other part knows that he'll probably just manhandle me. Not that manhandling would be a bad thing necessarily, but the guy has to earn stuff like that. I follow behind him, my steps as slow as I can possibly make them. He waits for me by the running track, rolling his eyes at my pace.

When I finally make it to him, he says, "Glad you could join me."

"I aim to please," I say dryly. "Now what? My wings are already sore from practicing flying earlier. I'm telling you, I can't do more. I have to practice in small bursts. You might have a cute little kitty cat tail, but these bad boys are heavy and take a lot of work to use."

He looks at me incredulously. "Cute little kitty cat tail?"

"Yeah. It's adorable," I say, watching it flit back and forth behind him. "Can I pet it?"

He makes a weird choking sound.

"Whoa. Are you gonna have a fit or something?"

"I...you..."

"What? Is petting your tail like a no-go? I haven't read the genfin rulebook. Is it off-limits? Too bad. It looks so soft. Maybe when I get out of here, I'll find some other genfin who will let me pet his tail. Or I bet Evert will let me pet his."

"Fucking hell."

"What's the big deal?"

He pinches the bridge of his nose with his fingers and takes a deep breath. "Just...stop talking."

"Okey dokey, kitty cat."

He shakes his head at me while I try really hard not to smile. "Anyway. You need to push your wings more. That's the only way you'll build up your stamina and muscles. But for right now, you won't be flying. You'll be running."

I stare at him and blink. I probably misheard him.

When he says nothing more, I copy his stance and cross my arms. "I'm sorry, did you say run? I can't run."

"You told us you ran when you were in the fae palace," he points out. "You ran from the beasts. And I'm pretty sure you nearly ran to the river when you were covered in shit."

I scoff. "Well, yeah, those times it was out of pure necessity."

He looks at me, unimpressed. "I could arrange a life or death scenario if you'd like. Would you like me to wrangle up some of those beasts in the forest and have them chase you? Or perhaps get a bucket from the outhouse?"

"I hate you."

"Believe me, the feeling's mutual, little demon. Now start running. You can stop when I say."

I look down at my clothes. I'm still wearing Evert's tunic and nothing else. It's definitely not running material.

"I'm not dressed for it," I tell him.

It's hard enough trying to fly in it without showing off my lady bits. I'm gonna flash everyone for sure.

"You'll be fine."

I look down at my feet. "I don't have shoes. I could get blisters."

"It's good to harden them up."

I look around, trying to find another excuse I can pluck from the air. "Umm...I trip. I trip a lot. I could skin my knees or something. That would hurt."

"I'm sure Evert would heal you. Now stop coming up with excuses and run."

Dammit. I'm losing here. I look around at the other guys, but they're pretending to do their own thing, too busy to rescue me from having to run. Chivalry is dead.

Then a thought pops in my head, and I snap my head back to Ronak.

"Boobs!" I shout loudly.

He looks taken aback at my outburst. I'm pretty sure the other guys are looking over at me, too. That word has a lot of power.

Ronak sighs. "What?"

I hold my boobs up with my hands as if I'm putting them up on display for him.

"Boobs. I have them. It'll hurt if I run. They'll be bouncing around like balls," I explain, tilting my head in thought. "Well... not *those* balls," I say, motioning toward his groin area. "But you get what I'm saying. Or maybe those *do* bounce around when you run, too? I have no idea. Do they?"

He looks at me as if I've grown two heads. I hear Evert start laughing. I'm not embarrassed, I'm actually really curious. I mean, their pants don't look tight enough to really hold everything together. But maybe I'm wrong? Or maybe Ronak has tiny balls, so it doesn't bother him? The way Ronak is watching me doesn't bode well for me to get any answers, though.

He rubs his eyebrows like I'm giving him a headache. "Demon, just run before I wrap my hands around your neck and start shaking."

I ignore the demon thing. I'm going to pretend it's a term of endearment from now on.

"Fine. But if my boobs hurt later, it's your fault."

"I can always massage them for you, Scratch," Evert calls over.

Such a gentleman.

"I'll pass," I say back. I totally wouldn't pass.

Oh, and his nickname for me reminds me to scratch my arm again. I tackle the spot of my old itch with vigor. It's incredibly satisfying knowing that itch stands no chance against my super awesome physical fingernails.

"Take that," I say to my arm.

"Stop scratching it, Scratch."

I sigh and drop my hand. I turn around and start walking along the track, because Ronak is still giving me a death glare and rubbing his eyebrows. I really have to pick my battles with this guy.

Most of the dirt of the track is smoothed out, so at least I won't have to worry about hurting my feet too much. I pretend to run by swinging my arms quickly at my sides, but my feet walk at a leisurely pace. Relaxing, even.

After about twenty steps, Ronak calls out, "Pick up the pace."

I roll my eyes even though he can't see, and I start to lightly wog. You know, the way you pretend to jog, but it's really no faster than walking, just bouncier? Yeah, that's my goal. Fake it. I'm super good at wogging.

"Faster!" Ronak shouts. Fucker.

I pick up the pace until I'm legitimately jogging. It's horrible.

My sore wings bounce almost as much as my boobs do. Gravity fights me with every step. When I get to the end of the track, I turn around to jog back, but of course, I get tangled up and trip. I try to find my footing before I fall and just barely manage it.

"Ha! Didn't fall!" I say triumphantly, already out of breath.

Of course, right as I'm congratulating myself on not falling, I trip again and go sprawling face-first to the ground. "Ugh," I groan as I spit dirt out of my mouth.

Evert is laughing again. He's definitely not in first place anymore.

"You okay?" I look up to see Sylred hurrying toward me. He puts his hands under my arms and hauls me up.

"Yep, stupendous."

He's trying hard not to laugh at me, I can tell. He's a nice guy like that. Still, his brown eyes are crinkled at the sides as he reaches up and wipes my cheek with the pad of his thumb to remove the dirt from my face. The touch sends flutters in my stomach.

"Okay?"

I nod and look down, checking myself for injuries. At least I didn't manage to make myself bleed. Yet.

"Better get back to it," he says. "Be careful."

"Right."

I turn and start to jog-walk again. After I finish two laps, I have to hold my boobs up with my hands because they're getting so sore, and my wings start dragging on the ground because I don't have the strength to hold them up. Good thing they're so pretty and soft, because they're a pain in my ass. And back.

The next time I trip, I stay down.

My breathing is faster than a gale force wind. I see a pair of boots come into view, and they stop right in front of me where I'm sprawled on the ground.

"Get up and keep running."

I never noticed how annoying Ronak's sexy voice was until this moment. I mumble something that may or may not have been a string of curses damning him to the deepest layers of hell, but who really knows?

"I said, get up and keep running."

I lick my dry lips and tilt my head up to look at him. "I can't, it's too hard. Why do people run? It's awful. Did you know people actually do this for fun? I saw humans do it all the time. There must be something wrong with their brains." I narrow my eyes at him and gasp. "Oh gods, you run for fun, don't you?" I ask. "What am I saying, *of course* you do. That explains why you're so unhappy all the time."

He kneels down in front of me and levels me with a glare. "Listen to me, demon. You have less than three weeks before we leave this island. We don't know what will happen to you. If you want a tiny chance of surviving this world, you need to be able to do basic shit. That includes running and flying. The prince is not going to stop looking for you, do you get that?"

I swallow. "Yeah."

"Good. Because it's true. I know him. He'll hunt you down. He'll kill you or use you. And if you can't figure this shit out, he's already won. If you can't run twenty yards, he will catch you. If you can't fly, he will catch you. If you can't take care of yourself out there, he will catch you. So pull out whatever pathetic strength you have inside and use that shit before you get yourself, or us, killed."

"Good gods, I hope you aren't in charge of the pep talks," I mumble.

With great effort, I push myself to stand up. I sway a little bit and my wings ache in protest, but I stay standing. I see Sylred standing nearby, looking worried. "Ronak, maybe you shouldn't push..."

"No," he says, cutting him off. "She's weak, and she has no discipline. If she wants to live, she needs to be better than this," he says with disdain.

I feel my wings ruffle, my hackles rising. Maybe I am weak,

but he doesn't have to throw it in my face like that. He'd be weak, too, if he hadn't had a body for fifty years.

"I don't give a shit whether she lives or dies, but I'm not going to get caught harboring her, and I sure as shit don't want her flapping her jaw when she gets caught and tortured. She needs to get control of herself before the prince captures her, and she screws us over."

I bite down my anger and harden my resolve. I'll do this, just to prove him wrong. Even if it kills me, I'll run just to shut his arrogant, bearded, stupid mouth.

Ronak stands beside me and tilts his head toward the track. "Get going."

So I run.

And run.

And run.

And trip.

And run some more.

I run until my legs are shaking so badly that I can't stay upright anymore. I run until my stomach starts heaving with overexertion. I run until my lungs are screaming at me, and my heart feels like it's going to jitter right out of my chest. I collapse in the sand. Again.

I'm covered in sweat, dirt, and probably some blood. My mind is imagining all the slow and painful deaths I could bestow on Ronak. Every time he yelled at me to keep going, I came up with another colorful way to make him suffer.

I particularly liked the one where I plucked every single strand of body hair from his body, one by one, starting with his beard and ending with his genitals. I'm relieved when I see a pair of boots stop in front of my face that don't belong to Ronak.

"That's enough. She's done for the day," Sylred says.

He casts me an apologetic look and scoops me up in his arms effortlessly, taking care not to crush my wings. I give him a groan of appreciation. I can't really talk because my tongue is too dry and my head is heavy with exhaustion. Still, as much misery as I'm in right now, I feel proud, too. I met Ronak's challenge and I didn't give up.

I'll probably want to die later, but for now, I feel alive.

CHAPTER 21

*Y*ep. I want to die.

Everything hurts. Even worse than when I fell onto this island, and that's saying something. But does Ronak give me a break? Oh no. He makes me fly and run again the very next day, and the next, and the next. Every day, for hours and hours, all I do is train.

I have bruises over bruises, and my muscles are so sore that I don't even remember what it felt like to not have them hurt. I'm lucky that at least Evert can heal my cuts and scrapes. I get a lot of them.

At night, I usually collapse on the rug in front of the fire, and I don't wake up until Ronak is barking orders at me at the crack of dawn to get my ass moving. Yeah, I pretty much hate him.

A week since starting training, I wake up and go through the painful motions of stretching my muscles before attempting to stand. It's embarrassing how long it takes. Ronak stomps around the main room for a minute before telling everyone to hurry their asses up and get to the training yard.

"I'm going to smother him in his sleep," I grumble.

Sylred smiles and passes me a piece of fruit to eat. "He's

rigorous, but we're a stronger covey because of it. Ronak knows that the stronger we are, the safer we are. It may not seem like it, but him drilling and pushing you is his way of caring."

"Huh. Could've fooled me. I thought it was his way of torturing me."

Evert smirks, coming out of his room. "Oh, it is. That asshole loves being an asshole."

Sylred shakes his head and turns back to me. "Emelle, I have something for you."

"What is it?"

He goes to his chair, picks up a pile of fur pelts, and hands them to me. "When Ronak hunted last week, I took some of the pelts and made you some clothes out of them."

I perk up. "You did?"

"It's nothing fancy," he says, scratching the back of his head. "Just thought it might be more comfortable than what you have now," he says. "I tried to fix your dress, but it was pretty ripped up, and the fabric was too fragile."

"Thank you! I'm going to go try them on right now. You're *totally* in first place now."

I rush into his room and quickly strip off Evert's shirt. I've only been able to spot clean it a couple of times since I have nothing else to wear, so I'm ready to be rid of it. I've definitely smelled better.

The clothing is the same dark gray color of the beasts that Ronak killed. The hair is sleek and shiny, and the leather is supple from the sun. I lay out all the pieces and see that he even made me panties that I can wear under the skirt. I pull those two pieces on first.

The skirt stops about mid-thigh, and my lady bits practically sigh at the soft cover of the underwear. Then I work on putting on the top. He made it so that it can be tied up in the back, so as not to interfere with my wings. I put my arms through the sleeveless top and then tie the back, securing it snugly across my boobs. This will be much better to run in. The shirt nearly makes it to the top of the skirt, showing just a peek of midriff.

Overall, I look like a fur-wearing badass. When I come out of the room, the guys have already left, so I take Evert's shirt and wash it before hanging it outside to dry. I'm sure he'll want it back, although it'll be sad that I won't be able to look at his bare chest anymore. Oh well, at least there's still Sylred.

When I get to the training yard, Evert looks over and whistles at me. "Gotta say, you look a hell of a lot better in that fur than the beasts did."

"I know, right?" I say, giving a little twirl.

Sylred walks over, looking me over. Unlike Evert, he doesn't look at me like he wants to undress me. His look is assessing and polite. "It fits."

"It's perfect," I tell him. I stand on my tiptoes and peck a kiss on his cheek. He gives me a dazzling smile.

"What the fuck?" Evert calls over with a scowl. "Why does he get a kiss?"

"Because he's a gentleman," I retort.

"Fuck that. You'd like it a little rough and mean."

And…my new fur panties are wet.

I sashay my ass over to the running track, but Ronak heads me off. His black eyes flit from my feet to my head, but he doesn't comment on my new outfit.

Instead, he surprises the hell out of me when he says, "No running the track today."

I let out a relieved sigh. "Oh, thank gods. I knew you'd see reason sooner or later and stop this madness."

I start walking away to sit down in the shade, but Ronak grips my upper arm and steers me toward the obstacle course.

I shake my head adamantly. "Oh no. Nope. Uh-uh. No can do, Not-First. I just crossed over to barely sufficient in the walking-running category. I am not ready for obstacles in my wake. I have obstacles enough as it is."

"You'll do the obstacle course three times, then you'll practice flying, then you'll get a break, then you'll run, and then you'll fly some more."

I wrinkle my nose in displeasure. "Yeah, I need to talk to someone about my schedule, because it sucks."

"Get your ass over there, demon."

"You know, for someone who quote-unquote 'hates me' you sure do talk about my ass a lot."

"Do you ever just shut up and do what you're told?"

"I've only been conversing for like, a week, so...no."

He growls under his breath at me. "Sylred! You deal with her."

Sylred nods and puts his spears away before walking over. He's already sweaty, but sweaty looks pretty sexy on his shirtless self. He waits for me by the obstacle course as I make my way over. When I reach him, I look over my shoulder to see Ronak with his arms crossed, watching us.

"Okay," I whisper. "Just act natural. Pretend I've said something hilarious and start laughing."

He just blinks at me.

"Okay, good enough. Now, I'll hop over that first obstacle log thingy, and when I give the signal, you pretend like I've just broken my ankle or something and swoop in to rescue me. Then we can both go back to the cabin and relax while gorging ourselves on food all day while these schmucks work out. Sound like a plan?"

His lips twitch before he looks over my shoulder and shouts, "Evert!"

Evert tosses down his makeshift sword and saunters over with a smirk. "Can't handle her, Tune? Don't worry," he says, clapping Sylred on the back. "I'll take it from here."

"Tune?" I ask.

"You know, his power."

"Ah."

"Come on, Scratch. You'll do the obstacle course with me."

I sigh. "Ugh, do I have to?"

He continues guiding me forward. "Think of it this way. Ronak thinks you're a useless, inexperienced weakling who's going to end up on the chopping block. Prove the fucker wrong."

Okay, his pep talk is much better than Ronak's was. "Fine."

He sends me a wink. "That's my girl."

His girl? My stomach just flipped over and started writing Mrs. Evert in its diary. I have to remind it that we're supposed to be playing hard to get and that I've been put on their no-sex list because of their covey link thingy.

The obstacle course has six parts. The first one is a series of logs lined up one after the other that you have to jump over. Then it goes to a wooden structure that's tilted so you have to climb up it using some notches in the wood. From there, it's a long jump to the ground, where you have to crawl on your stomach under a bunch of crisscrossing ropes before you haul yourself up again and race to a tree trunk set in the middle where dangling ropes wait for you to pull yourself up to the top. The last two are a balancing board and a crude-looking ladder where you climb up one side and down the other before reaching the finish line.

In a nutshell: It looks like torture.

Evert takes a swig of water from his waterskin, and I watch his Adam's apple bob up and down underneath his dark beard.

When he finishes and wipes his mouth with his forearm, he catches me looking and winks before tossing it to me. "Drink up, Scratch." I do, all too aware that his mouth was just where my mouth is now. When I finish and put the waterskin down, he lines me up at the start of the course.

"Try to keep up."

"Psh. I'm totally going to beat you."

He chuckles. "On my count. Three, two—"

"One!" I shout, cutting him off.

I sprint forward as fast as I can, leaping over one log after another. I hear him shouting at me about being a cheater, and my grin widens. I actually manage to jump over every log without tripping. It's a cupid miracle.

When I get to the climbing board, Evert is right on my heels. I stick my feet into various notches in the wood as I climb, and for once, my bare feet actually help me along. I can grip much better than Evert can with his huge boots. Once I reach the top, I jump down, using my wings to bring me softly to the ground.

Evert overtakes me as we rush to the crawling section, so I'm forced to watch him ahead of me as we crawl on our elbows and bellies through the soft dirt.

"Stop looking at my ass!" he calls over his shoulder.

"I'm not!" I am. "Besides, your ass isn't that nice to look at!" It is.

Once we pass under the last of the ropes, Evert and I jump to our feet. The tall tree stands sentinel, with ropes dangling from the very top of it. Evert grabs the first rope, and I go around the side and grab the other.

Using his impressive upper arm strength, his muscles bulging nicely, he effortlessly pulls himself to the very top, tapping it before he slides back down. I'm still dangling from the bottom. Try as I might, I can't pull myself up. My upper arm strength is exactly zero. I try to use my legs as leverage, but it doesn't work. Every time I try, I fall right back down without getting more than a couple of feet off the ground.

Instead of continuing the course, Evert comes to stand behind me. "Come on, Scratch. You can do better than that."

I blow a piece of pink hair from my face and stand up. I grip the rope again, ignoring my stinging palms, and try to haul myself up. My arms start shaking before my strength gives out, and I go falling down again. This time, instead of landing flat on my ass, Evert catches me.

"Hmm. We'll work on that one," he says, his hands on my waist.

"I can't wait," I say dryly.

He releases my waist and smacks my butt, making me yelp. "Don't get mouthy. Now get your ass to the next obstacle."

I rush toward the next one, stepping up onto the very thin balancing board. I have to concentrate to put one foot directly in front of the other, but I'm slow going, and I fall off almost immediately. I try to use my wings to help me balance, but if anything, they make me wobble even more because they're so damn heavy and big.

Evert makes me start over at the beginning every time I fall. I have to do this six times before I make it all the way to the end without falling. Walking in a straight line is seriously harder than it looks.

The last obstacle is the ladder. I climb it up one side and down the other, my leg and arm muscles shaky from exertion. When I make it to the bottom, I practically fall across the rope on the ground that marks the finishing line. Evert walks up, hands in his pockets as if he's just taken a nice, leisurely stroll, while I pant like I'm about to die.

"I hate you," I mumble.

He laughs and helps me up. "You're not very good at this." I give him the evil eye before trying to dust myself off. "But," Evert continues, "you're not hopeless, either. You did pretty well for the first few obstacles. You just need to work on your upper arm strength, balance, and stamina."

"My wings make everything harder," I complain. "I think I could've pulled myself up the rope, but my wings are too heavy."

Evert nods, studying my red wings as he raises his hand and traces a finger along the feathers at the top. The sensation instantly shoots a shiver down them, and my feathers ruffle up involuntarily. I slap his hand away. "Stop that."

He looks at me, amused. "Touchy, touchy."

Before he can catch on to what I'm about to do, I bend down and grab hold of his tail, petting it gently. He flinches back in surprise, and his tail flicks out of my grasp. I tsk. "Touchy, touchy," I say with a smirk.

He narrows his eyes and takes a step forward, forcing me to tilt my head up to look at him. "Touching a genfin's tail isn't a good idea, Scratch," he says, his voice dropping to a near whisper.

I have to unhinge my tongue from the roof of my mouth. "Why's that?"

I can feel the heat emanating from his body and smell his arousal. He leans over until his lips are nearly touching my ear. His warm breath tickles the side of my neck, making goose bumps spring up over my skin. "I'll tell you," he says huskily, "… when you make it to the top of the tree obstacle."

He steps back and crosses his arms, and I'm left swaying where I stand, my emotions going haywire and my body flushed from head to toe. I have to blink several times before my mind can form coherent thoughts.

I swallow and narrow my eyes. "Asshole."

He chuckles, flashing me his dimples and perfect teeth. "Just giving you the proper motivation, Scratch. Now come on, let's do the course again before Ronak crawls up our asses."

CHAPTER 22

I'm sitting on the ground under the stars, devouring a piece of beast meat while watching the guys around the bonfire. Sylred thought it would be a good idea to do something different, as a sort of break in our grueling days of training.

When I finish eating, I down a cup of water and lie on my back to look up at the stars. Evert and Ronak are arguing about their favorite types of swords. I'm pretty sure Evert is just arguing with him just for the sake of it.

I feel Sylred as he comes over and lies down beside me. He stretches his arms above him and rests the back of his head in his hands. Neither of us talks for a long time. The only sounds are the guys bickering and the fire crackling.

"Back in the human realm, they'd sometimes have these star-watching events. They could predict when there'd be shooting stars in the sky. People would flock to parks and rooftops to watch," I say quietly, still looking up at the heavens between the treetops. "Looking at stars always makes people feel small, you know? Even the humans would say so. It made me feel like they were kind of like me. That we were all looking up and feeling small, just mere spectators."

"It must've been lonely. Watching for all those years and never being able to be a part of them."

A small sigh escapes me. "It was."

Sylred hums thoughtfully. "Genfins are social by nature. Back on our island, there's usually at least three generations living under a single roof," he says. "And that's a lot, considering the size of some coveys."

I turn my head to look at him. "So all genfins form coveys?"

He nods. "Genfin boys leave their parents' home at a young age, when our powers begin to form. We leave to go live on another island nearby to find our covey match."

This is the most I've learned about them since I've been here. I'm almost afraid to speak, because I don't want to break the spell and risk him clamming up.

"I was ten when I left home," he continues. "I'd never been away from my parents or grandparents or brothers before. Going from family to an island full of strange pre-pubescent boys with a lot to prove wasn't easy."

I try to picture a young Sylred. I imagine him lanky and awkward, with a lopsided grin and kind eyes. "Why just boys?"

"Genfin females are very, very rare, and it's very, very difficult for us to procreate. That's one of the reasons our people form coveys. Multiple genfin males mate with a single female. It is our sworn duty to protect and honor her."

"And what's the other reason?"

"Our magic doesn't fully mature until we form a covey."

"Why not?"

He looks over at me with a shrug. "That's just how our magic works. We balance each other out. It's probably in part to ensure we can protect our female from any threat."

"Why are genfin females so rare?"

"Who knows? But for every three hundred boys, a girl is born. Then she is celebrated and cherished. Not all coveys get the honor of finding a female to form a mate bond with."

"Wait, do you three have a mate?"

Sylred swallows and then goes back to looking at the sky. I hadn't noticed that the other guys had stopped talking until this moment.

"Why don't *you* tell her?" Evert challenges Ronak. "Tell her if we have a mate."

I can tell by his tone that he's picking a fight. Sylred and I stand up and look over at him.

"Can we not do this?" Sylred says.

Evert stalks over until he's standing between Ronak and us. "Why not? We only have two weeks left. Let's hash this shit out once and for all."

"We've hashed this out plenty," Ronak counters.

"No, we haven't. I've been pissed, and you've been silent. So let's do it. Give Scratch the full picture," he says, turning his head toward me. "You want to know why we were banished? You want to know if we have a mate?"

I really do. I'm burning with the need to know. But Evert's cruel face makes me hesitate to answer. "I'll tell you. There was a female. Strong, loyal, kind. Viessa. She would've been good to us. If we'd claimed Viessa, we would be home right now, probably with sons of our own running around," he says. Then he points an accusing finger at Ronak. "But Strength here decided she wasn't good enough for us. Thought himself too highborn for a simple country genfin girl. So he rejected her. He sent Viessa away, without ever talking to us."

Based on the way Evert glares at him, I'd say that he cared for this Viessa. Probably still does. I stand up and take a few tentative steps to get between them. Not that I could really stop them from fighting.

"Delsheen's status and power made her a better match for us," Ronak argues.

"Delsheen," Evert spits, her name like a rotten swear word on his tongue. "Delsheen was a haughty, conceited twit who fucked any noble who looked her way."

Rage rolls off Ronak. I can feel his body temperature rise as his tail flicks up behind him. A low, guttural growl escapes his throat. "I was trying to do well by our covey."

"You were trying to do well by your ego! You threw Viessa away like she was a piece of trash, and worse, you didn't even listen to me when I told you that Delsheen was playing you. You're supposed to trust your covey, but instead, you've always been a fucking prat with a silver spoon shoved so far up your ass you think you have the right to lead us. Well, I don't give a fuck if your power is strength. You're a fucking pussy who doesn't deserve this covey. I'm glad Delsheen fucked the prince behind your back. I'm glad you lost your mind and tried to attack them. My only regret is being chained to your ass, banished on this island alongside you because of your arrogant stupidity."

Ronak is so furious that he's shaking. His whole body is taut, fists and jaw clenched, shoulders tight, eyes like darkness. Evert waits for a reaction. It's what he's always doing, I realize. Pushing buttons, trying to get to where they are right now. Ronak usually ignores him or Sylred intervenes, but not this time.

Just when I think Ronak is about to tell him off, finally have the argument that has so long been buried, Ronak turns on his heel and starts to storm away. But before he can, Evert grips his arm to stop him.

The second Evert's hand makes contact with Ronak's skin, it's like Ronak's flip switches. The barely contained rage that he'd been holding in suddenly unleashes. Ronak flips around, rears back, and punches Evert square in the jaw. Evert goes flying back, his body barely missing the fire, and lands in a heap on the ground. If that punch was landed on any normal person, I'm sure it would've killed them.

Before I can even shout, Evert is on all fours, ready to spring back into action, his tail rising high behind him like a panther. He rushes at Ronak, catching him in the stomach, and the two go down in a flurry of fists, grappling with each other before Sylred can rush over to try to pull them apart. But Sylred is no match for Ronak's strength, and he catches a hit to his stomach for the effort. Evert charges Ronak, shoving him to the ground.

When his back hits, Ronak sends out a kick, making Evert go careening backwards again. Without thought, I fly up and touch down right in front of Ronak, just as he gets to his feet.

He has his fist raised, ready to land another punch on Evert, so I stand on my tiptoes and put both of my hands on either side of his face. "Ronak," I say, forcing him to stop and look at me.

I noticed the change in Ronak's eyes when I saw him attack the beasts for me, but seeing them now, up close, makes me realize how feral these genfins can be. Instead of his usual black eyes, they've turned into a menacing iridescent gold. His sharp canines are bared, his tail twisting behind him, his body shivering with power. I can hear Sylred behind me, trying to grapple Evert to the ground, but I keep my focus on Ronak.

"Ronak," I say again, my hands not leaving his face. He struggles. I can see and feel the struggle inside of him to shut off the feral side of him. "It's okay," I soothe.

When his eyes try to find Evert again, I grip his cheeks and turn his face back to me. "Come back, and you can be your quiet, grumpy self, and I'll come up with all sorts of ideas to try and thwart your training schedules. Come back, and you can pretend to hate me, and I'll pretend like it wasn't hilarious when I Lust-Breathed on you."

His gold eyes stay locked on mine until I see the gold flash with recognition and then flicker away. His pupils dilate, the black irises return, and he takes a long, heavy breath as he comes back to himself, while his wild, feline side burrows back down inside.

"There you are, Not-First," I say with a small smile.

He reaches up and holds my wrists, even as I continue to hold his face. We stay like that for a few seconds, just staring at each other until he finally pulls my hands away from his face and lets go. I turn around to see Evert is gone. Sylred watches Ronak warily but sends me a small, reassuring smile.

"Okay?" he asks Ronak.

Ronak grunts before turning and walking away into the forest. I watch him leave.

"He'll be okay. He just needs to cool off."

I wrap my arms around myself, more for reassurance than from the cold.

"And Evert?"

"He's fine. It might not have looked like it, but Ronak was holding back. He didn't use his full strength on him. If he had, he could've killed him. But genfins are tough. It takes a lot to take us down."

I nod. I'm glad to know that they're both okay physically, but it's their emotional pieces I'm worried about.

Sylred nudges me. "You did good. No one other than me has ever been able to talk Ronak down once his animal side comes out."

"He won't hurt me," I say, surprised by my admission, because I can feel the truth in it.

"No, I don't think he would."

"So that's why you were banished here? Ronak attacked the prince?"

"Yeah."

"Guess we have more in common than we thought."

Sylred laughs lightly. "Looks like it. We were at the kingdom island to announce our match. During one of the balls, Ronak caught Delsheen in bed with the prince, and his feline side came out. He attacked them, but the guards intervened before he could do any damage. The prince wasn't allowed to execute him outright, so he sent him and our covey to banishment."

"And what about Delsheen?"

"The last time I saw her, she was standing beside the prince, watching our sentencing like she thought it was the best form of entertainment she'd ever seen. She loved the fact that males were fighting over her. Who knows where she is now. We don't exactly get gossip down here."

I can't imagine the level of betrayal that's stained their covey. And not just with the female, but with Ronak and Evert, too. I don't know if their bond can be repaired.

"Evert said something about trying to break your covey link," I say, remembering. "Are you really going to try to do that?"

A pained look crosses his face. "I don't want to. But I don't see how we can get back to where we should be as a proper covey. Too much has happened."

Hearing this makes me incredibly sad. "Is there something I can do?"

He gives me a small smile and places his hand on the small of my back to guide me toward the cabin. "We still have to make it out of the culling alive. Then we can worry about our covey link."

"You will," I say quickly. "You're all strong and smart. You'll make it."

"Thanks for the confidence boost, Emelle. Now, come on, let's get you inside before you get all hypothermic again."

"It was one time."

Afterward, when I'm lying next to the dying fire inside, bundled up with furs, I can't stop thinking about everything I learned. I know, beyond a shadow of a doubt, that if there's any way I can help them, then I'm going to do it.

Maybe everything that's happened, everything that's led up to me being right here, right now, was for this purpose. Maybe, just maybe, I can fix them. I'm a cupid, dammit. If I don't fix their hearts, who will?

CHAPTER 23

*T*he next day was tense. Ronak didn't come back to the cabin all night and didn't show up at the training yard until midday, which, according to Sylred, is unheard of. Evert wouldn't even look at him. The day after that, things weren't much better. No one was really talking, and even when I prompted the guys with funny jokes or sexual innuendos to try to snap them out of it, I barely got a response. What a waste.

By the third day, I'd had it. We were all back in the cabin after a long day of training. No one was speaking or sitting together at the table. Everyone tried to pretend to be busy with chores. Even Sylred, who always acted as the peacemaker, was in a serious funk.

I'm so upset on their behalf that I can't even finish my dinner. The horror of that alone was enough to push me over the edge. After listening to nothing but angry, stomping foot-steps and manly grunts for the past half hour, I get up and raid their pantry.

When I find what I'm looking for, I slam four cups on the table, along with the barrel of homemade mead. When you're banished on an island, you have to get creative with your booze.

"Covey meeting right now!" I yell, cutting into the silence like the crack of a whip.

Sylred appears first, popping out of his room. I wait a beat, but Evert doesn't come. "Evert, I'll flash you if you get out here right now!"

It takes less than three seconds for him to appear. He comes right up to me, wagging his brows. "Well? What are you waiting for?"

I coyly lift the bottom of my fur shirt and show him my belly before letting it drop down again.

He makes a face at me. "What was that?"

"That was me flashing you."

He scoffs. "You were supposed to flash me your tits. A deal's a deal."

"Nuh-uh. I said I'd flash you. I didn't say what I'd flash."

"Fuck."

I smile triumphantly as Sylred shakes his head at us. Ronak still doesn't come out of his room. "Not-First, you get your butt out here right now, or I'll come in there and breathe my Lust-Breath all over you!"

It only takes him two minutes to grudgingly comply.

"Sit," I say, pointing to their chairs.

The guys grudgingly take their seats. I stand at the other end of the table and start pouring the mead, passing the cups around until we all have one. "You all have a lot of bad baggage between you. I get that. But you are a covey, and that's more important than everything else."

When Evert scoffs, I shoot him a glare to shut him up. "Now. This is what's going to happen," I say, using my very serious, I-mean-business voice. "We are going to sit here and play a drinking game, and you're all going to like it."

"A drinking game?" Evert asks dubiously.

"Yes. A drinking game. Although I expect it won't be very much fun. It's called Dirty Laundry. You're going to get every-

195

thing all out there and air it all out. All your bad, stinky bullshit that you keep burying so you don't have to look at it. You're going to pull it all out, and then you're going to work through it, as a covey, and move on. You have the culling in less than two weeks. I know you guys don't want to die, and I don't particularly want you to die, either. So we will sit here and play this game until your dirty laundry comes out smelling like happiness and sunshine, or at least until you can stop hating each other. You get me?"

"This is stupid," Evert says.

"You're stupid," I snap back, because I'm super mature. "Here are the rules. You say one thing you feel mad about, and one thing you feel bad about, and then you take a drink. If someone else agrees with your statement, you both drink. The game ends when no one else has anything to say or you're too drunk to say it."

"We'll be here for a very long time," Evert mutters.

"Then I guess we better get started. I'll go first," I shoot back, grabbing the cup. "I feel mad that I was shot out of the sky with an arrow," I say, looking at Ronak. He meets my gaze, his face unreadable as always. "But, I feel bad about scaring you all into thinking I was here to cause you harm."

"We weren't scared."

"Eh. Agree to disagree."

I take a long drink. The alcohol burns and throws me into a coughing fit. "Gods, what is this?" I ask through watery eyes.

Evert smirks for the first time in three days. "I make it. It's not your average mead. I have to get creative on this island. It'll put hair on your chest, that's for sure."

I wipe my mouth, pointing to Sylred. "You're up."

I choose Sylred because he's the one least likely to fight me, and once he participates, I have a better chance of the other two following suit.

Sylred taps his finger on the table in thought. "I'm mad that my covey doesn't get along anymore," he says, not making eye contact with anyone. "And I feel bad that I can't fix things." He picks up his cup and downs the contents, grimacing slightly at the taste.

My eyes move down the table. "Evert?"

"This is fucking stupid."

"I don't care. Do it."

He rolls his eyes and makes a big show of crossing his hands behind his head and stretching his legs out in a fuck-all attitude. "You want to know why I'm mad?" he challenges.

"Yeah."

He hooks his thumb over his shoulder at Ronak. "Because that asshole didn't listen to his covey. He was too wrapped up in getting the noblest pussy he could find that he went blind to what was happening. A covey is only as strong as its link, and he's the one that ruined it, not me. When he told me to fuck off and went for Delsheen, even though I knew she was fucking us over, he chose her anyway, because he didn't want to lose face. He would've subjected us to a lifetime of fucking misery mated with her bullshit, and he didn't give a shit. A covey is supposed to be closer than brothers. We're supposed to make decisions together, but he always tries to run the ship just because he's the one with noble blood. And look at the good it did us. He got us banished for five fucking years."

He downs the cup, not even bothering to answer the second part of the game. My eyes fall on Ronak next. He's not looking at anyone, just staring at a spot on the table.

I clear my throat. "You're up, Not-First."

He doesn't say anything, and I worry that he'll refuse to participate or storm off. But to my surprise, he finally answers. "I'm mad at myself for what I did. With Viessa. With Delsheen. With the prince. With my covey. I've been mad at myself for every second of every day for the last five years. I know our covey is broken and that it's my fault. My guilt and anger eat me alive, and I haven't felt anything else for a long time. So all I can do is try to keep us alive."

Silence.

I swear, if one of my feathers popped off my wing and fell to the ground, we'd all be able to hear it, that's how quiet it becomes once Ronak makes his admission. He tosses his drink back and then goes for the barrel, refills his cup, and drinks another while we all watch him. Even Evert stares at him.

Sensing the need to step it up, I reach for the barrel and refill my cup, too. "I'm mad at all of you for screwing up your covey bond. And I'm really mad for any talk about you trying to break it up. You guys are family. I can see it, even when you're at each other's throats. You work together. You understand each other. Don't toss that away because of a few mistakes and a genfin hussy who didn't realize your worth. Show her and that pig prince that they didn't break you. Forgive each other and be the covey you're supposed to be, and then go into that culling and win."

I take slow sips of my drink, hoping it will make it go down easier. It doesn't. After I finish coughing, I say, "If you don't, I'll feel bad because I'll have to shoot all your asses with arrows for being too stupid and stubborn to move on. And take it from someone who's been shot by an arrow, it doesn't feel very good."

Evert smirks at me. "What, first you're our resident demon, and now you're our angel trying to save us?"

I shake my head, feeling the effects of the alcohol already swimming in my brain. "Nope. I'm your cupid, and I'm going to do what I do best. I'm going to fix your fucking hearts."

CHAPTER 24

*N*ote to my stupid cupid self: When drinking alcohol, you should stop after one, because your tolerance level is none.

You should not, under any circumstance, decide it's a good idea to agree to go against Evert on who can chug a cup faster.

You should also not decide to climb on top of the table to dance and sing songs from the human realm that you don't know the words to. Nobody needs to see-hear that.

And no, Evert's mead definitely does not taste better coming up than it did going down. Somehow, it's worse.

"How you feeling there, Scratch? Or should I start calling you Guts? You've puked enough of them up."

"Go away, Third," I grumble to Evert as I lie face down in the grass outside.

I have no idea how I got here. Everything went fuzzy last night right around the time I started to try to climb Ronak like a tree so that I could swing on his arm.

Evert laughs and kneels down in front of me, handing me a skin of water. "Drink this. I spiked it with some herbs that'll help your head."

It takes considerable effort to sit up, and I almost start puking again, but somehow, even amidst the dizziness, I manage to drink down the water.

"Good girl," Evert says, patting me on the head. "You know, you look pretty cute when you're hungover."

"Well, you look pretty stupid."

His grin widens. "There's that charm."

"I hate you."

He tsks. "Uh-uh, don't lie. Don't you remember what you said last night? You told me I am, and I quote, your 'freaking favorite, because you're funny, and you have dimples that I just want to lick.'"

I squint up at him and groan. "*Noooo.*"

"Oh yes," he says with his shit-eating grin. "You also claimed you would like to kiss Sylred's eye crinkles. Didn't know what the fuck you were talking about, but dude turned about three shades of red."

I put my spinning head in my hands. "Why didn't you stop me from embarrassing myself?" I say into my palms.

"Why would I do that? You were hilarious. You even pinched Sylred's nipples and told him you were glad you ruined his shirt in the shit pile so that you could ogle his chest all the time."

I drop my hands and glare at him. "Okay, you can shut up now."

"Oh, and you continued to play your dirty laundry game, where you admitted to feeling bad about sneaking into Ronak's room and filling his boots with squirrel shit," Evert adds, giving me a look. "Did you really do that?"

I try to stop myself from laughing, but it escapes anyway. "I don't know what you're talking about. I would never do something that immature."

Evert laughs. "Sure. I'm looking forward to you getting drunk in the future. That's the most fun I've had in years."

"I'm glad I could amuse you."

Evert picks a leaf out of my hair and wipes a smudge off my cheek. "I thought you should know," he says, his tone growing more serious. "That was a stupid game." I start to argue with him, but he cuts me off. "Stupid game, but maybe it was alright, too."

"Really? So you don't hate Ronak anymore?"

"Let's not get carried away," he admonishes. "But I am considering not hating him."

I can live with that. "Good."

"Ronak's still an asshole."

I nod. "Definitely."

"And I'm still going to talk shit mercilessly."

"I wouldn't want it any other way."

"But maybe, if we can get through the culling, I'll consider not strangling him in his sleep."

"Please, don't get all sappy on me."

He shakes his head at me and then taps my nose. "You're a snarky little thing."

"Yep. Now carry me inside and feed me. And then heat me up some bathwater and brush my hair and tell me I'm pretty."

"Yes to the first, no to the rest. I told you already, Scratch, I'm not the nice one in the covey. But I'm sure Sylred will be happy to wait on you hand and foot."

I pout. "Fine," I say with a dramatic sigh as I lift my arms for him. "You may pick me up now, but I can't be responsible if I throw up on you."

With a shake of his head, he scoops me up, and I lay my head against his chest, trying to keep it from spinning. It spins anyway. "I'm never drinking your alcohol again."

"That's what they all say."

Inside, the guys are still quiet around each other, but not in the hostile, I'm-going-to-throat-punch you way anymore. It's more like they're trying to figure out how to act now that they're trying not to hate each other. Evert was right. By the time he sets me in front of the fireplace, Sylred already has a plate of food for me, and he's carrying out hot coals to set up under the bathtub so that I can wash off my hangover.

"You're my new favorite," I tell him dreamily after I've eaten and am ready to go soak.

Sylred smiles. "All it takes is a warm bath, huh?"

"For now. But you shouldn't get comfortable in that role. Ronak could surprise us all and become my new favorite."

Ronak walks by just then. "Nope."

"Don't fight it. It's only a matter of time before you want that slot, Ro-Ro."

"Don't call me that."

"You got it, Ro-Ro."

He stalks outside with a shake of his head.

"I'll be sure to endeavor to stay in the top slot for as long as possible," Sylred tells me.

"You're a smart guy."

When Sylred has brought the last of the hot coals to warm the water, he leaves me to my privacy, and I soak in the tub. Inside. Next to the fire.

Taking a bath is *much* better with warm water and a crackling fire beside me. In fact, I'm on a cold bath strike from now until the end of eternity. I soak my sore muscles and wash my hair, using the soap Sylred left for me. It's the same soap that everyone else uses, so I end up smelling like the guys. I'm not complaining.

CHAPTER 25

*I*t's around midday when Ronak comes in the cabin. I'm curled up on the fur rugs, humming to myself and eating grapes on the floor in front of the fire. "What are you doing?" he asks, coming over to stand above me.

I toss a grape in the air and catch it in my mouth. "I'm practicing my hand-eye-mouth coordination," I say, chewing. "Your turn!" I throw another grape, trying to aim for his forehead, but the bastard moves and catches it in his mouth effortlessly. "Huh. You're adequate."

I toss another grape in the air to catch, but this one hits my nose and goes flying in the other direction. I frown up at Ronak. "You're distracting me. Go brood over someone else."

"You should be training."

"I have a pass."

He cocks a brow. "A pass?"

"Uh-huh. Stitch's orders. I get to relax today. You know, since I drank my weight in terrible mead last night and then puked it all up this morning. I'm taking a sick day."

He narrows his eyes and scratches his beard as he studies

me. I throw another grape at him. He catches it again. "Dammit," I mutter.

The other guys shuffle in, going for the table where I've laid out lunch for them. I'm super nice like that. They start stuffing their faces immediately.

Ronak is still studying me. "You have red feathered wings," he says suddenly.

I blink up at him. "Wow. The guys told me you were savvy, but I had no idea. What else have you perceived in that giant brain of yours?"

"And your ears aren't pointed," he continues in his strange assessment.

I stand up, tossing my braid behind me before popping another grape in my mouth. "Tell me more, oh Mighty Observant One. Dazzle me with your deductions."

"You don't have high fae wings. Theirs look more insect-like or reptilian. You don't have pastel-colored skin, although your hair could pass for a high fae. But out of all the fae, you look most like one of them, except you're too short."

I look at the other guys and then back at Ronak. "I'm sorry, is this the game where we just randomly spout off how the other one looks?" I ask. "Okay, my turn. You have a lion's tail. Your eyes get freaky feline when you wig out. Your bicep is bigger than my face. Oh, and you have smelly feet. Like all the time. It's embarrassing."

I look over at Evert. "Think fast!" I launch a grape at him, and it hits him on the cheek and then bounces away. "Ha! You lose."

He narrows his blue eyes on me, picks up a grape from his plate, and throws it at me. I jump up and catch it victoriously, throwing my hands in the air as I chew. "Victory!"

I throw the next one at Sylred, but it hits him so hard that it splatters against his chest. He frowns down at it before plucking it off. "Why are we throwing food?"

"Hand-eye-mouth coordination training," I say. "You didn't do so well, Second."

"Oh, I'm back to Second now, am I?"

I shrug. "Can't keep someone with such embarrassing grape-catching skills in first place. It just wouldn't be right."

"I can do much better things with my mouth than catch a grape," he says with a dazzling smile.

My face breaks into a huge grin. "Now you sound like Third!"

"No way am I in third place still," Evert counters. "And no way is he better with his mouth than I am, Scratch. Don't you forget that."

"You're both idiots," Ronak says, sitting down to eat.

"Well, this idiot is going to be the one she's begging to fuck," Evert replies.

"Ugh, don't be cocky. Besides, I do believe you all voted to keep your hands to yourself, isn't that right?" I look around at them. "Yeah, I heard you say that I'm officially off-limits to your covey," I admit, swaying my hips as I walk over to pluck more grapes from the vine on the table. "I think when you all go to the culling, I'll fly to your genfin island and find myself another hot covey to be with. I'm sure they'll all be happy to fight over first place with me. They'll probably be even hotter than you all, too. You're looking pretty scruffy with your beards."

"Fuck that. You'll stay with us," Evert says with a frown.

Inside, I secretly freak out like a schoolgirl with a crush. On the outside, I'm as cool as a cucumber.

Ronak clears his throat, making everyone look over at him. "Anyway, what I was trying to get to before all the grape throwing is that she doesn't look like any fae in the realm. The second she leaves here and someone spots her, word will get back to the prince. She sticks out too much. She might be able to pass for half human, half high fae, but not with those wings.

When he hears the rumors about a weird bird-demon-girl, he'll come looking."

"I'll just outrun him."

Everyone laughs. It's not a confidence booster.

"You can barely make it three laps without collapsing," Ronak points out.

I twist my mouth in thought. "Then I'll out-fly him."

"He has other fae that fly much better than you. I'm pretty sure his great-grandmother could out-fly you."

I huff. "Fine. Then I'll hide."

"The last time you hid, you ended up covered in shit," Evert says behind me.

I toss him an evil eye, but I don't think it works on him, because he just grins. "Then I guess I'll just turn myself in and become his personal cupid. I'll do everything he wants me to do. I'll start orgies in his ballroom, I'll make sure every fae marries whomever he wants them to marry. I'll spread Love and Lust throughout the kingdom. He'll eventually fall in love with me, because let's be honest, how could he not? Plus, I'll be secretly feeding him my powers over the months, just in case, slowly forcing him to be wrapped around my little finger. And then one night, after hours of sweaty hate-sex, I'll slit his throat in his sleep and stage a coup to overtake his throne."

Done with my speech, I look up at the guys. I toss up another grape, catching it in my mouth with a chomp. I smirk at their dumbfounded expressions. "There. Problem solved."

Ronak makes the first move by rubbing his brows with his fingers. I guess I gave him another headache. "Or…we could get someone to glamour you so that you can look more like a high fae and blend in better."

I cock my head to the side in thought. "Meh. My idea sounds more fun."

"I'm with Scratch on this one," Evert says.

I give him a brilliant smile. "Forget what I said before. You *are* in first place."

"I know I am, love. Why don't you take me into my room and prove it to me?"

I laugh, even as my face blooms with heat. "Cheeky, cheeky."

Ronak sighs at us. "So it's settled. We'll find someone to glamour her. Once we win the culling, we'll find someplace safe for her. She can't leave this island without a glamour. She'll be caught immediately."

"Party pooper," I pout. "But wait, you said you can't get through the barrier. How are you supposed to find someone to glamour me?"

"We aren't. You are."

"Come again?"

"You're the only one who's ever crossed over the barrier. Not even the high fae can do that. So you'll have to be the one to leave and come back. You'll do it the day before our banishment ends."

I don't like the sound of that at all. "Wait, wait, wait. You want me to go to another island alone and find some random fae to glamour me?" I ask anxiously. "You said that I'd be taken as soon as someone saw me!"

The thought of being captured does not exactly thrill me. "Then you'll have to be sure you aren't caught," he says, as if it's the simplest thing in the world. "Why do you think I've been making you train so hard?"

"Because you're a sadistic jerk who enjoys making me suffer?"

"That, and because you need to be able to do this."

I look to the other guys for help but find none. I throw up my arms in frustration. "Great. Don't worry about Emelle. I'll just go on this very dangerous, very terrible quest all alone, while you three relax here and forget to mourn me once I get captured and chopped up into little cupid heart-shaped pieces."

Ronak rolls his eyes and walks away, grabbing a leg of meat on his way out the door. "You'll be training all day tomorrow, so enjoy the rest of your break."

I ignore him as he walks outside and round a glare on the other two. "Okay, so you both just left me totally hanging on that one. I'll remember that," I say, tapping my temple. "A cupid never forgets."

"What song did you make Sylred sing last night because you insisted it was a duet?" Evert challenges.

I open my mouth and then close it again. I forgot. Dammit.

"That doesn't count. I was drunk."

"Looks like your reasoning is faulty."

"Oh come on, how cool would it be to overthrow Prince Pig? I'd wear a kick-ass crown and make people do whatever I said. I could declare a cupid holiday if I wanted. Did you know they do that in the human realm? It's named after someone else, but it totally counts. Oh, and I could decree it illegal for anyone to be named Ronak. And running. I could ban running. I could sit in my royal bed all day, eating my royal food and getting royal foot rubs. Being queen would be awesome."

"Sure, but I'm not bending the knee unless it's in the bedroom," Evert says as he takes another bite of food.

I tsk. "That's treason, Third."

"Back to third place already?"

I shrug a shoulder. "I'm queen. I do what I want."

He flashes a dimple before walking back outside, followed by Sylred.

After re-braiding my hair, eating more grapes, and cleaning up the table, I get bored, so I start cleaning the rest of the place, all the while daydreaming I'm queen of the realm. You'd think a small wooden cabin would be fairly easy to clean. You'd be wrong.

It's clear that none of the guys have ever done any type of cleaning since they built the thing. I use rags to scrub the walls and floors, and then move on to the table and chairs. When I'm done with those, too, I decide to sneak into their rooms and snoop.

I've already been in Sylred's and Evert's rooms, so I go into Ronak's. Unlike Evert's plain room and Sylred's room that's filled with musical instruments, Ronak's is full of handmade weapons that hang on the wall. Spears, staffs, shields, swords. Everything wooden and polished to a shine.

I find a nice small dagger hanging low and pick it up. It's only about the length of my hand, but it's wicked sharp, considering it's made of stone and wood. It's plain, but sturdy.

"What are you doing in here?" I whirl around with a shriek, and the dagger goes flying out of my hand. In the split second that I watch it careening toward Ronak, I know it's going to hit him square in the chest, and he'll die right in front of me, forever haunting me and causing me to faint at the sight of blood.

I'm already readying myself to start crying and performing first aid while forming an epic eulogy when he plucks it out of the air effortlessly before it can hit him. He holds it in his hand and just watches me still freaking out.

"Holy crap," I say, my hand over my heart. "Oh my gods. That was a close one. You almost died right in front of me. I nearly murdered you. I would have felt so guilty. I just cleaned all the floors, and I would've had to do it again because of the blood. That would've really sucked."

He cocks a brow. "It's going to take more than a tiny wooden dagger to take me down, little demon."

I scoff. "I beg to differ. I just saw your life flash before my eyes. Death was nearly imminent."

"You're a weird female."

"Does weird mean awesome in genfin-speak?"

"No."

"Hmm."

"You didn't answer my question."

"Which question was that?" I ask innocently. I try to scoot past him out the door, but he blocks my way.

"What are you doing in my room?"

"I was just admiring your wall décor," I say, indicating the weapons.

"I know every single weapon that I have in here," he says, frowning at me.

"Umm…congratulations?"

"Which means, if you take anything, I'll know it. Don't even think of betraying us."

"Geez, can't a girl snoop through a room without being accused of being a backstabbing liar face?"

He just looks at me. I sigh. "I didn't take anything, Not-First. But you're free to give me a pat down if it'll help you sleep better at night," I say with a smile, holding up my arms and turning in a circle for him.

He regards me coolly, eyes roaming down and then up. "Out."

I give him a two-finger salute that I'm fairly certain he won't understand. "Yes, sir," I say in mock-seriousness.

He steps aside for me to pass, and I skip back into the main room just as Evert comes in from outside. When he sees me leaving Ronak's room, he stops in his tracks. "What the fuck? Why were you in that asshole's room?"

"We were doing super sweaty sexy time stuff," I deadpan. "You caught us."

He narrows his eyes at me. "Bullshit."

Sylred comes inside behind him, taking in the scene. "Why are you staring Emelle down like you're pissed off?"

"Ronak!" Evert calls. "Why the fuck is Scratch coming out of your room?"

Ronak appears behind me. "Why do you think?" he asks.

Evert crosses his arms. "So she's suddenly fair game? What

210

happened to all that 'don't threaten the covey mate link' bullshit?"

Ronak and I both roll our eyes. It's a real moment.

"I didn't fuck her," Ronak says, like the very idea is preposterous.

I glare at him. Moment ruined.

"I am not *fair game*," I retort. "I told you, as soon as I get out of here, I'm going to find a better, hotter covey to love and adore me and service me in sexual favors."

Evert ignores everything I say and looks at Ronak. "You didn't fuck her?"

"No."

"Then why was she in your room?"

"I was looking at his *dagger*," I say suggestively, waggling my brows.

Ronak scoffs. "Demon, go snoop in someone else's room and stay out of mine."

He turns on his heel and disappears inside his room again, ending my fun. Evert is still glaring at me.

"What?" I ask. "Oh come on, I was just messing with you. It's not like any of you can really have sex with me, anyway. You have to go out and find a genfin mate, right? So don't mind me. Pretend I'm not even here."

"*Right*," Evert mocks. "We've only been stuck on this fucking island for five years without seeing a single female. Our balls are permanently blue, but yeah, we'll just ignore the hot female strutting around in tight furs."

"Good plan. Inconvenient, though. Guess your balls will just have to be blue for a while longer." Then I think of something. "Wait. Does that mean you're all virgins?"

Sylred chokes and starts coughing. Evert laughs. And laughs and laughs.

"Fuck no," he answers.

"So you had sex with people other than your intended mates?"

"Of course," Evert says. "We're genfin nobles because we're a part of Ronak's covey. We've been to plenty of fae parties, and believe me, fae aren't shy."

"Then why can't we...you know."

Sylred is the one to answer. "It has to do with our magic," he explains. "When we make a match with a female, we go through several rituals. We were in the middle of completing our rituals when we found out Delsheen was cheating with the prince, and Ronak attacked them, so things were cut short.

"At the end of the mating rituals, genfin powers become more powerful and coveys form a physical link with their mate. Because we didn't complete it, our powers didn't solidify in their enhanced form. We can't risk screwing anything up and destroying our powers further or weakening us more than we already are.

"We also can't risk not being able to bond with our future mate. We don't know what could happen. We've never heard of the mating rituals not being completed before, and since we've been cut off from our elders, we haven't had any advice on the matter."

That's a lot to take in. I've been lonely for a long time, and I know that with my loneliness, added together with my insatiable curiosity and general desire to participate in all things sexy, I perhaps have a skewed outlook. But no matter what I want or how attracted I am to these guys, I would never jeopardize their future. Despite our rough start, I want the best for them.

Most of the time. Usually. Nearly all the time.

"That makes sense. I promise I won't screw anything up for you guys." An idea occurs to me, and my eyes widen with excitement. "Hey! I can help you!"

"Help us?"

I nod vigorously. "Yeah. When you find a new mate, I can help you along. Nothing too crazy. I won't Love Arrow her if you don't want, but I can help you along with some Flirt-Touches and Lust-Breaths here and there. You have your very own love expert at your disposal. I'll probably have to really work the system to get her to fall for Ronak, because that guy is as prickly as a heat rash, but I can assure you, I'm very good at my job." I consider this. "Usually," I amend. "Sometimes. When I want to be. And when things work out." At least I'm honest.

"That's...nice of you," Sylred says.

I nod. "I know. I'm super nice. Now, start complimenting me on all my hard work at cleaning the cabin. I was scrubbing the place all day, you know."

They look away, as if trying to spot the tracks of dirt I scrubbed away. "Looks good," they say at the same time.

I narrow my eyes. "You can't even tell the difference, can you?"

"No."

"You're jerks."

"I can tell the difference," Sylred insists.

Evert rolls his eyes. "Liar."

"No, I can," Sylred says. "The floor is less...dirty. And the table looks...cleaner."

I flash him a smile. "Thank you. You're in first place."

Evert glowers. He's super sexy when he's sulking. He's about to say something that's no doubt sarcastic when he's cut off by a loud sound.

I'm trying to place the familiar noise when Ronak rushes out of his room. "The barrier is being taken down," he says.

All of the guys rush into his room and stock up on weapons. Ronak even tosses me the small dagger. "Stay here. Don't come outside. Hide in one of our rooms. If anyone comes in here that isn't one of us, don't let them take you. Run, fly, stab them if you have to. Just don't let them get to you."

213

I swallow hard, my eyes wide with fear. "O-okay."

Sylred puts a comforting hand on my shoulder. "Don't worry, Emelle. We'll take care of you."

The guys rush outside, and I slink to the window to look out, clutching the dagger in my sweaty palm. I hide behind the leaves that act as a curtain and watch through the gaps. The guys stand sentinel several yards away, looking out toward the forest, each of them no doubt stocked full of weapons.

I don't know how long we wait, but the moment that the last of the barrier falls away, I hear it. A terrible, wailing screech that seems to come from everywhere. Ronak yells something, but I can't hear anything over the sound of that terrible keening. I copy the guys' movements when I see them covering their ears with their hands. The sound is so loud that it feels like my head is going to burst. My hands do nothing to lessen the sound.

Suddenly, I see four female figures appear. They have dark gray skin and obnoxiously big eyes. I can see tears streaming down their cheeks, the drops landing on their cloaks. The sound is from their wide-open mouths, open so wide it looks like their jaws are unhinged.

Ronak is the first to move. He bends down until he's nearly on all fours, and then launches himself up in an incredible leap, landing directly on top of one of the fae. Raising a sword, he cuts her down in a single swipe. The other guys are already on top of the fae, too, but my vision is going fuzzy, and my head hurts so badly that I can't focus.

It feels like their sound has burrowed into my brain and is eating away at me like a maggot digging into rotten fruit. I feel something wet dripping down my neck and jaw, but I can't move to see what it is. My legs give out from under me, and I crash to the ground. I lie there in torment, clutching my head, pulling out my hair, screaming at the top of my lungs.

I just need the sound to stop. I can't think, can't breathe, can't move with it in my head. It digs its shrill claws into the very essence of my soul. I don't know how long I lie there.

I don't know how much time passes. But sometime between hearing the terrible shrieks, I start hearing a soft, calming music that drives away the screeches from my head.

My finger twitches and I try to open my eyes. My head is pounding, but I slowly recognize that someone is stroking my hair. The music continues to play, and when my vision finally returns to me, I see Sylred sitting in front of me on the floor, playing something that looks similar to a pan flute.

When he sees me looking, he stops playing and leans in closer. "Are you okay?" he asks, his voice soft and comforting.

My eyes are burning with tears, but I nod. "I think so," I croak. "What happened? What were those?"

"Banshees," Evert answers. I look up and realize that my head is in Evert's lap. "They're an annoying bunch of bitches."

My ears are ringing slightly, and I'm a bit dizzy, but Evert helps me to sit up. I wipe my cheeks and notice my hand comes away red. "What the..."

"Your ears started bleeding a bit," Sylred supplies. "Not too badly, though. We finished them off in time."

"What if you hadn't?" I ask.

"Then your brain would've bled out your ears," Ronak answers from somewhere in the room.

Evert shoots him a glare, and Sylred sighs when he sees my horrified expression. "Don't worry, Emelle. You're fine. They didn't do any permanent damage."

"Your music helped me," I say.

He nods. "I can counteract the banshee cries," he says. "But I didn't take any instruments with me outside. I should've. I didn't expect for them to send banshees. By the time I realized what they were, it was too late. I got to my instruments as soon as I could."

"How come you guys aren't as messed up as I am?"

"Genfins are strong," Ronak says with a shrug.

I blow out a relieved breath. "I'm glad you're all okay. I guess cupids aren't meant to go up against banshees. How did those things get past the barrier?"

"They didn't," Ronak says. "The prince sent them. This is why I was convinced you were a spy. Nothing gets in past the barrier without the high fae giving them access, and the only things that have ever come to visit us have been sent here to kill or hurt us."

"Ohhh," I say. "Your assholeness makes more sense now."

Ronak scoffs and tosses over a damp rag that Evert catches. Taking me by surprise, he starts gently cleaning the blood that leaked out of my ears away from my face and neck. I study him as he tends to me, in awe of seeing this gentle side of him.

As if he can read my mind, he catches me looking and smirks. "Don't get any ideas, Scratch."

"But my ideas are really good."

"Like your taking over the fae realm idea?"

"Obviously."

"I'll keep that in mind."

"How's your head?" Sylred asks. "I can find some herbs to help if you need something. Or if you're hungry, I'll get you some food."

"Geez, I should get knocked out by banshees more often. This is awesome."

Evert rolls his eyes, but I look over at Ronak expectantly. "Well?" I prompt him.

"Well, what?"

"Everyone else is being super nice to me. Now it's your turn."

"I think it was pretty nice of me to kill those banshees before they could kill you."

Such a gentleman.

CHAPTER 26

It's the day before I'm set to find a fae to glamour me. Ronak has everyone up at first light. I'm quiet and tense, unable to laugh at Evert's jokes or pretend that I'm not completely freaking out. I'm so nervous about leaving my safe little bubble with the guys that I feel like I'm going to puke every time I think about it. We all stand outside the cabin going over the plan. Again. Currently, the guys are arguing over which fae I should visit.

"The sirens could do it easily," Evert suggests.

"Sirens hate outsiders even more than genfins do," Sylred points out. "The elves are powerful. They're the best at glamour besides the high fae."

"And they're also the most loyal to the high fae," Evert counters. "Can't risk it. What about the harpies? They hate the high fae bastards."

Sylred shakes his head. "Their island is way too far away for her to reach."

They toss more ideas back and forth, but I watch Ronak. His eyes meet mine, and I know he's already decided where I'm going and that I'm probably not going to like it.

"Okay, Not-First. You can stop pretending to listen to their ideas. Where am I going?"

The guys stop talking and look from me to Ronak. As usual, he's wearing an unreadable expression and has his arms crossed in front of him.

He clears his throat at the attention that's suddenly on him. "She'll be going to Arachno."

Sylred's mouth opens in surprise, and Evert's expression turns incredulous. "Fuck no, she isn't!" he exclaims. "Are you trying to get her killed? Arachno is a crazy bitch."

Ronak stays calm despite Evert's outburst and talks directly to me. "Arachno is a very powerful gwyllion fae. She's not someone you want to cross, but she's our best chance at getting you the glamour you need."

"No," Evert says, shaking his head. "It's too dangerous. She'll kill Emelle without hesitation. We'll send her somewhere else."

Ronak finally turns to him. "Despite how much she's practiced, Emelle's flying is barely sufficient. Her wings know what to do, but her muscle strength is severely lacking. She'll tire too soon to get anywhere far.

"Arachno is banished on the island directly below ours. It's the only island she has a hope of going to and from in a short amount of time without being seen. Arachno might be a nasty piece of work, but she's also always up for a bargain, and we know what she trades in. As long as Emelle brings her something worthy, it'll be fine. Plus, Arachno's banishment island has a barrier over it, just like ours. She's least likely to run into any extra fae trouble there than if she were to go somewhere else."

Evert is still shaking his head unhappily. "I don't like it."

"Be honest," Ronak says. "Do you really think she can make it anywhere else, find the right person, not be seen or caught, and make it all the way back with a glamour?"

Evert clenches his jaw and runs a hand through his long black hair. "Fuck."

I would try to comfort him if I weren't so freaked out. I try to put on a brave face, but I'm pretty sure I'm just grimacing.

"Sylred, show her," Ronak says with a nod.

Sylred kneels down in the sand and starts drawing a map of the islands. "This is us here," he says, pointing. He draws another, smaller island below us. "This is where Arachno is banished. It should be the same type of barrier as ours, so you should have no trouble passing through. Look for a cave, or rock formations. She'll prefer somewhere dark and concealed."

"Okay," I say shakily.

"Don't make any other deals with her. Don't say anything other than what we specifically tell you. She's tricky and she won't hesitate to ensnare you," Ronak says.

"What am I trading her?"

The guys exchange a look. "Think she'll be satisfied with some genfin hair?" Sylred asks.

Ronak nods slowly. "Yes, but Emelle should bring more than that, just in case."

"We can use something from the banshee bitches," Evert says grudgingly.

Ronak nods and then frowns. "Dammit. I hate digging up corpses I just buried."

"You do that a lot?" I ask.

"You'd be surprised," he replies dryly.

We go over the plan, and the guys make sure I have my request memorized word for word before dispersing. Ronak and Sylred leave to dig up the banshees while Evert supplies me with weapons and then takes me to the training yard so that I can get in my last hours of practice flying before I have to leave tomorrow at first light.

We don't speak much. Evert just takes me through the motions as I make running leaps into the air, get as high as possible, and then touch back down. Sometimes I launch into the air from the ground. Sometimes, I leap off tall branches or the ladder from the obstacle course.

I also practice endurance by flying up all the way to the barrier and circling around as many times as I can before exhaustion and muscle spasms set in. As pretty as my wings look, they're incredibly heavy for my slight frame, and my wingspan is longer than my body.

Without wind currents to help carry me, I tire quickly. Evert stands by to watch me, handing me water whenever I need it and rubbing out the knots in my back and shoulders when the muscles lock up on me.

That night, the guys try to distract me with stories of them when they first met and formed their covey when they were just boys. I'd normally be eating it all up, but I'm too preoccupied with worry to enjoy it.

I end up curling up in front of the fire and pretending to sleep. I can't stand their worried looks that they send my way when they think I'm not looking. I barely sleep.

I toss and turn all night, and then before I know it, Sylred is shaking me awake. "It's time."

I sit up and braid my hair tightly. Sylred tries to force-feed me, but I can only tolerate a few bites before my stomach rebels. Evert straps two of Ronak's daggers on each of my thighs, where they'll be hidden under my skirt, and then ties a water-skin at my waist.

When I get outside, Ronak is already waiting for me. He hands me another leather bag. I have no desire to look inside since I know that it's filled with the contents for the trade I'll make with the gwyllion fae.

We go over the plan three more times before the guys are satisfied, and they all walk me to the edge of the island. It doesn't take very long for the edge to come into sight, but none of us speak as we walk. As we get closer, I can see the shimmering dome barrier end right at the island's rim. I stare at the edge, knowing I'm only minutes away from jumping off the side of it. Even with wings, the thought isn't comforting.

"Ready?" Ronak asks.

No. "Mm-hmm. Yep."

I feel numb when Sylred steps forward and gives me a quick hug. I barely have the wherewithal to pat him on the back. As soon as Sylred releases me, Evert stalks forward and forces me to focus on him by grabbing hold of my cheeks and tilting my head up to look at him. "If you don't want to go, just say the word, Scratch. We can figure something else out."

It's sweet of him to give me an out, and I appreciate it more than I can express. But I also know that if I want to have a chance at evading the high fae, I need to do this. Ronak's right. I don't blend in. At all. I stick out like a sore thumb, and the minute I leave this island, it won't take long for word to get back to the prince. And since I'm the only one who can fly and also pass through the barriers, I'm my only hope.

Evert studies my face like he's trying to get under my skin and read my thoughts. When he sees that I'm not going to back down and refuse to go, he sighs. "Get in, get glamoured, and get out. You understand me?" I nod with his hands still holding my face. He kisses me on the forehead before releasing me.

"Remember, don't make any other deals. Don't engage in conversation. Keep on track. She'll try to trick you. Don't let her," Ronak says.

"Okay."

"I should've trained you to use close-range weapons for self-defense," he says with a frown, looking down to where I have the daggers strapped to my legs. I pat the strap on my back where the quiver rests.

"I have the bow and arrow, too. I'm not completely defense-less. And a dagger can't be that hard to use. I'll just swing it around and hope I stab something."

His lip twitches slightly. That basically equals uproarious laughter from Ronak.

I turn back to the others, feeling like I have a huge stone stuck in my throat that I can't swallow down. "Right then. Guess I'll just get to it."

"You got this, Scratch," Evert says with a nod.

I really hope he's right. I turn my back to the guys and walk to the very edge of the island until my toes are touching the barrier and I can lean over and see the vast sky below. I look back over my shoulder one last time, memorizing the guys' faces. Just in case I don't come back, I want to remember them just like this. All three of them looking at me like they give a damn.

With a deep breath, I turn back around, and I dive off the island into the endless sky.

CHAPTER 27

*G*ravity reaches up with both hands and snatches me down like the needy bitch she is. I fall through air and clouds, keeping my body as tight as possible. Ronak suggested I fall for a good distance so that I don't tire myself, but I'll need to use my wings to gain control soon.

According to Sylred's map, the gwyllion fae's banishment island is directly below. Arachno has been there for nearly a century. When I asked what she'd done to be banished, the guys wouldn't tell me. I have a feeling I don't want to know.

As I'm falling, I notice a strange feeling come on deep inside my gut. It's almost like I want to hurl, almost like I've been stabbed, but it's neither of those sensations at the same time. It must be because I just tossed myself off the side of a floating island. How do I get myself into these situations?

When I start to see something below me in the distance, I unfurl my wings and catch a wind drift. After a bit of maneuvering, I start to soar on the breeze effortlessly. It's the first time I've been this high up since I fell from the prince's castle, but this time, I actually have some control over what I'm doing. All that practice has paid off. For a few moments, I simply enjoy coasting through the air. With the wind at my wings and the sun at my back, I've never felt so free before.

Tilting downward, I soar all the way down to Arachno's island. It's small and has a rocky, sparse terrain, very different from the guys' island. Once I get closer, I circle around it, searching for a space that the gwyllion might be holed up. She doesn't like the sunlight, so the guys believed that she'd be somewhere protected by the elements. When I see a larger rock formation, I head for it, passing through the barrier. I wouldn't even have noticed it if I weren't looking for it.

I fly down to the ground, proud of myself when I manage a perfect landing. I let out a big breath and try to fix the wayward hair that ripped out of my braid as I take in my surroundings.

"Okay, Emelle. Find the creepy fae, get glamoured, get out. You can do this," I whisper to myself. Except the weird pain in my stomach seems to expand just then, and a strange sensation trickles down my left arm, all the way to my fingers. I lift my hand in front of my face in horror, and I watch as my palm disappears from view. "What the..." I frantically move my hand around, as if I can shake it back into visibility like a reverse Etch-A-Sketch. I watch as it flickers back into view.

I blink at it, my panic forcing my breathing to quicken. Maybe it was a trick? Maybe my hand didn't really disappear? Except, if Arachno is as powerful as she's claimed to be, then perhaps she has some sort of spell over the island that's causing my stomach pain and the weird vanishing act? Whatever it was, it seems to have passed for now, although the weird ache in my gut is still there, but I mentally shove that away so that I can deal with my task. I'll just hope my hand stays visible for the remainder of the visit.

I approach the mountain of rocks as I warily look around. Unlike the guys' island, this one is eerily quiet, with all sounds of wildlife oddly absent. It's an unnatural, forced kind of quiet, and it's abnormally colorless here, too. The trees are sparse, the ground is hard, and even the wind doesn't seem to want to touch down here. The atmosphere is downright freaky, and it sets me on edge. As I tentatively make my way toward the rocky mountain, I feel the hair on the back of my neck rise up in warning.

Following Ronak's instructions, I carefully clear my throat to announce the scripted words. "Arachno, I've come to make a trade."

My voice comes out shakier than I would have liked, but hell if this place doesn't feel haunted. I wait, looking around the rocky hillside, trying to see into the hidden nooks and crannies that are shielded by endless shadows. Nothing happens. I walk further around the hillside, nearly tripping over the jagged, jutting rocks that make up the ground.

"Arachno, I've come to make a trade," I say, louder and steadier this time.

I wait for a few minutes, but still, nothing happens. I start to worry that maybe the gwyllion fae has been released from her banishment, or maybe she's died, or maybe the guys were wrong about this being her island. I feel panic stir inside me. If I can't get a glamour to hide my obvious appearance, then there's nowhere in the entire fae kingdom that I can hide where Prince Elphar won't find me. Maybe I can fly to another nearby island and find someone else to help? Maybe I can—

My trail of thought is cut off when I suddenly scream at the figure before me. She blended in so well with the gray rocky expanse of the hillside that I don't even know how long she's been standing there watching me.

She has gray skin that perfectly matches the rocks, and long, stringy gray hair that reaches her knees. But it's her eyes that really freak me out. Instead of two, she has many, taking up the entire expanse of her forehead. They're small, beady, and black, like a spider's. They all blink at different times. For some reason, I get really hung up on this fact and catch myself trying to follow each one blinking in succession like it's a game of Simon.

"A-Arachno?"

The fae raises a hand and curls her bony finger at me. With a hard swallow, I make my way toward her. As soon as I'm moving, she turns around into a hidden fissure between boulders, disappearing into the side of the hill. With one more look behind me, knowing I might possibly never see the sky again, I follow her in.

She takes me down through small, rough warrens until we reach a hollowed-out cave. It's obvious by the interior that this is where the fae lives. There's a fire in the middle with a bubbling cauldron on top, and from what I can tell, it doesn't look like she's cooking dinner.

There's a mess of random objects around, all of them dirty, all of it mismatched and strange. A pile of blankets sits in one corner, and there's a wall covered in a strange, white stringy substance from floor to ceiling. I can't tell what's behind the strings, but it's bumpy in certain spots and looks like there might be something trapped behind it. But perhaps the most alarming of her possessions are the jars of floating...body parts. There are dozens of them. Maybe even hundreds. Some of them look animal, and some look fae.

A cold sweat breaks out over my body like I've been doused in water, and I quickly avert my eyes. She stands in front of the cauldron, watching me with her many eyes, still not saying a word.

"Arachno, I've come to make a trade."

Slowly, her thin lips stretch out into a smile. I expect her teeth to be rotten or missing, so I'm thrown off guard when I see a set of dazzling white teeth, even if they are a bit sharp. It doesn't match with the rest of her haggard, unpleasant appearance.

"The little bird wants to make a trade," she says. Her voice is as rough as gravel and deeper than any female's I've ever heard.

I nod. Ronak warned me to only speak when absolutely necessary, and I intend to stick to that. This female may look old and grotesque, but I have no doubt that she's incredibly powerful. Even the guys seemed frightened of her, and they don't frighten easily.

She motions for me to sit down on one of the jutting rocks beside the fire, and she sits on another rock across from me. I'm secretly relieved to be sitting. The pain in my stomach has only grown since I first felt it, and I wrap my arm around my front to try to ease the discomfort. I check my hands, too, just in case. Still there. Whew.

"So, the little red bird thinks she has something to trade Arachno?" she rasps. "The little bird crossed into Arachno's barrier. The little bird comes alone. The little bird carries something she thinks Arachno will want. But the little bird is so scared she wants to fly away," she says, ending on a cackle.

I watch her guardedly as she laughs, keeping my mouth shut. She really likes to speak about herself in the third person. I have to sit on my hands to keep them from shaking.

I hear a scuffling noise on the far end of the room behind the stringy mess of a wall. I think I see one of the bumps moving, but I draw my eyes back to Arachno.

Reciting the rehearsed words, I say, "I need a glamour, and I have hair from genfin tails to trade for it."

I pull out the pouch Ronak gave me. Without looking away from Arachno, I reach in and pull out the hair from the guys' tails. There's a mixture of black, blond, and brown-haired tufts. Arachno's beady eyes zero in on the hair in my hand, and she slips out a dark purple tongue to lick her lips hungrily.

"Arachno has not had hair of a genfin tail. Arachno will accept this," she says.

When she reaches for it, I close my hand around the hair and pull back. "Glamour first," I say.

Arachno opens her mouth and cackles again. "The little bird is a fool for coming here, but maybe not such a fool after all."

"The glamour," I say again firmly, wanting to get out of here. Every second I'm here feels like I'm getting closer to my death.

"Stand," Arachno says, getting to her feet.

She steps forward, and I have to force myself not to move back as she reaches toward me and clamps onto my arms. A bright blue glow of magic bursts between our touch, but she's barely touched me when she suddenly snatches her hands away again, shaking them as if my touch hurt her. She narrows every single one of her beady little eyes on me.

Her voice turns angry. "What is she, Arachno? This little red bird has strange magic on her. Glamour will not work on her, no. Glamour cannot hold onto little bird, just like barrier could not keep little bird out," she says, talking to herself. "Some magic does not attach to the little red bird. But why? What is the little bird?"

"I—I..."

I was instructed by the guys to never, under any circumstance, tell her what I am. I have no idea why some magic works with me and some doesn't. Other magic, like when Evert heals me, and the cries of the banshees, has worked on me. But the barriers and the glamour don't. I have no idea why.

"I am...different," I finally decide to say.

Arachno sneers at me. "Arachno knows little bird is different. Arachno's eyes can see that little bird is different, the little fool! The little, lying fool thinks she can trick Arachno!"

I shake my head adamantly and hold my hands up to appease her. The last thing I want to do is piss her off. I was warned against making her angry. "No, no tricks," I promise. "I am different, but I only need to blend in better. No trick, Arachno. A trade. Just a trade."

Arachno stops pacing to look at me again, tapping a bony finger against her pointed chin. "Arachno cannot glamour little bird. Glamour does not stick to little bird. But Arachno can let little red bird hide her wings."

"Hide my wings?"

Arachno nods, making her stringy gray hair fall over some of her eyes. "Oh, yes. That magic should work on little bird. Different magic. But it will cost more than genfin hair. This is bigger magic, oh yes. Much bigger."

I carefully consider her words, worrying that this is a trick. "You'll do something to make it so that I can hide my wings and bring them back out whenever I want?"

Arachno nods. "Arachno can do this."

Hoping I'm not going to regret this but unable to see any loopholes, I nod. "Then I can trade you genfin tail hair and the tongues of banshees," I say, reaching into the pouch again.

I pick up the tongues that are rolled inside a strip of cloth and hold them out for her to see. She smiles with delight, her eyes locking onto the repulsive tongues. Much to my horror, Arachno bends down and licks one of them. Gross.

She straightens up and gives me her sterling grin again, seemingly satisfied. "Arachno will make this trade with the little red bird."

She turns around and starts digging through some of her possessions strewn throughout the cave. She starts systematically tossing things into the boiling cauldron, most of which I can't see. Jars shatter inside, droppers full of liquid go next, a box of ashes from a trunk, and a whole mess of other things I don't get a chance to see before she tosses them in.

Then she comes over and plucks a red feather from my wing without warning, eliciting a small yelp from me. She tosses that into the cauldron, too, and then begins to stir it all in a strange pattern, doing methodical types of mixing as she works. The mixture starts spitting and then begins to emit a bright red glow.

Finished, she tips the cauldron and pours the mixture into a jar, handing it to me. I close the lid and start to put it in the pouch at my hip, because there's no way I'm going to drink this here with her. There's no telling what it really is or what it could do to me. I'd better wait and do it in the company of the guys. Besides, I think I'm going to be sick. My stomachache is getting worse, and beads of sweat have collected at my hairline from the pain.

But before I can stow the jar away, Arachno shakes her head, stopping me. "No, little bird. Drink now, or it will not work. You drink. We trade."

Dammit. If I die from drinking this, I'm going to be so pissed.

CHAPTER 28

*I*n one foul gulp, I shoot Arachno's drink down.

A terrible burning sensation travels from the back of my tongue, down my throat, deep into my gut, and then up my spine, where it finally settles between my shoulder blades at the base of my wings. If I thought my stomach was hurting me before, it's nothing compared to this pain.

An agonized cry rips out of me, and I fall to the ground and writhe uncontrollably. It feels like all the bones in my back and my wings are breaking like dry branches, splintering off into uneven halves.

Arachno's face swims in front of my eyes, and it takes me a long time to realize she's speaking. With great effort, I focus enough to hear her say, "Pull them in, push them out, pull them in, push them out," over and over again.

Pull my wings in? I don't even know what that means, and I sure as hell don't know how to do it. Still, Arachno's chanting infiltrates the agonized shifting of nerves at my back.

"Pull them in, push them out, pull them in, push them out…"

With a scream, I focus on my wings and mentally *pull*. Envisioning them curling into my spine, safe and wrapped beneath my skin, I pull and pull and pull.

And just like that, the pain vanishes.

I gasp and sit up, nearly toppling over in the process because of the sudden weightlessness of my body. My wings are gone. Following instinct, I *push* them back out. With a snap of pain, I feel them break free from my body, and when I look over my shoulder, there they are again. A tired, shaky laugh escapes me as I look at them in disbelief.

My celebration is short-lived as Arachno pulls me to my feet, her sharp nails digging into my arms. "Trade," she says with a threatening sneer.

I hand her the pouch with the hair and tongues inside, and she greedily snatches it from my grasp. She plucks the tongues from inside and places two of them in a jar. She does the same with the hair, separating them by color.

Then, to my horror, she takes the third tongue, opens her mouth, and bites into it like a cheeseburger. "Oh gods…"

I can't help the dry heaves that escape me, and I'm forced to turn around, clutching my aching stomach. I try not to listen as she chews and slurps and sucks, but the sounds seem to echo off the walls of the rocky cave. To make matters worse, the tingling sensation is back, but this time, it's in both hands.

I look down in horror to see my hands flickering in and out of sight. "Are you doing this?" I ask in a shrill voice.

She ignores me, and when I hear her licking her fingers with satisfied "mmm," sounds, I turn back around and begin to make my way toward the exit. "Okay, then. Glad you enjoyed the… tongue. Pleasure trading with you. Have a nice banishment."

She finally looks at me and zeroes in on my flickering hands. She swallows down the last of the tongue and licks her lips with a creepy smile. "Hmm. The little red bird has strange magic in her. Arachno can tell the little bird about the magic."

I stop in my tracks and turn around to look at her. I'm pretty sure that she's now slurping down a strand of my guys' tail hairs like it's a spaghetti noodle. Yuck.

The pain in my stomach grows so intense that it makes it difficult to breathe, and now the disappearing flicker is spreading, reaching all the way up to my elbows as my limbs come in and out of visibility.

"What do you know?" I croak. "What's happening to me?"

Arachno smiles and sidesteps around me. I'm all too aware that she just got between the exit and me. With every step she takes closer to me, I back away. Arachno opens her fist and shows me one of my feathers crushed inside her hand. She must've plucked more than one when she used it for the potion. She lifts the feather and puts it into her mouth, swallowing it whole.

I clench my teeth. "My feathers were not part of the trade," I snarl.

Arachno just smiles wider as she picks a string from my feather out from between her teeth like a piece of floss. "Arachno can taste every magic. Every taste makes Arachno stronger. Arachno can taste what you are. Little bird is not fae. Little bird does not belong here, oh no. Does not belong here at all. Little bird cannot stay."

Even as I hold myself around the middle with invisible arms, bending over slightly from the pain, I stare at her. "What do you mean I can't stay?"

Arachno smiles widely. "She will fade. Oh, yes, little red bird will fade away. It's already started. Her anchors keep her here, but she is too far away from her anchors, now, isn't she? Little bird should not fly so far away from her anchors. Stupid, stupid little bird."

Dread fills me like cement, solidifying in the pit of my stomach and hardening my mind.

"It will not last, either," Arachno goes on. She plucks another strand of genfin tail hair from her pocket where she must have stashed some away and sucks it down. She rolls her eyes in the back of her head in euphoria. "When the genfins' mate bond forms, they will not be little bird's anchors anymore. Cut away, she will fade. Oh, yes, little red bird will lose her anchors and fade away."

My body trembles, but I don't know if it's in pain, horror, fear, or a combination of all three. When she keeps advancing on me, I accidentally back all the way up to the sticky, stringed wall. It's only when my wings and back touch the tacky substance that I realize what it is.

A web.

The bump behind the wall of web moves when I come into contact with it, and I jump against it, startled, but I realize then that I'm stuck. The second I realize it, Arachno realizes it, too, and she starts cackling again. "Little bird is trapped," she says in singsong. "Arachno will taste the little red bird as she fades away."

Terror washes over me but only for a second. The next second, I'm reaching down to the dagger strapped at my thigh and ripping it out. I stab at the web behind me using the limited mobility I have, but it's enough to get my right side free.

The dagger gets snagged in the web, forcing me to let it go. I close my eyes and concentrate, *pulling* my wings back into my body. With a sharp jolt of pain, my wings disappear. I try to jump free, but Arachno is suddenly there in front of me with a dagger of her own. She aims it for my heart, and I manage to stop her from stabbing me just in time, my hands coming up to hold off her arm and wrist.

She's much stronger than she looks. It takes all my strength to keep her from plunging the blade into my heart. There's movement behind me, and out of the corner of my eye, I see something snatch onto my left-behind dagger and pull it deeper into the web.

"Little bird flew into Arachno's web. Little bird's wings will taste very good, oh yes," Arachno hisses in my ear.

I can see my terrified reflection in her black spider eyes as she tries to bear down on me. I don't have the strength to release one of my arms to try to get to my second dagger. I'm barely keeping her at bay as it is. It's strange to fight against her when I can't see my limbs. Maybe I can use it to my advantage.

"Will little bird's blood be as red as her wings?" Arachno snarls in my face. "Will little bird's bones crunch? Will her skin melt in my mouth? Will her invisible fingers taste strangely?"

I flinch when she brings her head close to mine, and she runs her long, purple tongue up my cheek, making me shudder. "Oh, little bird will taste so nicely."

I scream at her, my arms shaking with the force of trying to hold her off, but I'm losing quickly. My energy is draining, and inch-by-inch, her blade gets closer. But then I'm suddenly falling back, and Arachno is falling with me.

I barely have the wherewithal to roll out of the way so that she doesn't crush me with her blade as she falls on top of me. Before she can get her bearings, I shove her off of me and leap up, only to stare wide-eyed at a male covered in webs, his face deathly pale and gaunt, his hand clutching my dagger.

His wild eyes flash behind me, and he's suddenly launching himself at Arachno, knocking her back down again. He shoves her screaming, flailing body into her web wall and uses the dagger to cut some of the web away to wrap it around her until she's stuck hanging there. She wails at him, her face flushed red, her whole body thrashing but unable to get free.

I'm standing frozen at the scene when the guy grabs hold of my arm (the visible part), turns, and forces me to run. I stumble but he keeps going, forcing me to scramble to get my feet underneath me again as I sprint after him.

"Which way?" he asks, panting.

I look around, trying to remember which way we came in from the underground passageways. "Left," I say.

Still holding my hand, he races forward, pulling me with him. I direct him every so often until we're finally outside again, and I take in huge gasping breaths of fresh air. Arachno's screams can still be heard echoing after us.

"Come on," he says, forcing me to run again.

I really hate running, but since my wings aren't out, it's a little easier without their added weight and bulkiness. We race away, but the guy makes us double back several times in different directions. I don't say a thing. I'm too busy panting for breath and dealing with the pain in my stomach to do anything except put one foot in front of the other.

Finally, we reach the very edge of the island where the barrier shimmers at our feet. We both struggle to catch our breath, and I curl over, both because of my screaming lungs and my screaming gut.

"You okay?" the male asks.

I tilt my head and get a good look at him for the first time. He has white hair and gray eyes, and the softest shade of silver for skin. But it's the two curved horns coming out of the top of his forehead, curling down behind his ears, that hold my attention. They're gray and thick, holding back his long hair and ending just at the base of his jaw.

"What are you?" I ask before I can stop myself.

He tilts his head at me. "I'm a Cernu. What are you?"

"Umm...half high fae, half human," I answer carefully, hoping he'll buy it.

"Human, hmm? Interesting."

"Yeah, that's me," I say, still catching my breath. "Super interesting."

Gods, my stomach hurts. I'm trying to hide my hand behind my back, too, because I don't think he's noticed that it's invisible yet.

"Thanks for the dagger," he says with a smile.

It's obvious that he's the shadow of a very handsome fae. With a few dozen good meals in him along with a long bath and web removal, he's probably a heartbreaker.

"Thanks for taking out the spidery bitch," I say.

He places a hand on his chest in introduction. "I'm Belren."

I try to stand up, but I can't quite straighten out. "Emelle," I say in greeting.

He nods and looks around. I reach to my waterskin while he's not looking and push it into his chest before quickly snatching my hand away again. "Here. Sorry, I don't have any food."

He takes the waterskin and starts downing the water, his throat bobbing up and down. He stops and wipes his mouth with the back of his arm before trying to hand it back to me.

"No, you have it."

He looks like he wants to argue, but we both know that his need is far greater than mine. He takes another long drink before stopping himself. "Thank you." He motions to my arms. "What happened there?"

"Oh, umm…" I look down at my hands, even though there's no point because I can't see them. It looks like I have stumps for arms. "Some kind of magic spell," I answer vaguely. "How long have you been stuck there?" I ask, deflecting attention away from me.

"I don't know, to be honest. Days? A couple weeks? I don't think too long or she would've eaten me by now, but she already had something else in that web that she's been working on for a while."

"Gross," I say with a shudder. "What are you doing here?"

"Pissed off the royals, what else?"

"You were sent here as punishment?" I ask, surprised.

He nods, taking another drink. "Got myself into a situation and got carted off here. Didn't know it was Arachno's island. I would've fought a hell of a lot harder. They knocked me out and left me here. She found me and dragged me back to her cave," he explains. "Crazy bitch talked to me all day long in the third person about which parts of me she was going to eat first. She likes to make her victims dehydrate and starve first, apparently."

"That's awful."

"What about you? Why were you sent here?"

"I wasn't. I came here to do a trade."

He looks at me like I'm insane. "I couldn't hear everything you were saying through the web, and I thought I must've heard wrong. I can't imagine anyone coming here willingly," he says, studying me. "How'd you get through the barrier?"

"I...have a magic that lets me pass through."

His eyes grow excited. "Could you get me out?"

I shake my head and bite my lip. "I'm sorry, I wish I could, but I can't. It only works on me."

His face falls, but he tries to hide his disappointment. "That's okay. They're constantly lowering Arachno's barrier and bringing her gifts, just like they brought me. As soon as they come next, I'll get out of here." He flexes his shoulders, and a pair of silver wings jut out from his back.

"I like your wings," I say.

He looks at me with amusement. "Thanks. "You have a pair of your own, I'm guessing?"

"I do."

He nods. "You should get out of here. I'm going to keep eyes on Arachno and then settle in somewhere to wait it out. It won't be long before I'm out of here, too."

"Are you sure?"

He nods. "Yes. Like I said, they bring her gifts every few days, and she's due for another one soon. They like to let Arachno play with those who have displeased them. Get out of here. Just promise me you won't come back, no matter what the hell you're desperate enough to trade for."

I laugh lightly. "I promise."

He holds out my dagger, but I shake my head. "Keep it. I have another," I say.

He nods and starts to walk away. "Good luck, Emelle."

"You too, Belren."

When he's out of sight, I *push* my wings back out and then launch myself off the island. I'm ready to get the hell out of here. It's way harder to fly back. For one, I don't get to just fall. This time, I have to use all the strength I have left to beat my wings up, up, up. The wind fights me until I finally hit a pocket of air where I can coast.

My stomach is in such terrible pain now that I can do little more than take tiny, gasping breaths, and I can feel the invisibility tingles spreading further up my arms, all the way to my shoulders now. My vision swims with black dots, and I know I'm not getting enough oxygen for the energy I'm exerting, but I can't stop. If I stop, I'll fall and never reach the guys. And if what Arachno said was true...

To distract myself from the pain, I count every flap of my wings. One, two, three, four. One, two, three, four... Sweat drips down my face, and I have to wipe it from my eyes so that I can see.

When the bottom of the island comes into view, a sob of relief escapes my lips. The bottom is jagged with rough rock and packed dirt, and I can see giant tree roots sticking out all over. With the last of my energy, I make it to the edge of the island and hurl myself through the barrier, rolling across the grass before landing in a crumpled heap.

The familiar sights, smells, and sounds of the forest fill my senses just before three big genfins come charging toward me from different directions. I don't know who reaches me first, because it seems like they're all upon me in the next second.

"What the fuck? Where are her arms?"

The moment one of them touches me, the pain deep in my

gut disappears with an internal whoosh, and then it's just gone, like it was never there in the first place, and both of my arms pop back into view.

I look up to see Evert rubbing his hands, watching as they fizzle with magic before petering out. "What was that? Your arms were gone, and then I touched you and... What the bloody fuck, Emelle?"

I rub my hands together as if comforting myself that they're really there. I take a relieved breath, happy to be back, happy to be rid of the hurt, and happy to be completely visible again.

But my relief is washed away with the cold, hard truth of Arachno's revelation. She was right, I'm not meant to be here. I know it. Every other cupid knows it. Hell, even the guys know it.

The fae prince magic-blasted me into this world. Me, a cupid, an entity only ever meant to exist in the Veil. And if Arachno is to be believed, I would've faded right back into the Veil if it weren't for one thing. Well, actually, not one. Three.

I look up at the three faces crowded around me. They're the ones keeping me here. I landed on their island, and they touched me. They were the first people to ever touch my skin, still crackling with the magic blast from the prince. That's what magic they felt that day. That's why they can sense me. Instead of sinking back into the Veil, they're somehow keeping me tethered here. *They* are my anchors.

But if they complete their mating rituals and solidify their covey magic, their bond to me will break. Without my anchors, I'll float away, back into the Veil and back into where I only exist to myself.

CHAPTER 29

*T*he problem with finding out something as intense as my very existence hinging on the lives of three other people is the conflict that goes along with that knowledge. Tomorrow, their five-year banishment ends. The barrier will drop, and they'll be taken to the kingdom island where they'll be faced with fights to the death.

If the fates smile down on them, they will survive and all counts against them will be wiped away. They'll be restored to their previous positions of nobility and power, and their lives will continue. If they fail, they die.

So, I'm nervous enough as it is. I'm worried for their well-being and for their futures. Add that worry to the fact that my life literally depends on theirs, and that leaves me in a mess of thoughts and emotions. No matter the outcome, I'm up Cupid's Crap Creek without a freaking physical body to paddle.

If they lose in the culling, they die, and I lose them and myself. They might be asshole genfins, but I've come to think of them as my asshole genfins. It would kill me if anything happened to them.

But if they win, then they'll go back to their lives, choose a new mate, finish their genfin power ceremony stuff, and I'll lose the only anchors that are keeping me bound to the physical world.

As I look around at the guys as they eat around the dining table, I know I can't tell them the truth. It wouldn't be fair to them. Which is why I lied and told them that Arachno hit me with some strange invisibility spell before I left.

As much as I want to break down and tell them everything that Arachno said, everything that I've figured out, I can't. I can't guilt them into changing their plans for me. It wouldn't be right.

If I told them the truth and they chose a mate anyway, it would wreck me, in more ways than one. If I told them the truth and they decided to not choose a mate in order to help me stay, then they'd eventually end up resenting me, maybe even hating me, and that would wreck me, too. So I can't tell them. I just can't.

Not that I want to fade back into the Veil. Hell no. I'm just going to have to find a different way. I just have no idea how the hell I'm going to do that.

"Emelle?" I hear Sylred's quiet voice, and it breaks me from my thoughts.

I look up from my place on the ground, finding that all three guys are watching me. "Yeah?"

"You're quiet."

I try to put a smile on my face, but I know it's forced. "Sorry."

"Did something else happen on that island that we should know about?" Ronak asks, his black eyes cutting a hole through me.

"No."

Sylred tilts his head in thought, as if he's trying to figure me out. I can see the concern in his brown eyes and in the way he combs his hand through his blond hair.

"Are you okay?" Sylred asks.

No. I am definitely *not* okay. "Mm-hmm. Yep. I'm fine."

"Scratch."

My eyes dart to Evert. His blue eyes narrow on me, and he has his serious face on. "Yeah?" I ask, trying to sound innocent and casual.

"You didn't eat," he points out, looking down at my still full plate.

"Oh, umm. I'm not hungry."

"Exactly," Evert replies. "You're *always* hungry. You're hungry even after you just ate. You're hungry first thing after you wake up. You even get up in the middle of the night and start digging through our food stores like a little mouse searching for crumbs. So, we'll ask you again. What's going on?"

"Nothing. I'm just tired."

The guys share a look. I wish I knew what they were communicating with each other when they do that. It's like they can carry on an entire conversation without uttering a word.

"Are you worried about tomorrow?" Sylred asks gently.

I pounce on that. Partly because it's true, and partly because I don't have any other excuse to give them. "Yes. Very."

"You don't need to worry about the culling." He sounds so sure. Cocky and confident.

"It's called a *culling*, for gods' sakes. That's not a good name."

Evert chuckles and rolls his eyes like I'm being ridiculous for worrying about them. "Scratch. Come on. Give us a little credit. In case you haven't noticed, we're fucking badass."

"Hmm. Can't say I noticed that, no."

He smirks at me, and seeing his dimples makes me want to burst into tears and throw myself into his arms, because I really am terrified of tomorrow. I'm terrified of them leaving me behind in one way or another.

I wish I could hit pause and keep them all here with me on this island, where nothing exists except the four of us. I know that this island has been their punishment, but for me, it's been a gift.

When the first tear escapes out of my eye, it's like it snaps something inside me, and before I know it, they're flooding out of me. I cover my face in my hands, unable to stop the miserable sobs that escape me.

"You made her cry," I hear Ronak mutter.

"What the fuck? What did I do?" Evert asks.

"Just shut the fuck up."

I feel a body move next to me, and I know it's Sylred as soon as I feel the up and down motion of his hand as he rubs my lower back where my wings would normally be. It's strange to feel him touch there.

"It's okay," he whispers soothingly.

I nod and get myself under control. I drop my hands away from my face and take the offered cloth that Sylred hands to me so that I can wipe my eyes and nose.

"Just...win. Okay?" I plead, looking at each of them. "You have to win."

"We will," they all say.

I take a shaky breath and stand up with Sylred's help. I stand on my tiptoes and give him a kiss on the cheek above his blond beard. I move around to Ronak and lay one on his cheek before he can resist, teasing his hair before I walk away.

When I get to Evert, one side of his mouth is tilted up in a smirk. "Trying to have your way with all of us, eh, Scratch?"

"Do you ever shut up, Third?" I reply.

I lean down to plant one on his cheek, too, but he turns his head at the last second, forcing our lips to meet as he steals my very first kiss.

I'm so shocked that his lips are on mine that it takes me a few seconds to realize that we're kissing. His tongue teases my lips, wanting entry inside, and of course I open like a burst dam, because...*dayum*.

The second his tongue is inside, he takes over like he owns the place. Swirling, sucking, nibbling—my brain can no longer form coherent thoughts, and heat shoots right down into my core.

My tongue takes on a life of her own. She doesn't just dance with his, she bumps and grinds like she's a drunk chick in a nightclub.

Finally, after what feels like years and years of the most amazing first kiss in history, I feel his mouth pull away from mine, and I mewl—*freaking mewl!*—like a pouting kitten when his lips leave mine. I snap open my eyes—*when the hell did I close them?*—and stare at him in surprise, my lips swollen from the assault.

The bastard grins at me. Smugly. "Who you calling Third?" he asks with a wag of his eyebrows. "Looks like I just won first place."

All I can do is stare at him. It's embarrassing how much self-control it takes to not launch myself at him and make him kiss me again.

"I think you broke her," Sylred says with a quiet chuckle.

Ronak smacks Evert on the back of the head, but Evert just laughs. I have to shake my head and clear my throat in order to form thoughts and be able to respond again like a functioning person.

I yank on the hair on his beard, making him grimace. "That was a naughty trick."

"Oh, believe me, love. I have much, *much* naughtier tricks than that."

Sweet cupid's bow, my lady bits are dribbling.

Okay, so he kisses like a kissing god, but I really want to knock that cocky look off his stupidly sexy face. Two can play at this game. I lean down until my lips are grazing his ear, displaying my cleavage at just the right angle in front of his face and whisper, "So do I."

With that, I straighten up and walk away to my spot in front of the fire, leaving the guys chuckling at a flushed-face Evert, who stares after me with hunger, his scent filling the air.

"Something wrong?" I hear Ronak jab at him.

Evert stands, fixing the front of his pants, and grumbles something about taking a walk out in the cold night air. I laugh as I lie down on the furs, burrowing myself inside their warmth. I just had my first ever kiss, and it was *amazing*.

For now, I'm one happily stupid cupid. For now, my guys are safe. For now, they are my solid anchors keeping me here. For now, everything is okay.

Tomorrow? Yeah, tomorrow is a different story.

End of Book One

ACKNOWLEDGMENTS

Thank you to my family for being so supportive of my dreams and for your unending love.

Thank you to my readers for choosing my books to read out of countless others. I hope it offers happiness and an escape.

XOXO —RK